NEGOTIATIONS BEGIN

Ryven smiled, but there was something else in his expression. "Do I repulse you?" he asked softly.

There it was again, that tension. Xera tried to be careful with her words. "I'm not comfortable with this subject. Our people are at odds."

"I was speaking of us."

It was hard to look at him. "I don't want to have a relationship with you."

He looked thoughtful rather than offended. "It's like a council for peace talks, isn't it? Neither side wants to give away their concessions too early. The pace is slow and drags on for days. Sometimes a man can go mad from the tension."

She glanced up, surprised at his admission. Saw those amazing eyes.

He stepped forward. "I've never had much patience for delays, so I'll see if we have one goal in common right now." He took her in his arms and kissed her.

No Words
Alone

Autumn Dawn

LOVE SPELL NEW YORK CITY

A LOVE SPELL BOOK®

December 2008

Published by

Dorchester Publishing Co., Inc.
200 Madison Avenue
New York, NY 10016

ISBN 10: 0-505-52801-0
ISBN 13: 978-0-505-52801-8

Printed in the United States of America.

10 9 8 7 6 5 4 3 2 1

Visit us on the web at www.dorchesterpub.com.

ACKNOWLEDGMENTS

I'd like to take a moment to appreciate the following people:

First, thank you, God. When I prayed for my book to be well received, I had no idea how fast you'd work!

To my editor, Chris Keeslar, who looked past the absentmindedness (Lord of XXX!) and saw potential.

To Alissa Davis, who placed the first call. What a morning!

To my agent, Ms. Wheeler, who took the call from a giddy author with a bad connection with gracious calm.

To S. Grant, for the timely advice. I owe you one.

To John, my husband of fifteen years. You are the fantasy, love.

No Words Alone

Chapter One

"Looks like they want to talk."

Xera's gaze followed the engineer's to the cadre of silent aliens. The shifting tones of their black and gray uniforms made them hard to focus on, almost as if the cloth itself repelled the eye. She didn't see any wounded among them, but they'd probably left their injured aboard ship.

She wiped at some ooze above her left eye, smiling grimly as her black and tan uniform sleeve came away smudged with blood. Two ships had crash-landed on this planet, crippled from the battle they'd just fought, but Xera's craft had done more crash than land. Her ship's crew's casualties were heavy, and they were down to less than twenty able-bodied personnel. She counted sixteen men in the enemy group.

"Why don't they do something? They're just standing there," the engineer, Cort, muttered. Stocky, more comfortable with machines than men, he gazed at the aliens with distrust.

The captain of Xera's group said nothing, just stood there in a sweat. She knew better than to mistake the fierce frown on his face for courage under fire. The man was a coward.

"Captain Khan? Do you want to talk to them?" Cort persisted.

Captain Khan's bulldog face contorted with rage. Vietnamese, with a round head and meaty body, he'd clearly worked his way to the top by intimidation and bluff. It certainly hadn't been because of his massive intelligence. "Shut your mouth, Cort! I'm still captain here." He looked back at the aliens for a moment then gestured to one of his officers. "Genson. Go see what they want."

Genson gave him a wild look. "Sir, perhaps the translator—"

Xera, the translator, braced herself.

Captain Khan sent her a scathing look. The two of them had butted heads often enough that he didn't trust her to slide under his thumb on command. Those he couldn't dominate, he pushed to the side as useless. "You're an officer—they'll recognize that. Get moving."

Xera looked away to hide her disgust. Genson didn't know a word of Scorpio, which she herself had been learning for the past two years since graduating from the academy. Whenever the Galactic Explorers uploaded new findings on the language and customs of the race known as Scorpio, she'd been on top of it. So little was known about the alien race, and she'd been fascinated. Unfortunately, the GE didn't share her curiosity— or at least not her professional reasons for it. It hadn't taken long for Xera to realize her employer was a planet-hungry entity bent first and foremost on keeping the worlds it discovered under its control. In the Scorpio, they'd found a powerful race intent on maintaining their liberty and the privacy of their territory.

The humans had named the Scorpio for their home planet's position in the sky, in the belly of the human constellation of the same name, but also because of the alien race's stinging reprisals. Scorpio were known to shoot first and not bother with questions. Everything known of Scorpio language and customs had been decoded from damaged ships and survivors of small clashes. The fates of these captured prisoners rarely came up, though the GE maintained that they were traded back to their people in return for certain concessions. The two groups weren't involved in a full-scale war yet, thanks to the Interplanetary Council's diplomatic intervention, but this little skirmish might change all that.

Not that the IC had much control over the GE's actions, no matter their official position as peacekeepers. Officially a forum for government representatives from different planets to work toward peace and harmony, it lacked the funds and support to accomplish much. The governments and cultures involved rarely agreed on anything for long, which made it ineffectual in controlling conglomerates like the GE.

Genson walked reluctantly across the dun sand, probably swearing to himself with every step. He halted about two paces from the leader and spoke. The leader shot him down.

Xera's group jumped and pointed their guns at the aliens, who looked back at them with arrogant unconcern. A few bursts of gunfire bounced harmlessly off some unseen force field. The Scorpio made no move to return fire.

"Hold! Hold!" Captain Khan shouted, waving his hands. "We don't want to provoke them."

"But sir—," someone protested.

"I said hold it! Let me think." His thoughts must have been rapid, and full of self-preservation, for he turned to Xera. "You. You're the translator . . . you go talk to them."

She looked at him for a moment. Voicing the thoughts in her head would get her thrown in the still-smoking brig. This wasn't the first time he'd queered a deal then sent her in as translator to try to salvage it. Unable to quell a trace of mockery, she asked, "Any special messages for them, sir?"

Khan's eyes narrowed. "Don't screw this up, Harris-d, or I will bust you down to kitchen help. Find out what they want."

"Yes, sir." She gave him a jaunty salute and strode toward the alien line with her usual high energy. Fully expecting to die, she figured she might as well look proud doing so.

As she got closer, though, her stride slowed in surprise. She hadn't expected the leader to look so, well . . .

He was tall, his black hair cut close with military precision. One of his ears was pierced with a golden starburst, and there was a hands-free communication set around his ear. This close, his uniform ceased shifting colors, remained dull, gray-black combat attire.

Coldly handsome, he had a strong face, a piercing expression. His eyes were what threw her, though. Three paces away from him, she could see his irises were flame orange, tinged with gold at the edges.

Brimstone eyes.

Genson's body was in her way. She spared him a brief look, enough to see that he was very dead, then stepped around him, refusing to talk over his body. Since that brought her face-to-face with the man at the leader's left, she raised her brows inquiringly and glanced between them.

The leader finally growled in the Scorpio tongue, "Why do you look to my second? I am the leader here."

She adopted a polite expression and answered him in his language. "I don't know your customs. It seems you kill those who speak to you first." She contained a flash of rage at Genson's death. Of course, her captain was as much to blame as this man. If he'd followed protocol and sent her in first, this might not have happened.

"I will not speak to an underling. Bring your captain back or don't come at all."

She inclined her head, then bent her knees and grabbed Genson's wrists. He outweighed her by fifty pounds at least and was deadweight besides, but she managed to drag him twenty feet before some of the guys from her side broke ranks and ran to help. She would have liked to drop him right at Captain Khan's feet, but knew she'd have to settle for letting the men help. By the look on Khan's face as she walked up, she'd made her point anyway.

"Sir," she drawled, adopting her mildest expression. "He won't speak to underlings."

Her captain's face turned red. "He spoke to you!"

She shrugged. "That is what he said." She could almost see Khan's mind work: Stuck on a barren planet, half his crew dead, finite supplies and no way of knowing when or if they'd be rescued . . . They knew nothing about this place, except that the GEHQ wanted it. If the aliens were willing to make some kind of alliance, they needed to accept.

He stared at the Scorpio. "You'll need to translate."

At last, a sensible command. After all, she didn't want to die, either. "Yes, sir."

They crossed the sand halfway, then stood and waited. The alien leader and his second approached.

The leader glared at Khan. "What is your name and rank?"

Xera translated, then waited. Khan surprised her with a nudge when she didn't volunteer the information in return. The word for *captain* escaped her, so she said haltingly, "He's the leader of those in our ship—*Captain* Khan. My name is *Lieutenant* Xera Harris-d."

"He has no other rank?"

She frowned over that, then asked her captain, "You don't happen to be a prince or something among your own people, do you?"

Khan moved as if he'd like to hit her but thought better of it when he saw the alien leader tense. "Just ask him his name!"

She looked back at the Scorpio. "He asks your name."

The alien didn't look satisfied with this reply but said, "Commander Ryven Atarus, of the High Family."

She passed this on, then spun out her captain's curt, "What do they want?" to "Commander Atarus, you wished to speak to us?"

The Scorpio's eyes narrowed. "This planet becomes a death trap after dark. There are nocturnal creatures here that would feed on all of us if we stay. The ships are not strong enough to safeguard anyone. The danger is great enough that we will ally with you long enough to reach shelter. If all go, some will survive."

Captain Khan didn't like that news. "What kind of creatures can get inside a closed ship? Solid steel should keep them out."

"We need to seek shelter anyway, sir. If there is water where—"

"Your job is to translate," Khan snarled at her. "Do it!"

Xera sighed and faced Atarus. "What kind of animals can get inside a sealed ship?"

The commander's eyes traveled to their damaged spacecraft. "What's left of *that* will not keep them out."

She rather liked his tweaking Khan's tail, but she needed an answer that would move her captain, so she guessed, "Small winged creatures, and very large animals . . . I'm not sure how to translate."

Now Khan looked worried.

"We must leave now. If you are coming, come. If not, stay and die." Commander Atarus walked away.

Chapter Two

Commander Ryven Atarus watched the aliens arguing with a jaded eye. They had about five minutes until he took his party to the shelter and left them to their stupidity, but he hadn't been lying: the greater their numbers, the better their chance of survival. It was the reason he'd allowed them to remain armed. This upped the risk to his men, but they would all need weapons if they were to survive long enough to get to shelter. Until then, he'd let the humans maintain their fragile taste of equality. Once they reached the fortress, things would be different.

"They don't like each other," his brother Toosun murmured. "See how the woman stands? She is defying their leader." There was a note of satisfaction in his voice. He'd clearly found the human captain stupid, too.

Ryven had to agree with his brother and second in command—he hadn't missed Captain Khan's move to strike the translator, though perhaps he'd been provoked. The woman had certainly seemed cocky enough while striding up to them earlier, neatly sidestepping her fallen comrade. It was her act of courage in dragging away the body that had reluctantly impressed him, though. Not many males would dare such a thing, putting their back to an enemy.

Odd, too: from what he'd seen she was angrier with her captain than she was with him. Not that he regretted killing the man; he and this woman's people were at odds, and he would use every advantage to intimidate his enemies.

Toosun absently rubbed his left bicep, probably trying to build heat. The planet's atmosphere had been cool to start with and was getting colder. By nightfall, the desert would be dangerously cold. Toosun's dun-colored hair was short like his brother's, and it allowed an unwelcome draft.

Ryven turned to his men. "We've waited long enough. The antigrav sleds are loaded—let's move."

They hadn't crossed two dunes before the aliens caught up, many of them breathing hard. Ryven kept his gun loose in its holster but said nothing as they joined the column, following two lengths back with Khan and the woman in the lead.

She was attractive, in an exotic way. Even with the blood smeared on her skin, she showed well. Short, black curls framed a determined face. He'd never seen blue eyes before, and they'd take some getting used to, but her body . . . the height and strong shoulders hinted at stamina. He hoped the trimness meant she'd conditioned her muscles— she was going to need it.

It was just after noon and they had five hours of hiking through sand ahead of them. His men had plenty of food and water, but he didn't know about the humans. The men he didn't care about, but the woman . . .

"Brirax, Delfane," he said softly over his crew's communication network. "You will keep an eye on the woman. She'll tire by the time we are done, and there are the other dangers to watch for."

"Yes, sir," they responded at once. Covertly, he watched them slowly drop to the rear of the group. By the end of the march, they'd be walking next to her.

Satisfied he'd met the demands of his conscience, he turned his mind to keeping his men alive.

They'd been walking half an hour when the first man went down. Xera watched in horror as their galley master sank out of sight, sucked down a sinkhole. Screaming, the man begged for help until the sand closed over his head—too rapidly for them to save him.

"Avoid that spot," Atarus called out, and walked on. Too stunned to translate, Xera stumbled forward when the guy behind her prodded her.

"B-but shouldn't we . . ." she began, trying to look back.

"No time," one of the aliens said. Their two groups had slowly closed the gap between them as time wore on, and now there was barely any space between them. Like Atarus's second, this Scorpio had brown and gold eyes and dun hair. "Here, take this rope. Tell your people to pass one among them, too, if they have it. If another goes down, we may save them."

May save them. She wasn't sure if this was just the Scorpio way of speaking, Scorpio idiom, but she would have been more comforted by a *will save them.* This didn't stop her from grabbing the cord the aliens had strung amongst themselves, however. They had more than one, she saw, which kept them from being forced into a single file. She began to especially envy the ones pulling antigravity sleds: as long as they held on to the tethers, they would be safe from sinkholes.

"Your name?" asked the alien who'd passed her the rope.

She drew a breath. "Lieutenant Xera Harris-daughter. Harris-d for short."

He repeated the name, mangling it. "Brirax," he said by way of introduction. He gestured to another alien, a red-eyed one, who'd dropped back beside them. "Delfane."

"What do they want?" Captain Khan asked suspiciously. He'd stayed in Xera's vicinity, an unusual move for him.

"They suggested we pass around a rope." She held up the end she'd been given in illustration.

Captain Khan grunted and immediately barked out an order, only to find his men had already found a rope and were forming a line. He growled in annoyance at that sign of independent intelligence, but took hold himself.

Xera looked around at the desert. Other than a few dun rocks scattered here and there, she could see no danger—but that meant nothing. "Brirax, besides sinkholes, what other perils do we look for?"

"Biters," he said, looking grim. "Our eyes can see them, but yours will not. Even we can be caught if we crest a dune and come right on them. It is almost too late then."

She looked at his bright eyes and asked, "How is it you can see them when we can't?"

"Camouflage, for you see only colors. We see heat and colors."

"Heat and colors? Infrared?" she mused aloud in her own language. That information had never made the GE intel website. Maybe no one had ever noticed.

"What's that?" Captain Khan demanded sharply.

She blinked at him, then explained. His eyes narrowed, and he muttered something under his breath.

"What's one look like?" she asked the aliens.

Brirax's eyes shuttered. "Small, like a man's fist. They travel in families and attack at once. Flame or laser spray is the cure, but one bite will paralyze a man for hours. They eat him alive. And quickly."

Xera shuddered. Even Captain Khan looked horrified when she translated. "Pass on the information to the men—," he began.

Brirax spoke quickly, interrupting. "You'd be wise to keep this to yourself if you're contemplating otherwise. Your men might flame each other trying to kill something they can't see. Let us deal with the biters."

Xera stared at him, unsure.

"Our commander is serious about making shelter," the alien added. "We can't waste any men, not even yours."

Captain Khan started to yammer at her, but she shook her head and held up a hand so she could listen to Brirax's next words.

"Tell your people about the larger menace, the flyers. They have leathery wings and round mouths full of teeth. These they can watch for, and they will start to fly at dusk. There are also burrowers, armored worms you can wrap your arms around. We can sense these coming, so if you see us shoot the ground—"

He'd barely gotten the words out when one of his companions swore and blasted the earth. There was a screech, a hump of sand shivered, then stillness.

"A burrower," Brirax confirmed over the hubbub. "If you feel the ground vibrate under your feet, jump away."

Xera rapidly translated to her crewmates, yelling to be heard over the group's clamoring. Men started watching the ground and the skies.

"Keep moving," Commander Atarus called out from the front of the line. "We don't want to be unprotected in the desert when night falls."

Their pace quickened. Nobody thought sleeping on this sand was a good idea.

"I still don't see why we left the ships," Captain Khan complained. "These things wouldn't have been a danger to steel hulls."

Xera passed on the question.

"The flyers secrete acid that can eventually eat through a ship's hull. The only thing impervious to it is solid rock. The shelter we're going to is carved into a mountain. There's fresh water there, also."

The mention of water temporarily mollified

Captain Khan, but Xera had questions of her own. "Do you expect to be rescued?"

Brirax was silent, letting her draw her own conclusions. Her captain wanted more information about the shelter, but Brirax would only say he'd never been there.

Xera decided to save her breath for walking. Her situation wasn't good, and it wasn't just the sand working its way into her boots that worried her. If they were stuck for weeks or longer in this sandbox, she had a problem—and as the only female on the planet, it was a rather big problem. Men got lonely in space. This was bad enough normally, when at least they had hope of pulling into port. She'd had practice fending off horny crewmates for years and had learned to brush off their suggestions and flirtations; it was expected that females who signed on with the GE learn to take care of themselves. Oh, outright harassment was frowned on, but captains overlooked anything else.

But stranded for months, maybe years . . . Under the right circumstances, some men would be tempted to take what wasn't freely given. She didn't trust her captain to defend her rights, and she wasn't sure about the rest of the crew. Some of them had been fairly aggressive in the past.

Ironically, Genson had been one of the better men among the crew. Older, with a wife and daughters, he'd been a casual friend. He would have been a good man to have at her back.

She looked ahead, her eyes narrowed on the alien leader, Commander Atarus. If he was capable of that kind of random brutality, what else might he do? For now they had a common foe, but there was no telling how long this fragile truce would hold. She was going to have to sleep with one eye open.

Six hours later, she would have been happy to sleep at all. It was getting cold, and they'd lost two more men, both human. It had been because of the biters. The aliens had started flaming the sand and her side had panicked. One man died, caught in the flame spray of his own comrades; the other had run back the way they'd come, trying to escape. He'd failed. By the time they'd reached him, his eyes had already been savaged, he was paralyzed and bleeding from multiple wounds. Captain Khan had refused to carry the "deadweight" with them. The man's buddy protested violently against his abandonment, but had finally given in when the aliens started moving off, losing interest in the drama. He gave his friend a mercy bullet in the brain.

By this time, Xera was shivering with more than cold. The ground had moved under her feet not an hour ago. Delfane had swung her out of the way when she lurched, and Brirax had fired into the ground. If they hadn't been beside her . . .

She swallowed and focused on continuing to move her feet. Sand was murder on the legs.

"We're close now," Brirax told her. "See that huge rock rising out of the sand? Less than a mile to it." He glanced with concern at the darkening sky.

Xera eyed it too, thinking of flyers.

The Scorpio picked up the pace. Xera staggered, her tired legs protesting. Delfane put a hand under her elbow, steadying her. She didn't have breath for thanks, using it all to keep up the jog. Brirax scanned the sky while Delfane kept his eyes on the ground. She let them have at it—at this point, all she could do was run on.

The rock got closer, but then—

"Flyers!" The cry started out in Scorpio, but was taken up in her language as her side caught sight of the beasts. Winged terrors, black against the sky, swooped toward them from the direction of the giant rock. There were scores of them, spreading out like storm-tossed leaves coming from every direction.

Xera tried to run, but her tired muscles betrayed her. She tripped over a wind-rippled hillock of sand and twisted her foot.

But her end was not to come so soon. Delfane and Brirax snagged her arms and ran for it, firing at the sky. A flyer crashed down right in front of her, delivering a glancing blow that staggered Delfane. He would have fallen if Brirax hadn't reached over and steadied him. The beast thrashed, nearly tripping Xera with its wings, but her two protectors lifted her over it and they were away.

Thirty yards to the rock, and one of the Scorpio went down under a flyer, screaming. The beast was shot, but too late. Twenty yards, and another flyer latched onto a man from Xera's crew. This flyer was killed in time, and the man, though wounded, staggered on.

Ten yards . . . and then they were there. They put their backs to the rock wall and fired up at the flyers until Commander Atarus yelled, "It's open! Hurry!"

Xera was nearly trampled in the rush to get inside.

Someone turned on a hand torch, and somehow they got everyone through. At last they slammed the door on the winged creatures, safe . . . at least from the monsters outside.

Chapter Three

The sealing of the door triggered lights to blink on. Squinting her unaccustomed eyes, Xera looked around.

They were in a tunnel, six feet wide and forty yards long, its rock walls lined with a series of recessed tubes providing illumination. The Scorpio were already moving forward, sleds, injured and all. Unwilling to rest so close to the doors, even the weariest of Khan's crew followed.

Xera took a step and staggered as pain shot up from her foot. She must have been too scared in the mad rush to safety, or too pumped full of adrenaline, to notice how it hurt. She was feeling the pain now, though, along with many smaller aches she'd shut out in the madness.

"There's heat in your right foot," Delfane said, glancing down. "Hold on." He swung her up on a sled without asking permission. Perched precariously on several tarp-covered parcels, she gritted her teeth and tried to ignore the surge of pain that electrified her leg. Sitting wasn't much better than standing, not with her legs swinging as they were.

At the end of the tunnel they entered a two-story cavern a little longer than it was high. The floor was solid dun rock, and the atmosphere was a surprisingly comfortable temperature. Stone stairs ran up one wall and opened onto a second-story balcony. Dusky light filtered down from that level, making Xera shudder. Surely there weren't windows up there! Some things she didn't need to see.

The Scorpio did a quick reconnaissance. Satisfied that they were alone, they made camp.

Xera slid off the sled and hobbled over to a bench carved into the wall. Exhausted, she drained her water bottle and then tackled her boots. She had to get the injured foot out before it burst the leather, and there was probably enough sand in there to build her own beach. Even her eyes were gritty with it.

It took an effort to pull her boot off without whimpering. Once free, her foot throbbed with a vengeance, doubling with the pain of her blistered, raw soles. She pulled off a sweaty sock and hissed at the feel of the cool air on her tender skin. What she wouldn't give for some warm water and antiseptic! Instead, she lay down on the bench and closed her eyes. Maybe she should be grateful just to be breathing.

She must have slept, for she was woken by a nudge. Blearily, she wiped grit from her eyes and looked up. It was Brirax.

"You need to tend your injuries. You can't afford gangrene." He handed her a bottle and a packet of gauze. "There is medicine in the water. Use it to clean your wounds."

"Thanks," she muttered as he walked off, still

groggy. It was tempting to go right back to sleep, but he was right. A nap could wait until she made sure her limbs wouldn't rot off.

She sat up stiffly and washed her feet, hissing every time the gauze made contact with a sore. Walking was going to be painful for the next few days, what with all the blisters, but it was comforting to know she wouldn't be the only one sore-footed. While she was at it, she swiped at the gash over her eye and washed her face. She was unable to see what she was doing, but such ministrations were probably better than none at all.

Finished, she glanced around, seeing many other tired, dispirited souls. These were in the human camp, really. While the aliens were quiet, they didn't seem overly distressed. But, of course, this was their turf.

Ryven had watched the woman lie untended for a half hour before he intervened. It had been a small thing, to send the medicine, but he shouldn't have had to do it. Among his people the most badly wounded were attended first, then the women and children. Warriors with minor hurts would delay their own comfort.

This protocol was in contrast to that of the humans. The square-headed human captain hadn't bothered to see to the only woman in his group. He'd immediately flopped his body down on a bench and let his men tend themselves for a good ten minutes, only rousing himself to give orders when hunger stirred him. His group's translator, possibly one of his best assets, he'd ignored.

There was another difference: Ryven hadn't

needed to order his men to make camp. They knew what was necessary to do and did it.

His people were stronger than humans; he could see that now. While tired, they had not suffered nearly as much on the march. He would almost have been impressed by what the humans, with their limited physiques, had managed to do . . . if they hadn't neglected their woman so. She needed ice for that foot. Even from here he could see the faint heat signature, an angry, painful-looking red.

This time, he chose to take it himself rather than send Brirax.

Xera looked up, mildly surprised to see the alien leader. He plopped a cold pack onto her foot. "Use this."

"Okay," she said slowly. While the gesture had not exactly been gentle, she appreciated the ice, if not the source. She would not forget that this man was a killer. In all fairness, though, he had no reason to love her people. She forced herself to accept that, too. "Did you need something?"

His face gave nothing away. "We've activated the temperature control system. The thermal grills for cooking are on line. You will be allowed access to water, but your people will have to forage for their own food—we will not share our rations. Whatever you brought in your packs will have to suffice, though we will show you how to seek what food can be gathered. If you are diligent, you will not starve."

Well, *there* was great news. "Anything else?"

He walked away.

Apparently not. She sighed. And things were about to get worse. She wasn't looking forward to talking to her captain, but here he came.

"What did he want?" Khan demanded, eyeing her ice pack suspiciously. He shifted his weight from foot to sore foot.

She relayed the information Atarus had provided. "Did you want some water now?"

"Water?" he shouted. "Water? What I want is to get off this blasted rock!" His piggy eyes narrowed. "Did he say if a ship was coming for them?"

"I have no idea," she admitted, wishing she did. It would change a lot of things, knowing there might soon be more of the Scorpio. She didn't relish being a prisoner of war. "I don't think they'd tell me if they did."

Khan grunted at her. "You seem mighty cozy with them."

She looked at him tiredly. "Sir, I'm the only member of our crew that speaks their language. I'd be happy to coach you and everyone else on it, though. God forbid I should drop dead and leave you all with no idea what they're saying or plotting."

Captain Khan grabbed her shirt in a rough grip. "Watch it, Harris-d. If we are stuck on this sandpit, we won't be seeing any more of the GE. Rules of discipline be damned, I'll jump at the first chance to teach you to watch your mouth. Remember that." He released her with a shove and walked away.

With mixed emotions, Xera watched the man stalk off. Granted, she could probably kick his butt if she needed, but not if the crew backed him up. Besides, doing that would just invite being attacked in the dark one night, which would of course end badly. She wasn't inclined to pick a fight, and the alternative was lying low.

Swallowing against that bitter reality, she lay back down and stared at the ceiling. God help her if the GE didn't show up to save them. Much as she hated their politics, her employers were the only thing likely to save her from what was coming.

It was morning by the time she woke. Groaning at her stiffness, she glanced at her watch and saw she'd slept for almost twelve hours. She was surprised she'd been allowed to rest so long, but a look around showed everyone else was moving slowly, too. She gingerly sat up. It was amazing how comfortable even a stone bench could be when you were dead tired, but she was paying for lying on it with even more aches.

Someone had thrown a survival blanket over her during the night. She brushed it aside, thankful for the thin material's added warmth. She'd had one in her pack but had been too exhausted to dig for it last night.

She had to limp along the wall, using it to steady herself as she sought out Brirax. He saw her coming and met her halfway.

"I need to know where the . . . *bathrooms* are," she told him, trying not to be embarrassed. For some reason it was harder to ask an alien this question. It didn't help that she didn't know the exact words to use.

His brows drew together. "What?"

She sighed. "I drank too much water."

His face cleared. "Follow me." He watched her

hobble for two steps, and then motioned her to stop. "Wait." He hurried up the stairs to the balcony where the Scorpio had moved all their stuff. He came back down with a laser rifle, which he handed to her. "It's unloaded."

"Thanks," she said, surprised by his generosity. The weapon made for a cumbersome cane, but it helped get her across the room to where she needed to go.

In the area the Scorpio indicated, there were several doors right next to each other. She went through one and shut the door, then took a quick look around. There was a seat and something that looked like some kind of composting unit. There was nowhere to wash her hands, however. Finished, she opened the door and asked Brirax about it.

"Run your hands in front of that stone," he instructed, pointing to an area in the back of the restroom. "The energy kills the . . ." She didn't exactly understand what he said, but she got the drift. He added, "If you would like to cleanse your entire body, press the stone and stand there for a count of seventy." He closed the door to let her check it out.

It was like a solar shower, and she didn't even have to undress to use it. She'd heard of the concept but never experienced one. Green rays surrounded her, dissolving the dirt and oils from her clothes and body. In slightly over a minute she was as clean as if she'd never been chased through a desert by monsters. Even her muscles felt better, as if she'd had a long, hot bath.

"Cool," she told Brirax as she stepped out, using the Scorpio word without thinking.

"The temperature was cold?" he asked. "I will have to inspect it."

She laughed, realizing her mistake. "No! It was a compliment. I think your technology is wonderful."

"Oh." He looked as if he hadn't understood all her words, but seemed to process enough. "I will show you where to get water. Gather your crew after that and we will explain how to forage."

Commander Atarus acted as their guide. Captain Khan and all of her crew followed along for the tour. It was tiring, hobbling around the cave with stiff muscles and a bum foot. Xera finally broke down and accepted an offer from an ensign to be a human crutch. He'd seemed especially eager to help her, but she was too grateful to be wary.

The water was no big deal—it came out of a faucet in a wall alcove. The foraging was harder. They had to descend some stairs that opened out into a lower cavern. It was cool down there, populated with fungus and shadows. Something crunched under her feet. Atarus shown a flashlight at her boots and she yelped. The ground was swarming with fat slimy things.

"Ah! Worms! And bugs!" She tried to move away but just stepped on others.

"Protein," Atarus corrected with some amusement.

She stared at him. "You've got to be joking," she said in her own language, too grossed out to use his.

"What's he saying?" Khan demanded. "What are all these worms doing here?"

"Dinner," Xera said softly, feeling sick.

Her words caused an uproar. Atarus just looked at the humans with aristocratic unconcern until the noise settled down. He waved a hand at the fungi. They looked like pulpy fans and grew on the stone columns, floor and walls. "The stone fungus is edible once cooked, and this lichen makes a tea that will provide valuable nutrients." He indicated a glowing green plant that resembled dead leaves. Xera wondered if she'd start glowing, too, if she drank anything made of that stuff.

Her ensign crutch was a braver man than she. "Can't be worse than Mom's cooking," he said philosophically, and began gathering ingredients.

Xera felt sick. She started to hobble to the stairs. Step, *crunch*. Drag, step, *squish*. She shuddered. Reaching the steps, she hurried up. Brirax, Delfane and their captain had been either slow to leave or were waiting for her. They didn't say anything. Atarus wordlessly placed a hand under her elbow and supported her as she climbed.

"Tired?" he asked as they reached the upper cavern and blessed light.

Not a bug in sight. She sighed gratefully and tried not to think about the condition of her boots. "Some."

Shocking her, he swung her up into his arms and strode off toward her bench. None of her crew was there to see it, and his own people didn't seem fazed.

"What are you doing?" she gasped, panicked. She struggled, but he was even stronger than he looked. Was he going to try something now that no one was watching?

He set her down on her bench. "Stay off the foot if you want it to heal. There is little for you to do now but translate, anyway."

She gave him an unfriendly look. "I don't like being carried."

"You do not seem to like bugs, either, but you will eat them," he said, unconcerned. "What is the name of the man who helped you down the stairs? You should have him for your help."

"Ensign Trevor, and I won't need help long."

"Good." He walked away.

She watched him go, her gut still swirling with unease. She began to wonder how much of Delfane and Brirax's help was his doing.

She was still wondering a little while later when Delfane brought her a bowl of gray soup. "What is it?" she asked warily.

"Don't ask," he advised her.

She closed her eyes, took a deep breath and told herself it was mushroom soup. Of course it was. It wasn't bad, really.

He handed her a mug of faintly glowing green tea. His eyes crinkled with amusement. "Your face reminds me of my daughter when she tries something new. Her face always twists just so."

Surprised, she asked, "You're married?"

"Yes. Drink your tea."

Cautiously, she complied. It wasn't great, but it was drinkable. Kind of reminded her of kelp.

"Good. Now you will finish the soup and translate the making of it for your people."

It was a lot easier to finish the soup than it was to explain to everyone else how it was made. She turned a little green, much to the amusement of the Scorpio. She saw several of them laughing to each other and talking quietly but animatedly as they gestured in her direction. She'd have thought they were jerks, but noticed that several of them were eating the gray soup, too. Maybe they thought she was finicky, or they were making the best of a less than gourmet meal by cracking jokes. Even Atarus seemed amused.

To her surprise, her own captain slurped the slop right down. Must not be a picky eater, she assumed, or he just liked a full belly.

Afterward, she gave language lessons. Occasionally she had to ask an alien for confirmation regarding the meaning of a word. They seemed willing enough to talk to her, if especially aloof around her crew. The feeling was mutual.

Well, she reminded herself, the two groups *had* been shooting each other out of the sky just yesterday. Feeling more like an ambassador than an interpreter, she often stood between the two races, using her body as a kind of buffer.

It was tiring work, and she excused herself after an hour to hobble back to her bench. She lay down, inserted her earbuds and listened to music. The device was small enough to fit into a necklace and contained millions of files, many of which she'd still never heard. Now, given time and the lifetime warranty on the battery, she might just get a chance. She shoved that image out of her mind as soon as it formed and concentrated on other things. It had been a gift from her sisters on her last birthday and contained many family photos. She flipped through them as she listened to music, feeling wistful. She missed them and wondered what they'd been told about her disappearance. They'd worry. For that matter, she was worried.

The downside of teaching everyone the language was that she was helping herself out of a job. She didn't think it would change her situation, though. What might? She couldn't think of anything, so she concentrated on simply doing her job. Any intel she might get from the aliens about their culture or language would be a powerful tool if she ever got back to the GE. To cheer herself up, she imagined herself being in high demand as an expert on the Scorpio race. Of course, not knowing when they might be rescued, she might find out more than she wanted to know about their mating habits. . . .

Stop torturing yourself, she ordered herself sternly, and sat up. There'd been no comb in her pack, so she tried to untangle her hair with her fingers. The motion was soothing and it gave her something to do.

Ensign Trevor must have noticed. He came over and offered his comb. "Here. I don't need it." His hair was cropped regulation short.

She smiled gratefully. "It's short now. Give it time. But, thanks." She couldn't see what she was doing while she combed, but at least she now had a prayer of undoing the rat's nest.

Trevor sat down on the bench next to her. "Quite a hike yesterday, huh? Felt like I'd been sucked into a horror movie."

"It isn't over. There's still the food," she said with a grimace.

He laughed. "Yeah. At least there *is* food." He let his gaze trail aimlessly around, clearly stalling. At last he spoke. "Look, Harris-d, I was thinking we could do each other a favor."

She stilled. He didn't meet her eyes, or he

might have flinched at the suspicion there. She'd had too many come-ons start with that very line.

"You've really got a bad situation here, and I'm sympathizing with that. Being the only woman and all." He looked at her out of the corner of his eye. "I was thinking maybe I could help you out." She waited. She'd thought he was all right, maybe a little geeky, but he was no different than the rest. He was making a play for her. She wanted to hit him for trying to take advantage. In her present mind-set, that was the only way she saw his offer.

"It would really help if you had a guy on your side, you know. I'm willing, if you like." He got a little red-faced. "If the others thought you were taken . . ."

"So you want sex in exchange, is that it?" she asked coldly.

He flinched. "Well, it would be nice, but I'm not trying to force you or anything. I just thought I'd offer. It's not like we . . . I mean . . ." He stumbled to a verbal stop, his face glowing red.

She couldn't speak right away, didn't trust herself. She'd always had a temper, but she had common sense, too. He stood up. She almost let him walk away. "I'll think about it," she choked out.

He paused, looked over his shoulder. "Okay," he said.

He hesitated, then moved on. Xera gripped the comb so hard it bit into her hand. Suddenly she didn't care about her hair.

"The first one's approached her," Toosun observed softly. He was sitting with his brother, and the two men watched the quiet scene unfold across the room, just as his brother had predicted. Ryven also watched the way Xera just sat there, staring at her feet after the human ensign left. It was a dead giveaway.

"Yes," he said. He continued sharpening his blade. The eight-inch knife had the same shifting coating as his uniform and was already razor sharp. An enemy would not see it coming in the dark.

"Will her captain permit her to go to another man?"

"That one? He'll let her service anyone who asks, then demand her for himself when he wants her. She will not be permitted to refuse." Ryven's eyes were shuttered, deceptively focused on his task.

"We will keep watch, then. If she chooses a man of her own free will, do we still intervene?"

Ryven looked at him. "In this situation, will any choice of hers constitute free will? Even if it did, it would not change my plans for her."

Toosun nodded. "The men are settled, then. Shall we start with drills this morning? They need to stay busy."

"Yes. After they've bled off some energy, they can participate in more language studies with the translator. Also, ask for volunteers to do recon outside the shelter—we need to know more data about our environment, need to see if there's any recoverable equipment outside. If your group finds remains, burn them with lasers. Burial is too hazardous now. You have one hour. If you do not return on time we will send out a search party, but anyone left outside at dusk is expendable."

The brothers held each other's gazes. They had done this often enough that nothing else needed to be said. They had love but also duty. It had always been that way.

"We'll recover what we can and stay on the rocks. That should keep the diggers at bay, and the flyers are sleeping until dusk."

"Just don't walk into any caves," Ryven said dryly. After a moment he added, "Ask the humans if they're brave enough to go."

Toosun grinned. "The translator won't tell them my exact words."

Ryven flashed a brief smile in response. "Be discreet, then. I would rather our numbers be even— not that they impress me as warriors."

"No. I will ask her." Toosun hesitated. "What about their weapons? Will we take them soon?"

Ryven knew his brother wouldn't question the wisdom of his decisions directly, but he was sure his men were all wondering. "We will wait a little longer. Let them think they have nothing to fear—it will lull them." There had been enough casualties. There would come an opportune moment, and then he and his men would act.

He hadn't forgotten his objective—the interlopers would pay for their indiscretion. They were trespassers, and would be treated as such. Even the woman would learn her place . . . as soon as he decided what that place should be. It seemed a waste to send a woman like her to prison. He darted a glance her way. He had to think about the possibilities.

Xera eyed the Scorpio second in command, Toosun, and contemplated what he'd just said. As she didn't feel like hobbling over to her captain

just then, she caught Khan's attention with a gesture. It wasn't hard—he'd been watching her with
alarming frequency, especially whenever one of
the Scorpio spoke with her.

"What?" he demanded as he approached. "You
too lazy to bring a message to your captain?"

She gestured to her bound foot. "I'm still recov-
ering, sir. It'll heal faster if I stay off it."

Khan's small eyes gleamed with nasty satisfaction. "So you're only good for sitting on your butt
or lying on your back, eh? That's about . . ." He
broke off as the Scorpio shifted toward him, just
enough to make him wary.

"The Scorpio are making up a reconnaissance
party," she explained quickly, keeping her voice
even. "They want to know if any of us are brave
enough to accompany them. They plan to be gone
an hour."

"Brave enough?" Khan snarled. "Any of us are
braver than a stinking, filthy alien. Cort! Trevor!"
he bellowed. He looked at those two men, who hurried over. "Get ready for a recon mission. I want to
know what these guys know at all times! Grab any
gear you happen to see lying around outside."

The men paled but hurried to do what he said.

Captain Khan turned to Toosun and eyed him ar-
rogantly. "What else do they want?" he asked Xera.

She kept her sigh to herself, though she was
suddenly exhausted. In his own language she told
Toosun, "They are getting ready. Is there anything
else?"

Toosun looked at her and ignored her captain,
who practically breathed down his neck. "My lord
has told our men to watch out for your safety. It is

not our custom to see women mistreated. If you become afraid, you may move your sleeping place to our side of the shelter. You will not be disturbed or harmed." He gave her a slight bow of his head, then turned and looked down at Khan.

Faced with the Scorpio and his superior height, much of the captain's bravado leached away. Khan turned his back and stalked off.

A dark expression flashed through Toosun's face. It was leashed but not gone when he nodded to Xera and returned to his own men.

Xera took a slow breath, then exhaled. She'd just been offered protection by people she knew nothing about. Unfortunately, she knew too much about her own kind. She'd better be down to zero options before she took such a huge risk. She took her laser rifle crutch and hobbled over to sit by a few of her human companions. They were fiddling with a radio, clearly waiting to get reports back from the imminent reconnaissance mission. In response to the few curious looks they shot her, she said, "You might need translation help on that." She wasn't going to give Khan another chance to say she was useless.

The communications officer nodded and handed her a headset.

Chapter Four

Xera didn't envy Cort and Ensign Trevor as they followed Toosun and his crew outside. Both humans and Scorpio lined the entry tunnel, ready to blast anything that came through the door, though the shelter's sensors had reported nothing deadly beyond. A flash of light appeared as they exited, then darkened to artificial light as the heavy doors closed on the sun outside. It didn't take long before Ensign Trevor reported, "We found a boot . . . Scorpio make."

There was grim silence in the room as everyone heard the transmission. Xera remembered the Scorpio who'd gone down under a flyer.

"There's a ripped pack. We're gathering the goods. Doesn't seem to be anything else."

There was apparently a path carved into the rock that wound up to the top of the shelter, and the team followed it. Toosun explained the path was for maintenance on the solar array, and Xera translated. The top of the rock opened up into a rough plateau.

"Good place to land a ship," Cort reported tersely.

Captain Khan tensed.

"You can see for miles up here," Ensign Trevor broadcasted. He was looking through electronic binoculars. "Not that there's much to see. Desert, rocks, sand."

"Same thing as yesterday," Cort affirmed. "There's a few other rocky hills scattered here and there, but that's it. This rock isn't very big, either. Maybe the size of a football field. Makes you wonder why they bothered to build a shelter here at all."

The hour of reconnaissance passed quickly and uneventfully, but it provided a much-needed distraction. The men made it back to the shelter with no problem.

"Sandstorm looked to be kicking up," Cort remarked as he entered.

"Tell me about the landing pad," Kahn demanded. "Any sign of recent use?"

Cort shrugged. "Hard to tell."

"What I want to know is if they have a ship on the way," the captain snapped. "For all I know we're sitting ducks, with no way to know if or when our own distress signal will be answered."

His crew tensed. However brief their truce here, no one wanted to be a wartime guest of the Scorpio. POWs had no guarantee of fair treatment, no matter what the GE claimed.

"They killed Genson," one of the men added bitterly. "We've got no call to be trusting them."

Xera couldn't argue; everything her companions said was true. She didn't like where this was going, though. The building tension could lead to bad decisions, maybe get somebody killed.

Khan looked at her. "Harris-d, you're going to

question them. Ask them about the planet, about its resources. Ask 'em why a shelter was put up in this place, find out everything you can. Be careful about it! They don't need to know we're suspicious."

"Yes, sir," she said soberly.

"The rest of you, keep your eyes peeled! We don't need any nasty surprises. From now on, two of you will be on active watch at all times."

Xera limped back to her bench and waited a while before approaching the Scorpio. It was hard to view them objectively—they had been kind to her. There was no telling what would happen to her or her crew on an alien ship, though. They could end up under the authority of someone who was less lenient, with harsher views on the treatment of captive females. She hadn't been home in three years, and she wanted a chance to see her sisters again.

The Scorpio didn't seem disturbed by what the recon mission had revealed. Singularly and in pairs, they now performed martial arts drills. Doing so, they made her years of study look like kid stuff. She held a black belt in two different disciplines, and she had no doubt any one of these guys could take out her old masters without breaking a sweat. They were unbelievably fast. She could only be grateful that their space technology was roughly on a par with that of her own people, or they wouldn't still be here.

She waited until Delfane was finished with his kata and had taken his turn in the ray shower before approaching him. He saw her coming and waved her over to a bench.

"That was impressive," she said. As she settled

down, she winced. How long would it take this foot to heal? It was killing her whenever she failed to keep it elevated. "What do you call your martial art?"

He said something unpronounceable.

"The . . . killing way?" she translated hesitantly.

"Close. Your foot is better?"

She sighed. "It hurts, but it won't kill me. I'm sorry for the loss of your crewman."

He nodded but offered nothing else.

"This is a very cruel planet. Why did your people bother building a shelter here? Our scans showed some minerals, but nothing that couldn't be found on an asteroid. Even these oceans are filled with poisons."

He shrugged. "It lies within our boundaries. Claiming it is our right."

The GE would argue that, but Xera wasn't about to. "Sure. I'm just glad I won't have to live here. . . ." She trailed off, let a touch of genuine anguish color her words. "At least, I hope I won't."

It was a perfect opening, but he seemed uninterested in pursuing it. Instead he asked, "You have family?"

She looked away. "Sisters." She couldn't help a twinge of longing. One more year and her tour would have been up. She could have gone home. She'd never regretted her wanderlust, her desire to see the stars. She was independent enough that long separations hadn't bothered her, but that was when she'd had e-mail and pin beam available to send messages. She might want her space, but she liked to keep in touch with those she loved. Now that the tether had been cut, she realized just how much she'd valued the connection. She didn't know if she'd have chosen to go home after her service was up, or settle elsewhere, but she'd never thought to lose all touch with her family.

She drew strength from her family; they were her lifeline. Her older sister, Gem, had especially had a knack for encouraging her. Now that Gem was out of touch, Xera would have to exercise her little-used faith to believe that things could be all right.

Just thinking that positive thought brought a surge of courage. "I haven't seen them in a long time." It was impossible to miss the wistfulness in her voice.

"I miss my family as well." He smiled and showed her a holo-projection from his wrist computer. It showed a woman and child. The girl was aged six, perhaps, had shiny black hair and elfin eyes.

"Cute kid," Xera said appreciatively. "I hope you get to see her again."

His eyes shuttered as he closed the file. "Yes."

Toosun approached. "Xera Harris-d, our lord has requested that you give him and our crew language lessons, as you do for your own men. It would be best if we all understood one another, and it will help give structure to the day."

She glanced at Khan. "With my captain's permission. He may want some of our men to listen, also, to speed their own learning."

"That is permissible."

So Xera spent more time teaching, and learned a few things as well. Their society was patriarchal and monotheistic, for the most part. Superiors were allowed to speak first, according to Scorpio etiquette, unless the speaker was given prior permission. In a hostile situation, such etiquette was particularly important.

Chagrined, she wished she'd known that before Genson had been sent to speak with the Scorpio; it would have prevented a needless death. As the translator, she accepted part of the blame as her own. Her training was supposed to help prevent such things.

The Scorpio sat in a semicircle around her bench, with a few of her own crew clustered toward the back of the group. While an uneasy mix, the two races did cooperate while practicing simple sentences. There were even a few smiles as they managed to butcher each other's words. Some sounds were simply unpronounceable to both groups, and even Xera had a hard time pronouncing the syllable *frth* (with a rolled *r*, no less), without spitting. For their part, the Scorpio seemed unable to say *v*. Even so, progress was made.

Captain Khan made no move to learn the language, but Ryven Atarus was not so reserved. He listened closely and made rapid progress, rarely forgetting a word. After an hour, he dismissed any men who wished it, but he stayed, himself, along with three or four others, to learn more.

"The water is bad," he said to Toosun with a creditable accent. "Do not drink it."

"Your cooking is bad," Toosun replied with a grin. "I do not like fugs."

"Bugs," Xera corrected with a laugh. "You do not like bugs."

He smirked. "Neither do you," he said in his own language.

She'd been surprised to discover that he and Ryven Atarus were brothers, but she could see the resemblance now. Although Ryven was his superior, they still teased each other like siblings. Toosun was the only one permitted to do it, though. No one else dared.

"How do you say *blue eyes*?" he asked. "Your people have the oddest eye color, like hard gems."

She told him, and then added, "Us? You seem like the odd ones, with your eyes like fire." Her gaze darted to Ryven as she said it.

Toosun laughed. "Yes, he does have pretty eyes. Very like a girl."

Ryven gave him a cold look. "None have mistaken me for such."

"Yes, you are very brave," Toosun allowed, but a smile still lurked around his mouth.

Ensign Trevor had stayed behind while the rest of Xera's crew had wandered off. Now he edged closer to her, disliking the camaraderie, perhaps. "You look tired, Xera. Maybe you'd like to go eat?"

She looked at him. He was being doggedly protective, as if she'd already accepted his offer of companionship. His familiar attitude chafed. She might be just a lieutenant here, but she was also a successful, respected businesswoman back home. Her family owned a thriving tavern, and she'd had her share of employees under her. She didn't like the ensign's attempt to take charge of her. If she admitted it to herself, it was probably the reason she was still single. "I would like a drink, if you wouldn't mind bringing it," she allowed. Her voice was cool. He didn't seem happy with her answer, but he left to fetch some glowing tea anyway.

"You don't like him," Ryven observed.

How could she answer that? She decided not to.

"Your captain doesn't wish to learn our language," the Scorpio leader continued. "He seems tense."

"Our being here is an awkward situation," she replied, as diplomatically as she could.

"Are you expecting a ship to come rescue you?" he asked, casually, as if the question weren't central to both their universes just now.

"Hope is important," she said smoothly; then she changed subjects. "How will you occupy your men after dinner? You seem to keep them busy."

He accepted the new path of the conversation. "They will play games. I encourage them to think of this time as a brief holiday. It is better for morale."

"*Is* it a brief holiday?" she asked pleasantly. "How wonderful for you."

"You make assumptions," he replied, a gleam of pleasure in those brimstone eyes. "But in a way that makes me smile, so I cannot rebuke you. And here is your friend, back with your refreshment. . . . Your people may take part in our games if you like."

Xera soon discovered that the games included such silliness as slug racing, yet the men also competed in sprints, long jumps and rock tossing, the goal being to toss rocks of varying sizes onto chalk circles on the floor. She tried her hand at the latter game with surprising success.

Ryven Atarus watched with his arms crossed. He'd been observing a slug race with critical appraisal and happened to glance her way. "Acceptable—for a woman," he offered haughtily. Humor lurked in those remarkable eyes.

"Yeah, if I could just turn this into a career," she quipped. She reached for another stone. "I can see it now—the money, my name in lights. People will flock to see the great rock tosser!" She succeeded hitting another circle, and her competitors made her back up a couple of paces.

Her crewmates mostly watched from the fringes, reluctant to engage, though one or two others joined in. Ensign Trevor was always near at hand. She was tempted to throw a rock at his head.

Captain Khan watched her darkly from the shadows. He'd probably accuse her of fraternizing with the enemy, but how else was she supposed to get information? She'd have to report to him after the games—maybe *that* would sooth his antsy twitters.

She warily limped toward the edge of the room after the rock toss. Khan's eyes bored coldly into her as she approached, and he didn't invite her to sit. "You stink of the enemy," he sneered.

"Sir, you ordered me to spy on them," she said quietly. "I can't do that from a distance."

"And did you find anything useful, or were you just giggling through the games?"

"I've only got impressions, sir. No one would say if a ship was coming." There was no one near them to hear their conversation, and she wished she had witnesses. It seemed the captain was trying to pick a fight, or nerving himself up for something worse.

Oblivious to her concern, Khan spat, "I have an impression, Harris-d. I think you're flirting with

our enemy, just waiting for a chance to jump ship
and save your own hide. I see the way you look at
that murdering bastard, and I say you're planning
treason."

Her head jerked up. "What? You're wrong, sir."

"Am I?" he hissed. "I've known what you were all
along, Harris-d. You're nothing but an opportunis-
tic whore, aren't you? You know what we do to
whores where I come from, Harris-d?"

"Get arrested by them for harassment, sir?" she
said through bloodless lips. She felt stiff with shock
at the force of his attack. Much as she despised
him, she hadn't seen this coming. Officers didn't
act like this.

She barely saw his fist coming, either. Her dodge
was slow but mostly effective; she was only grazed.
Her weak foot screamed as she forced it to take her
weight, stepped back and slammed her rifle butt
into his throat. Even knowing that there would be
repercussions, she drew it back and rammed it hard
into his knee. There was a crunch. He screamed
and went down, clutching the joint.

Hard hands suddenly grabbed her, wrenched
the rifle from her grip. There was a babble of
voices as her crew surrounded her.

"Arrest her!" Captain Khan screamed, writhing
on the floor. He erupted in a stream of curses as
his men tried to help him up. Xera hoped she'd
broken his friggin' knee.

"What happened?" Cort demanded. "Why'd you
attack him?"

"You saw what happened! He attacked me!"

"You must have said something," Cort insisted.
"You always say something, Harris-d."

She opened her mouth to defend herself, then shut it. She wasn't going to help anything when she was angry.

Besides, there was a growing pool of silence around her. Men stilled. She looked over her shoulder and saw the Scorpio had gathered behind her.

"What happens here?" Ryven Atarus asked quietly. He looked much as he had the first day she'd seem him: cold, deadly. The starburst in his ear winked with deceptive light, and those brimstone eyes nearly glowed.

She turned to face him as her captors did, though she noticed their grips loosen.

"This is our business," Cort answered, unable to understand what was being said. The intimidation of the Scorpio commander was plain enough, though. The engineer licked his lips. "We'll deal with it." The silence stretched uncomfortably. "Translate, Harris-d!"

She looked at him as if he were stupid. "How will you know what I tell them? If they do something you don't like, then you'll blame me." She was shaking from the aftereffects of adrenaline and couldn't help her cheek—it was all that was getting her through.

Cort's eyes narrowed. "If you don't speak and they attack, I *will* blame you."

Grimly, she said to the Scorpio, "This is a matter for my people." She told Cort what she said as she said it, in case it might help save her hide.

"Your captain attacked you," Ryven remarked. "We witnessed this."

"Yes." She was very slow translating, as emotion choked her.

"We will not allow you to be punished."

She was speechless for a moment with the force of her thoughts. It took a prod in the back from Cort for her to translate. After she did, there was heavy silence.

Eyes on the floor, Xera said to the Scorpio leader, "You are making this difficult for me. My people will say I am a traitor."

"Then we will not give you a choice."

It happened too fast for her to track. She saw two Scorpio lunge for her. In seconds she was released from her former captors and drawn to the rear of the Scorpio ranks. Brirax and Delfane flanked her. None of her crewmates dared move.

Ryven looked at them as if they were nothing, less than nothing. "Confiscate their weapons. Leave only what they need for survival."

"You can't do this! You can't meddle in our affairs!" Captain Khan protested from the rear. Someone had pumped the captain full of painkillers and plopped him on a bench.

Ryven's smile was cold. "Confiscate their painkillers. From now on, they must come to us for this medicine. You may leave the antibiotics and such."

Xera felt dizzy. The Scorpio commander was going to let Khan suffer as punishment, and Khan would never forget it. Nor would he forgive his men being disarmed. He'd want revenge.

Ryven turned his back on his enemies as his men followed orders. Xera had to wonder if this was just the opportunity he'd been waiting for all along.

He stopped in front of her but addressed his

men. "There is heat in her ankle again. Take her to the balcony and ice it. Check her feet as well."

Delfane swung Xera into his arms and headed for the stairs. She didn't bother to protest, knowing she'd waste her breath. Most of her crew's attention was on the Scorpio going through their packs, but one or two glanced her way with accusing eyes. Khan was one of them.

Once up the stairs, Delfane sat her down on a woven fiber mat on a bench set along one wall. It seemed luxurious compared to the stone bench that had been ruining her back. There was even a boxy pillow to accompany it, and a brown blanket that looked like rubber folded at the foot.

Brirax appeared with a cold pack for her foot. "Do you need help to take off your footwear?"

Xera stared at him a moment, then slowly reached down and unfastened her boot. Shock had rendered her momentarily docile. She didn't know what would happen to her now, but she would choose her battles.

It seemed clear as time passed that nothing bad would happen. The men treated her with courtesy, tended the healing blisters on her feet and then left her alone. As the evening wore on, the lights were dimmed and she could see out through the thick glass that separated this bunker from the outside. The black shapes of flyers traced across the unfamiliar stars, searching for food.

The stars. Somewhere out there, up in that sky, was her family. It took a long time for her to turn her back on those winking lights and fall asleep.

Chapter Five

She was not permitted to speak to her companions. It might have been for her safety. It might not.

Xera stood on the balcony level and watched as the other humans went about their business under guard. The bottom level had been turned into a prison, and the top tier was the command center and Scorpio living quarters. She saw several Scorpio males with laptops conversing over headsets. It wasn't hard to tell they weren't talking with one another.

A ship was coming. A Scorpio ship. Xera closed her eyes and tried to ignore the rush of fear. She hadn't been harmed since coming up here, but she still didn't know what the future held.

"You did a good job of defending yourself last night." Ryven Atarus paused nearby at the railing of the balcony and looked down.

"I wish I hadn't had to. This will make my life difficult if I ever get back home." She slid a look sideways. "I don't suppose you have plans to return me there."

He looked at her almost curiously. "I have no such plans."

The full force of those eyes left her breathless. She looked back at the lower level. "What are your plans, then? What will happen to them?"

"Do you care?"

Startled, she said, "Why wouldn't I? I spent a long time on board with them. They are my crew."

"Who left you to your captain's mercy?"

"We don't know how that might have played out."

"You are overly optimistic."

"It beats being negative."

The Scorpio commander's answer was silence. He gave her a slight nod of his head in farewell and went about his business.

It was a long day. Xera hobbled to the ray shower, listened to her music and occasionally walked around the balcony, holding the rail. The Scorpio seemed to hum with anticipation.

Finally she went to bed. The flyers were out, but they seemed a lot less threatening with a thick sheet of glass between her and them. She had no desire to venture outside to play, though. Once had been enough.

She slept.

Someone shook her arm almost as soon as she fell asleep, it seemed. "What?" she asked groggily.

"The ship is here."

That got her up. Still fuzzy, she let Delfane hand her boots. Scorpio were already moving past her bed, armed and carrying packs. Brirax and Delfane hustled her along with them down the stairs. She could see her crewmates being escorted down the long tunnel. There were a few protests at going outside unarmed.

"What about the flyers?" she asked, feeling anxious herself.

"We won't let you get eaten," Delfane assured her. "The ship is here, and there are more men outside providing cover. The flyers don't have a chance tonight."

They stepped outside into a chill night wind. As promised, there were no flyers in the sky. Maybe they'd been frightened away by the flood of light bathing the nearby rocks and surrounding plain.

The stairs would have been difficult if Delfane and Brirax hadn't helped. Xera let them steady her and hopped as best she could, determined to walk on her own.

They reached the flat top of the rock outcropping and moved to one edge. Her first view of the ship stole her breath. Sinister black and monstrously big, it glowed with blue lights through the many portholes and the bridge. The ramp was down and also lit. Many Scorpio were on the plain, and the air hummed with the sound of the ship's massive engines.

Xera shivered in the cold wind as fear of the unknown hit her. What would happen now?

Ryven Atarus showed up at her side. "Follow me."

The four of them walked up the ramp and into the ship, down a busy hall and took a lift to the bridge.

"Atarus!" a male Scorpio greeted them as they stepped out of the lift. "Trust you to survive a crash on the most hostile planet in the galaxy!" He clapped his friend on the shoulder and then looked at Xera. "What's this? You managed to come out of it with a beautiful woman as well? Am I the only one who crashes with flatulent, snoring men?"

This new Scorpio was tall and broad-shouldered, with brown hair cut very short. One of his ears was pierced with a golden starburst, and there was a hands-free communication set around his ear. He was obviously this ship's counterpart to Ryven.

Ryven smiled. "Shiza. You deserve to crash with only men. This is the translator to the alien ship, Lieutenant Xera Harrisdaughter. She is injured and would like to rest."

"Of course," Shiza said, instantly solicitous. "Is a doctor needed?"

"After a rest. My men will escort her to her room to finish her sleep cycle." Ryven paused and looked at her, as if giving her an opportunity to speak. But what did he expect her to say—thanks for the ride?

He nodded to her and her escort, and then turned to Shiza. "How proceeds the recovery team? Our ship was not too badly damaged. . . ." Xera missed the rest as she was led off.

She was happy to see her room had a real padded bunk, not a steel slab or something equally obnoxious. Rock had been bad enough.

Sufficiently tired that the lack of a porthole didn't distress her, she listened as Brirax gave her a brief rundown on the lavatory and water dispenser. She was surprised that there were even a few supplies left inside for her—a new hairbrush, for one. A glance in the mirror told her she needed it desperately. He left her with a pouch of rations and wishes for a good slumber.

Sleep be hanged, she dove into the ration pack before the door was closed. There were various food bars, a pouch of dried fruit and some kind of sweet dried vegetable that she instantly loved. It sure beat the pants off slug soup.

Maybe it was the endorphins of actually having real food choices again, but she was able to lie down after that and nap.

She woke to the sound of an electronic tone. Wondering what it was, she sat up and looked around, then remembered. Ah, yes. She was hitching a ride on an enemy starship. Lovely.

The tone ceased as soon as she got out of bed and stowed the blanket and pillow. She used the lavatory and the ray shower, wondering idly if it were possible to do both at once. It didn't take long to brush her pageboy, and she smiled, amused to think some women spent hours in the bathroom. They wouldn't last long around here.

A new tone sounded at her door. It was Delfane, and he was there to escort her to breakfast.

They entered a galley full of males, and Xera had to take a breath to steel herself against their curious stares. It helped that the room smelled wonderful enough to make her salivate. Delfane handed her a tray, and then helped himself. She didn't ask what anything was, unwilling to ruin it. Instead, she just dished up a tiny bit of everything.

He grinned at her overflowing plate as he juggled his own. "I don't like slug soup, either." He then found them a quiet table off to the side, and she saw that most of the men were filing out of the room. They must have arrived at a shift change, and she wondered if that was deliberate. She quelled the natural urge to ask what time it was: it hardly mattered on a ship that operated on an artificial clock.

The food was good, for the most part. There was one odd-tasting purple vegetable, but she quickly removed it from her mouth. It was metallic and bitter, and she couldn't imagine anyone willingly eating it.

"Very like my daughter," Delfane said dryly.

She made a face at him. "Will you be seeing her soon? I bet she'll be excited to see you." Her mouth started to tingle and go numb, and she frowned, wondering if it was something she'd eaten, and if so, was it a normal reaction?

"I talked with her and her mother last night," Delfane said with a relaxed, satisfied smile. "We will reach our home planet in two days. I hope I will not have to leave again for a long while."

She nodded politely, not really listening. The numbness had spread to her throat, and she was having trouble breathing.

Delfane looked at her sharply. "Are you well?" It took only a moment of observation to answer his question. He stood up with a spate of rapid-fire speech into his headset and hauled her up by one arm. By that time she was seriously fighting for air.

She was a little fuzzy on what happened next. Maybe he carried her to the med lab. She did notice when she was laid down on a padded table, but spots danced before her eyes, distracting her. There was a sharp poke, and slowly faces above her started to resolve into individuals. Delfane she knew, hovering in the background, but the others above her were strangers. Glad she could breathe, she decided she didn't care and closed her eyes, the better to suck in sweet gulps of oxygen.

"Severe pulmonary distress," she heard someone explaining.

"Yes, we can see she's not breathing—what I want to know is why." That was Ryven Atarus's curt voice.

"Let them do their job, my friend. See? She is breathing better now," came Shiza's voice.

Instead of answering, Ryven began to grill Delfane.

Which was all very interesting, but Xera's back hurt from all the wheezing. She decided it must have been something she ate—maybe that awful purple thing.

"I think it was breakfast," she croaked out in her native tongue. She still wasn't thinking clearly.

"What?" Ryven came to stand over her.

She frowned in concentration and repeated herself in his language. "Yucky purple vegetable. My mouth started to go numb right after I tried it."

"Yucky?" he repeated with a frown.

"She called the slugs that," Delfane put in helpfully.

"What did she eat?" the medic wanted to know. "This could be an allergic reaction. We're still downloading the medical information recovered from the alien ship's wreckage, and it hasn't all been translated. I don't know what else this might be."

Delfane rattled off a list of foreign objects. "The only purple thing we had was yur root."

Yur root. She was never eating it again, she decided with a grimace.

It turned out she *was* allergic to the alien root and one or two other foodstuffs she'd have to take care with. The medics ran a full diagnostic on her, which took quite some time. They even had the audacity to kick Ryven and their captain out at one point, as the pair was getting in the way. Delfane was allowed to guard the door.

The medics also sent a team to test the other humans for allergies, just in case.

On the bright side, the medics had a healing accelerator for her foot, and they promised it would be as good as new in a day or two. They also gave her a special wrist bracelet with a medic alert symbol and patches that would deliver medicine to her bloodstream if her body went into allergic shock again.

Ironically, she was cleared to leave sick bay just in time for lunch.

"I'm not sure I'm hungry," she said warily to Delfane as she walked out of the chamber. She was barely limping, thanks to the healing accelerators, and not looking forward to facing the cafeteria line.

"Don't worry. Lord Atarus has instructed us to join him and the captain for a private meal. Your food will be carefully selected to eliminate potential . . . misfortune."

"Who knew my most dangerous enemy on this trip would be the food?" she muttered in her native language.

Ignoring Delfane's curious glance, she looked around. The hallways here were quieter than they had been when she first entered the ship. There was some kind of nonslip surface like rough rubber underneath her.

"Why is he so interested in me?" she asked after a moment. She didn't really think Ryven's underling would answer, but she wondered. She hadn't been interrogated or sexually importuned, for which she was profusely thankful, but she was also confused. Was she remaining braced for something that would never materialize? "He treats me like a guest. Am I not your enemy? Does he have a family?" she couldn't help adding after a moment. *A wife, for instance?*

"Ask him yourself. We're here," Delfane said without inflection.

An automatic door opened in front of him and Xera, revealing a private cabin. Ryven Atarus was there, as well as Toosun and Captain Shiza. They were all seated at a table but rose when she entered.

Shiza smiled broadly at her. "Ah, the beauty awakens! Are you well again, Lieutenant?"

She inclined her head. "Thank you, I am well."

"We have food here that will not sicken you," Ryven put in. "Join us at the table and we will talk."

The notion of talking made her a little wary, but she smiled pleasantly and sat at the small table anyway. Delfane remained outside the room.

She was much daintier about eating this time. The question still turned over in her mind why the Scorpio were being so nice to her. It began to worry her. To distract herself she looked around the room, which was comfortable but not extravagant, with two couches and two overstuffed chairs that looked like they doubled as storage. They filled the tiny sitting room. The only other furniture was the table at which the group currently sat. The walls were caramel with coffee-colored trim, and red, black and gold accents. She glimpsed a bed through an open door in a room she assumed was Shiza's cabin.

They let her get halfway through her meal in silence before Ryven spoke. "Your room was comfortable?"

"It was, thank you."

"You seem comfortable with Brirax and Delfane."

This time she answered slowly. "They are pleasant enough. I have wondered if they are bodyguards or guards. Perhaps you mean them to be both?"

"Perhaps I do." He considered her. "You have a unique position here, and in your crew. You are the only one who speaks our language, and you are . . . polite. You seem to possess discretion."

She blinked. Discretion demanded that she not reply.

"The other members of your crew, including your captain, will be treated as hostages. We will bargain with them." He looked at her with utter gravity. "Another captain would simply treat you as spoils of war."

She stilled. She might have paled.

Shiza smiled pleasantly at her from his place beside Ryven. If he was the captain involved, she could see what he would do.

Ryven claimed her gaze and spoke again. "I am in a position to offer you more."

More? What did "more" entail? Marriage? A bed

in his harem? Was she brave enough to slit her own throat?

"My people have a custom of selecting their own ambassadors from other races. We have need of one from your race. I will suggest to my father that we give you that position."

Okay, that was a lot to think about. Perhaps relief was premature at this point, but Xera felt it anyway. To be an ambassador sure beat being an after-dinner snack.

"Who is your father?"

"One of the rulers of our people. He governs the second continent of our home planet, Rsik."

Which made Ryven a very important person to have on her side. She thanked God he thought she was sensible. "I see." She debated blathering on about being honored and decided against it, not sure what the etiquette here was. She didn't ask what would happen if his father refused—she didn't want to know and suspected it would be bad. She took a discreet, steadying breath. "How soon until I meet him?"

His gaze moved over her. "We will have a few days to practice first. You have much to learn about our customs."

A rebellious brow quirked up at that. "If I have made mistakes, it was not deliberate."

"Yes," he agreed, which left her feeling uncomfortable. She picked at the rest of her food, too wound up to enjoy it now.

"Should you be accepted as an ambassador, you will be given much respect. Regardless of what happens, it is not our custom to mistreat women."

She didn't dare comment on that. She lacked

information, and he had been kind to her, an enemy of his people.

"You will not be allowed to return home."

The food on her plate got a little misty as her eyes teared up, but she bit the inside of her cheek and mentally kicked her own butt. She'd been prepared for that. It was nothing she didn't expect.

And yet it hurt so much. To never see her family again . . .

"Delfane has an electronic book for you to look at it. It has many things you will want to read about our culture, and further language studies. You may go if you like."

She rose and nodded without meeting anyone's eyes. Feeling oddly stiff, she left the room, hoping her face was as frozen as it felt. She didn't want anyone to guess at her turmoil.

Delfane took one look at her face and looked politely away, but not before she saw a flash of sympathy. So it did show, then.

Xera made it to her room before she broke down and cried.

"I think you nearly broke her by reminding her she'll never go home," Shiza commented. He took a sip of wine.

"I would do her no favors to let her keep illusions," Ryven said grimly. "She will realize she is fortunate in the end."

"Especially since she will not be your 'spoils of war,'" Toosun pointed out. "She seemed particularly horrified by that idea."

Ryven gave him a cold look.

Toosun looked away and scratched the back of

his neck. Casually, he asked, "What will you do with her if Father refuses?"

"You know he won't."

"Very well, he won't. Will you keep first claim to her? Her rank would make her nearly your equal, and she will be sought after."

"Mm," Shiza put in thoughtfully.

Ryven's eyes slid darkly to him. "I haven't decided."

"Give it some thought," Toosun urged. "I might be interested if you're not."

"You don't need another woman," Ryven scoffed. "They follow you like iron filings to a lodestone already."

"As they do you."

"You are too young for a wife."

"I'm two years younger than you. You're thirty-three," Toosun pointed out, as if his brother had forgotten.

"This is a matter for another day," Ryven said irritably. "We have other things to discuss." He steered the conversation to another path, away from the exotic alien woman.

Chapter Six

Xera cried, moped and had a nap. Afterward she felt good enough to sit up and scan the e-book. What she read made her cringe.

She should have been addressing Ryven as "my lord," or "commander" at the very least, though she did not recall ever using his name or title to his face. The next time she saw him she would have to acknowledge his rank. Rank was very important to his people. A man might not be looked down on if he didn't have it, but he'd better acknowledge those who did. Toosun also ranked as a lord.

Their society was governed by twelve lord governors, each of whom ruled an equal portion of their home planet, Rsik. While the title was hereditary, any governor who was found unfit to rule could be cast out, the title passed on their sons. Those who served in lesser positions were elected by the voters in their precinct.

There was a list of some of the Scorpio society's laws, and she saw that their code of conduct basically mirrored her own, but they had very harsh laws for offenders. It was a very bad idea to commit a crime against them—they didn't take it well.

There was some entertainment media in the e-book, and she watched a few shows to get a feel for how men and women interacted. The women were very respectful to the men, but not subservient. There was some humor, but always a line that wasn't crossed. Heroes treated women well, sometimes even tenderly. Villains often ended up dead.

Women were definitely not warriors, and they didn't serve on warships in any capacity. Xera also saw with a wince that they tended to have long, often elaborately coifed hair. That didn't bode well for her—she'd never had long hair and didn't want it. She hoped Ryven didn't plan on giving her extensions to please his father. The robes she saw the women wearing would be challenging enough. They were colorful, feminine and looked somewhat oriental in design. There tended to be a lot of feathered headdresses. On the bright side, many of the long tunics had pants under them, and she could handle that.

She declined Brirax's invitation to escort her to dinner. She just wasn't hungry enough to face a crowd. A little later he brought her a tray and set it silently on the bedside table. She knew he waited just outside the door, probably taking on the nightshift. She wondered if he and Delfane would remain her bodyguards for long, or if she'd be assigned new ones on the planet. Which reminded her: she'd been so busy that she'd forgotten to look up anything about any planets to which they could be going. Of course, they might be heading for a moon or even a space station.

Suddenly she couldn't sit still one more moment. She could study when she had to, but right now she needed to move. It had been days since she could do more than hobble, and she was in the mood to sweat. It would be good for her to work off some of her anxieties, and she could do it better in a bigger space.

She went to the door and opened it. Brirax looked at her, alert.

"Is there somewhere I could go to exercise? I've been inactive for a long while, and it would be nice to do something."

He studied her, then spoke into his headset. He was quiet for a moment, probably listening, then nodded. "Follow me."

They went down two decks and walked what seemed like half a mile through corridors until they reached a large gym. There was a lot of unfamiliar equipment and only a few men using it. Brirax led her to a treadmill and showed her how to turn it on. Xera started out at a brisk walk, careful not to reinjure her foot.

"What time are we docking tomorrow—early or late?" she asked.

"Early," he answered. He still looked unusually alert, as if she might try something desperate.

She couldn't imagine what she could do in a ship full of aliens in the middle of nowhere, so she ignored it. Maybe he had a better imagination than she did. "Are we going to a planet or a moon?"

"A planet."

"What is it called?" she asked, though she already knew. It would get him talking.

"Rsik."

Boy, he's talkative, she thought wryly as her machine inclined. "Is it winter or summer there?"

"It is winter where we are going."

She sighed. She hated winter. "Are they long, the winters?"

"They last three months."

"I guess that's not bad, then." She could handle a little snow. "Do the summers get hot?"

"At times."

"Are women allowed to own property? Do they live alone sometimes?"

He looked at her curiously. "Of course. It is more common for a single woman to live with her parents, though. It is more economical."

"Is it very expensive to own a home or property?"

He considered. "Why would a single woman wish to? It would be very lonely without family."

"For the same reason a single man would live alone," she said somewhat tersely. "Sometimes family drives you crazy."

He didn't look convinced. "Many single men live with their parents. A household might contain three generations. Often the houses are just built onto as the family grows."

She frowned. "Is land scarce, then?"

"That's simply how it's done."

She saved her breath for a couple of miles, then finally slowed the treadmill to a slow walk as her foot twinged. She was getting sweaty, so she reached for the top button of her uniform jacket, preparing to remove it.

"Don't do that here," Brirax snapped, with a quick look around.

She frowned at him. "I'm hot."

"It's not seemly," he said sternly. "Women do not remove clothing in public."

"I have other layers underneath."

"You will not do it."

She frowned, knowing she'd have to figure this culture out quick. It was good that she'd encountered this now, though this prudish attitude rankled. On the bright side, Brirax was treating her like a woman of his culture, and that might be a sign of acceptance.

"Let me see if I understand. If I had left my room in my short-sleeved shirt, would that have been okay?"

"Yes."

"So it's the undressing, not the showing of skin that's the problem."

"You should not show too much skin. It's . . . not good." He looked uncomfortable with the subject.

She sighed, prepared to sweat. "Can I roll up my sleeves, then?"

He hesitated. "That might be permitted." He still looked away as she did it, though. That didn't bode too well for bikini season. "I'm guessing men and women don't swim together, then? What with skin being an issue and all." She studied the workout area and headed for an empty space at the side of the room.

"Swimming is different."

"I see." She dropped and counted out thirty push-ups in her head, then rolled over and did v-splits. She alternated push-ups with other exercises until she'd done one hundred of them. Her foot was throbbing by the time she was done, just enough to make her quit. No sense pushing it.

Brirax looked faintly impressed. "I watched when you attacked your captain. You trained for war, then? Our women do not."

"Don't you allow them to defend themselves?" She didn't want to answer any questions about her own martial training—she never knew when his ignorance might be to her advantage, because while she liked him, he was still her keeper.

"Most have men to protect them."

"There is not always a man around to do that. Sometimes, a man may not think it's necessary to protect a woman from another man." Ryven, for instance. She had a feeling he could do quite a lot and get away with it.

Brirax was silent, and she suddenly felt tired. "I'm done. Let's go back."

Lord Ryven himself came to fetch her in the morning. She was told they had landed at their destination.

"Good morning, Lieutenant Harris-d," he said in her language.

"Lord Ryven," she greeted him, noting the use of her rank, and the way his eyes warmed when she used his own title. It seemed they had both been studying, for she had never taught him a morning salutation. The Scorpio never used time references in their greetings.

"We have landed on Rsik. It is cold out this morning. You will want to put this on." He handed her a coat.

She studied the dull gray material. It was at least two sizes too big, and she wondered from whom he'd borrowed it. Was it his? She noticed he wasn't wearing one. "Am I supposed to go to my room to put this on, or is putting on clothes different from taking them off?"

He actually grinned. "You may do whichever you like in my presence, but no one objects when a woman protects herself from the cold."

Was he flirting? Confused, she shot him a suspicious look, but she couldn't tell. Alien humor was hard to fathom. She put on the jacket and wrapped it closed over her middle to accommodate some of the extra fabric. The sleeves swamped her hands, but she didn't push them back, knowing it would protect them from the chill.

He sized her up, amusement still lurking in his manner. "Come. Let us have you out and done with the cold before the coat swallows you. We have transportation waiting to take us to my father."

She wondered at his good mood. Was he just happy to be home, back with his people and safe?

Captain Shiza and Toosun appeared, as well as a handful of others. She kept her eyes open as they walked, never knowing when observations might serve her later. There wasn't much to see along the route other than long hallways and a lift. In no time they were at the ramp. A blast of cold air from outside made her shiver.

Xera walked down the ramp and then froze in surprise. It was snowing, with banks surrounding the landing area and gently mounded on rooftops. That wasn't the surprise, though. The snow was pale lavender.

Ryven had stopped by her side. "What is it?"

"The snow is purple!" she blurted, unfamiliar with the word for the precipitation's exact hue.

He exhaled in amusement and gave her a slight nudge in her back. "Take a closer look." There were ranks of soldiers on each side, but it was hard for Xera to care about that when she was busy looking at snow swirling around her feet. She held out a hand and caught a few flakes on her coat, but they quickly melted into nothing. "Weird," she said under her breath. Weird but wonderful. She wondered if the snow stained things when it melted. Maybe that's why these people wore so much gray.

Then again, she was on a military base—or assumed she was. There were no civilians to be seen on the tarmac, only buildings like fat silos with decks and mushroom roofs. A transport was waiting for her party at the tarmac edge, and she stooped to grab a handful of snow before she climbed in. As it melted in her hand, a lavender cloud of gas was released.

"I give you a coat to ward off the chill and you choose to bring the chill with you," Ryven remarked, but he sounded amused.

A glance at him confirmed it. "It melts clear! What is this cloud that comes from it? It's not contaminated, is it?" She dropped the snow to the floor in sudden consternation.

He laughed. "It won't hurt you. The gas is a natural part of our planet and often colors our snow."

"No, it won't hurt you—unless you get lost in it," Toosun added, after he finished chuckling. "Or it gets under your collar when thrown at you." He and Shiza grinned at each other, probably recalling childhood exploits. It was odd to think of these soldiers as carefree youths.

"Is it always this color?" Xera asked. A glance out the window of the transport showed loads of freshly fallen snow, with more continuing to fall, making the world a lavender blur.

"Sometimes it's pale blue or even white," Ryven said. "I have seen it pink once or twice."

Pink snow. Xera shook her head and stared out the window.

It was only another moment before they pulled to a stop. They got out at the entrance to a steel and glass building. She didn't get a good look at the busy city around them before she was ushered inside.

A delegation was waiting for them in the lobby. A man of middle years and middle height bowed to their group.

"Kenji," Ryven acknowledged him. "How is my father?"

"My lords. Lord Governor Atarus is eager to see you. He bids you to come to him directly. He has refreshments waiting."

Ryven nodded. They all walked to the side of the room and rode an elevator to the top floor. As they stepped out, he told Kenji, "Toosun and Shiza will go with you. I will be there shortly."

"Of course, my lord."

While the rest of them headed for the set of golden doors directly in front of the elevator, Ryven took Xera two doors down. Three women waited for them inside. He nodded to them, then looked at Xera. "This is your aide and two of her assistants. They will help you to make a favorable impression on my father. Listen well and do whatever they tell you. You have one hour."

Xera watched the door close behind him, then turned and looked at the females. Awkward. Guessing she was supposed to be the senior member of the group, she said warily, "Hello."

A graceful young woman in a burnt orange robe stepped forward. "My name is Namae. We have little time. If you would come with me?"

Since she had no desire to upset the lord governor and blow her chances to be something other than "spoils of war," Xera nodded and followed along. Though she had recently showered, she took a bath to "get the smell of space off her." Namae had a toiletries kit and gave Xera a crash course, then dressed Xera's hair, murmuring about its lack of length as Xera sat wrapped in a sheet of fabric. "Still, it is thick and wavy. It will grow," she said consolingly. The aides were dismayed by the condition of her hands and nails, and murmured over her poor feet as they gave her the world's quickest pedicure. Xera wasn't sure what they'd been told about her, but the women exuded sympathy. Maybe they thought she'd had a rough life.

Whatever the case, Namae was full of helpful tips about how to handle the governor. "Allow him to speak first, of course. He appreciates feminine grace and beauty like any man, so that will help you. You are handsome in an exotic way. Lord Ryven also said you were to look to him if you were unsure. He intends to guide you." A current of excitement went through the ladies as she said that.

Xera wondered what was afoot. She decided to play the sympathy card. "I know little about your culture, and I admit to being nervous about Lord Ryven. He won't . . . hurt me, will he?"

Namae looked horrified. "Of course not! Lord Ryven is known as a champion of women. He is adored! You will be safe with him." She blushed. "Well, as safe as you wish to be."

"He's a womanizer, then?" Xera made sure to sound tentative, unsure. She didn't want to offend these ladies.

"It is more often the women that pursue him," Namae offered. "He is very handsome, and rich, of course. He is known for his bravery in war. Not only is he a lord, but a commander of a starship as well. Who wouldn't want him?"

Xera added "spoiled" to the list of things she knew about Ryven. Clever, ruthless, a killer, a womanizer. The adjectives concerned her.

"We have clothes waiting for you," Namae said as she completed applying Xera's makeup. "The ship's medics sent your measurements here after they completed their scans. I have never chosen colors for such fair skin and unusual eyes, but it was an enjoyable exercise. Everything should be the right size and the colors flattering, but we will know better when you try things on. Let's attempt this one first."

She moved to a rolling clothes rack filled with garments in dark pumpkin, russet, emerald, white with sky blue, indigo and pink. Xera seriously doubted she'd look good in anything on that rack. She hadn't worn pink since she was an infant, surely, and had unilaterally rejected it since adulthood.

Namae held several garments up to Xera's face and murmured to herself. She finally chose a sapphire blue tunic with slit sides and sleeves. It had a silky, sky blue pajamas-type garment that went underneath and gently swirled around Xera's legs and torso. After months of wearing a serviceable uniform, the clothes felt indecently silky and light. There was a wide gold sash for the waist and a wide collar made of brilliant blue, gold, green and red beads, bracelets and rings. Even Xera's slippers glittered with beads.

"Where did all this jewelry come from?" she asked, bewildered. "This seems extravagant."

"We want the lord governor to see you as we wish you to be," Namae said as she fixed a headdress with long trailing beads in Xera's hair. "Never underestimate the power of dazzling beauty."

Xera was allowed her first look in the full-length mirror. She gasped, hardly recognizing the image. She looked exotic, frighteningly feminine with her waist cinched with the sash and her irritatingly large breasts tamed by the wrapped top. Why hadn't she tried harder to find clothes that made her look this good before? Maybe she'd told herself that she was too busy, or maybe she didn't have Namae's talent. "You're good," she said frankly.

Namae smiled. "Our hour is up. There will be an escort to Lord Ryven now."

Xera wasn't surprised to see Brirax outside the door, but she didn't recognize the other three men. Brirax didn't say anything, but his eyes made a quick scan of her as he bowed slightly. "Come this way, Lieutenant Harrisdaughter."

She didn't feel like a lieutenant as she moved along in her slippers, trying to relax. The silky underclothes were terribly distracting on her bare skin. She prayed that didn't show.

The golden door opened. Xera walked as gracefully as she could through a foyer and into an inviting living room. Three of the four men inside rose to their feet as she entered. She couldn't tell from Ryven's eyes what he thought of her transformation, but he moved forward and took her hand in a proprietary manner. "Dangerous woman," he murmured. "Come, meet my father."

Chapter Seven

The rough timbre of his voice made Xera shiver. His slow, deliberate movements, as if he were savoring the moment, didn't help. Ryven led her before the older man sitting on the throne. Frankly, the man looked old enough to be his grandfather and must have sired him at a late age. He had a surprising amount of white hair neatly tamed on his head, and a thin, delicately groomed Fu Manchu that trailed down past his chin. He looked somewhat like a tanned catfish with fiery eyes.

His robes were simple brown, with a black-belted waist and a cream-colored undertunic. The room was decorated with similar, Zen-like simplicity. The floors were tiled in tan stone with a black mosaic, and pillows for sitting lined the room. The chamber featured light filtering through the rough-hewn beams, giving it a tranquil look.

Those keen old eyes, so like Ryven's, studied Xera. "If this is a sample of the women that serve on human battleships, I think we will be more careful about taking our prizes. You are a beautiful woman, Lieutenant Xera Harrisdaughter."

She lowered her face as heat fired her cheeks, unable to help herself. She wasn't used to compliments or such frank appreciation. "Thank you, Lord Governor."

"Hm. Sit. Refresh yourself." The Lord Governor Atarus looked at Ryven. "I think you have not told me the half of your adventures, my son. You mentioned her spirit, but not those magnificent blue eyes." He looked back at Xera. "I am told that your captain attacked you, that you broke his knee. Why did you allow him to live?"

Caught off guard, she had to think about that. "Our laws . . . if we had been rescued by a ship of our own and I had killed him, I might have been found guilty of murder. It would have been my word against the rest of the crew's."

Those eyes bored into her. "But you were not found by a ship of yours."

"No . . . Lord Governor." She was beginning to see this man for the canny old warrior he was. She'd have to be careful and guard her tongue or he'd trip her.

"You hesitate when using my title."

She frowned thoughtfully. "I have to remind myself to not simply call you 'sir.' We do not have lord governors where I am from. Also, I feel I am pronouncing the words badly and am trying to do a better job." There *were* some awkward syllables in there.

"Is that how you would address the ruler of your country? As 'sir'?"

"Yes . . . Lord Governor."

He relaxed into his chair. "You may call me 'sir.'"

She also relaxed, relieved to have gotten so far without mortally offending him.

"Drink," Ryven said, and handed her a chilled glass. "He has not eaten you yet, and I suspect he will not."

"Thank you, my lord," she said rather gratefully. She couldn't detect any spirits in the drink, but decided to go slowly, just in case. She didn't need to make a drunken fool of herself, especially now.

The talk turned to lighter things. She let the men speak and merely observed, trying to learn more about them. That worked for perhaps five minutes.

"I have never known a woman to be silent unless she is frightened or angry," Lord Atarus observed. "Which are you, Lieutenant?"

She blinked. "I am observing, sir. There is more to being a translator than speaking the language."

"Is this your passion, then, or your job?"

She hadn't thought about it in a long time. How did she feel about it? "Flying was my first love. I joined the Galactic Explorers to be a pilot, but was assigned to language services instead. I hated it at first, but now . . . I like knowing what those around me are saying. It has been a useful tool." And yeah, she did feel a little smug now and then knowing that she heard things her captain didn't understand. She'd had an essential role to play, and it had felt good.

"I didn't know you were a pilot," Ryven murmured. "What can you fly?"

She shrugged. "Small craft, officially, though I've spent many hours in a simulator." Flying fighters and large craft, but she wouldn't add that unless he asked.

He didn't have a chance, for his father had more questions. "Why did you learn our language? Surely you had many to choose from."

True. At the time there had been many more practical choices. "It was exotic, I suppose. I liked the way it sounded, the . . ." She couldn't think of the word. "It is beautiful to hear." Although she'd heard it shouted, growled and clipped in the last week, she still thought it was one of the most lyrical languages she'd heard. It was almost impossible to make ugly.

The old man looked pleased. "Do you have many suitors on your home world?"

He liked to hop around subjects like a grasshopper around stones. Xera replied, "Er, no. I haven't been home in a long while."

"Elsewhere?" he persisted.

She stared at him. "I've been very busy, sir." What with getting shipwrecked and all. She just hoped he wasn't asking for his own benefit. Too late, she thought about inventing a man, but doubted it would be useful here. Long-distance relationships were not going to help. Judging by the incredulous or scoffing looks around her, business should have been no impediment to her love life.

"It seems your captain was five times a fool," Shiza said candidly. "Had you been on my ship—"

"You may have been the one with the broken knee," she interrupted in warning. Shiza held her eyes, for she had been very rude in so speaking. She didn't back down, though. She couldn't hear what he may have been about to suggest without fighting adrenaline.

Ryven touched her shoulder, lightly. She stiffened as she met his gaze, but slowly the tension eased in her, almost as if he drained it.

"You will not be harmed," he said quietly. "You do not need to defend yourself from Shiza." He looked at his friend, who relaxed back in his chair. His expression was still arrogant, but the man dropped the subject.

Lord Atarus looked pleased. About what, she couldn't guess, so Xera let her eyes fall on her drink. It made a useful distraction. She'd always had a hot temper, but few things sparked the full fury of it. No matter how tame they liked the women here, she just couldn't hold her tongue over things like that without a beating. He should know better than to talk about women like that. She really didn't like him.

"I have appointments this afternoon. It would be best, Ryven, if you would settle your lieutenant at the palace. We will speak again later."

"She is hot tempered."

"When threatened, yes."

"Beautiful enough to keep a man home."

Ryven waited.

"I will consider your request." His father waited a moment, than added as if prompting him, "I am pleased." He seemed slightly anxious, as if afraid his son would not do the thing he was hinting at, would not fulfill the wish the father had held for years now.

Ryven just smiled. "As am I, father. I will see you again soon." Their transport was waiting to take them to the palace, and he had already sent Xera and her escort down.

Toosun smirked at him as soon as they were out of their father's hearing. "It's cruel of you to taunt him."

"It builds character," Ryven said blithely.

"You are going to do it, then?" Toosun asked too casually. Curiosity must have been burning him from the inside out.

"Perhaps."

Toosun punched his arm playfully hard. "You may be the elder, but I can still beat it out of you."

Ryven smirked. "Do not distract me, younger. I have important plans to make."

Toosun just growled.

When she had been told she was going to the palace, Xera envisioned a European castle or even something Arabic. She had not anticipated the mass of dark crystals thrusting themselves toward the sky like a black starburst. On approach it appeared windowless, bleak and without entrance. Monstrously huge, it towered for more than seventy stories and had to be a mile in diameter. It looked as if it had burst from the living rock.

She drew a sharp breath in amazement. She'd never heard of anything like it. How did people live here?

Their transport came in fast, revealing a series of unconnected crystal spikes before it slowed and rounded a last spire. A seemingly natural crevasse between crystals opened into an entrance that loomed larger the closer they got. It swallowed

their craft into a tunnel lined with lights, like the
glowing spots of some enormous underwater sea
monster. Instead of into a dark stomach, however,
the transport emerged into a sunlit shuttle bay.
Xera couldn't see the sky and it had been overcast
outside, so it wasn't immediately apparent how the
area could be so well lit. She could easily see that
the central shaft rose all the way to the ceiling, and
as their craft rose up the different levels she could
see shuttle bays on each.

They were only a few levels from the top when
their driver slowed and pulled into one of the
bays. Perhaps she looked as dazzled as she felt, for
Ryven looked at her and said in amusement, "Are
you all right?"

She blinked and reminded herself not to gush.
Now was not a good time to look overwhelmed.
"I . . . I'm fine. This is some place you've got here."

He smiled. "There is more to come."

She could hardly imagine. Ryven and Toosun
got out, and she slid out after them, allowing
Ryven to take her hand and help her. She barely
noticed that he didn't return her hand, that he
tucked it into the crook of his arm instead. There
were other transports parked there and people
came and went from them, but not many. It was by
no means crowded.

Ryven led her to the exit. A glance back showed
her aide and attendants supervising the unloading
of Xera's new things from the other transport.
The hallways ahead were wide enough to let three
people pass comfortably side by side, and decorated with Venetian splendor. The whole was filled
with sunlight.

"This can't be true sunlight, can it?" she asked Ryven. "We're inside a huge black crystal! It must be your technology that does this, but I wouldn't know where I was if I hadn't kept my eyes open."

His eyes gleamed with pleasure. "We are on the lord's level. You'll have a suite of your own for now. It should not take more than a day or two to have a decision made about your position. Meanwhile, I have time. I'll show you around the palace after you've seen your room." He stopped before a door and opened it. The first thing she noticed was the spaciousness; the second, the curving wall of windows looking out over a winter garden. As she got closer, she saw that the view was of ground level, an impossibility considering how high up they were.

"It's a hologram," she said, somewhat disappointed. Very pretty, but no more real than a picture.

He smiled and opened a balcony door. He reached out, scooped up a small handful of lavender snow and slipped it neatly down her shirt.

Xera shrieked. Most of the melting lump slipped down her back, but some slid between her breasts and down her belly, then lodged against her sash, and she couldn't get it off.

Ryven glanced up at the attendants who poked their heads from her bedroom and they quickly disappeared. "Allow me," he offered, and slid his hand into the back of her shirt to whisk away the offending snow. He didn't fumble around while he was there, but then he didn't have to. The feel of his hand sliding against her skin was enough to make her stiffen with shock.

He tossed the remains of the snow outside. "As you can see, it is a real garden, helped along by a little technology. It is over one hundred years old."

Her brains were scrambled. She felt alarmed, but didn't have time to analyze the source of it, if there was only one. The moment called for a reply, but the only safe one she could think of was a complaint. "My shirt is wet."

"You may change it if you like. I think they're finished putting away your wardrobe." He didn't look the least bit apologetic.

Well, why would he? she thought as she stalked to the bedroom. He was a man, and men liked putting their hands down women's shirts, even if he'd been rather circumspect about it. She didn't care for the knowledge that he'd enjoyed it, though. She didn't want to look at him in that light, didn't want him to view her in a sexual sense. She wasn't going to play with him. She was a "guest" here for who knew how long, maybe even the rest of her life. That's what they'd said.

The thought made her flinch. It didn't help when her attendants looked at her with wide, questioning eyes.

"I need a new shirt," she said stiffly. "Lord Ryven got snow on mine."

Namae looked at her carefully. "You sounded frightened, mistress."

Xera frowned. "I was . . . surprised. I didn't expect him to be playful."

The others relaxed. Namae helped undo the stubborn sash and chose a cream and blue tunic to replace the damp one. At a quiet word from her, the others left. Namae solemnly looked into Xera's eyes.

"Yes?"

Namae looked down thoughtfully. "You have had a very strange meeting with our men, have you not? You met them as an enemy."

Xera wondered where this was going. "Yes," she said warily.

"Have they hurt you?"

Surprised, Xera blinked. Honesty forced her to admit, "No. They have even protected me at times." And they had saved her life, and tried to secure a high position for her. It made her question some of the tension she was feeling now.

Namae nodded. "I think you could be safe with Lord Ryven, if you allowed it." She bowed without waiting for an answer and hurried away.

Xera stared at the carpet for a moment then nodded her head. Namae might not be older, but she seemed kind and sensible. It really was better to go on without fear.

Ryven took her to the public pools and showed her the place where families swam, and the separate pools for single men and women who were of age. She was frankly baffled why it was okay for unmarried sexes to bathe together when the Scorpio were so strict in other respects. How was it okay for them to be naked together when it wasn't permitted to remove a jacket in a man's presence? It was going to take time to figure out. Meanwhile, she could not see herself swimming in public anytime soon.

They toured the grand public library with its glossy crystal shelves full of books and media, and he explained as they walked the halls and took the occasional lift that there were recreation areas, sports arenas and shopping malls, and where they were located on the various levels. They had theaters and art museums and many more amusements when she had the time. The only place she and Ryven lingered was the large summer garden located in the heart of the Lord's level.

It was a place of incredible beauty. Intellectually, Xera knew that part of the sky and plants were holograms designed to fool the senses, but the sky still seemed to stretch forever. The illusion was even more convincing because so many of the aromatic flowers and herbs were real, the light so changing, chased by the occasional cloud shadow. Vegetables were interspersed with flowers and grown closely together in beds bordered by low hedges or stone walls. Everywhere she looked there was beauty, and she felt as if she'd been transported to some rich country estate.

"This is amazing! How far does the garden really reach? It looks as if you could walk here for days and never see it all."

"You could. It's as big as it looks."

"But how could it be so huge? How did your people build this place, this palace? It looks impossible from the outside, and even more so from here."

"Perhaps we are not the savages you think." His words broke the music of the moment, as if a song were cut off midword.

Xera looked at him. Was this a test? Impossible to know from his impassive face. "I've never thought you were savages."

"Never?"

She thought about it, gave honest consideration to anything she might have seen him do. As she did, a memory stirred. "You killed Genson."

"I saw your face when you looked at his body. You made a special effort to return him to your people."

"It was a life wasted. He was a decent man." And yet it seemed so long ago now, with too many experiences layered over it to find the original emotion.

"Was he a friend?"

She struggled with the feelings his questions brought up. "He was a comrade, a crew member. We weren't close, but he had family." Family that would be grieving him, and she felt for their loss. Her own family would grieve, too. She was never going home.

He nodded, his eyes steady on her. "Our cultures are very different at times. You will not believe what I was trained to find just, and I don't always understand you. I think you are honest at heart, though. That is rare."

She considered the times he'd protected her, given what he had for her comfort. "You're not completely repulsive, either," she agreed reluctantly. She even smiled a little at the joke.

He smiled, too, but there was something else in his expression as well. "Do I repulse you?" he asked softly.

There it was again, that tension. She tried to be careful with her words. "I'm not comfortable with this subject. Our people are at odds."

"I was speaking of us."

It was hard to look at him. "I don't want to have a relationship with you."

He looked thoughtful rather than offended. "It's like a council for peace talks, isn't it? Neither side wants to give away their concessions too early. The pace is slow and drags on for days. Sometimes a man can go mad from the tension."

She glanced up, surprised at his admission.

He stepped forward. "I've never had much patience for delays, so I'll see if we have one goal in common right now." He took her in his arms and kissed her.

Xera stiffened. His kiss dispensed with the formalities and cut right to the heart of the matter. There was no power struggle, only acceptance or denial.

Her body chose acceptance: without her mind's input, it softened for him, opened and received. She'd moaned her need into his mouth before she'd even had a chance to alert her defenses.

And then it was over. Meeting adjourned.

His eyes burned into her as his chest rose and fell against hers. "That was all I needed to know."

They didn't say anything else. She was too shaken and he was too aroused. Together they left the garden, two adversaries who had met their match.

Chapter Eight

Xera spent much of the afternoon in turmoil. She hadn't wanted Ryven to kiss her. She was afraid of what would happen now.

He hadn't given her any hints when he'd taken her back to her apartment and left her there, and he hadn't tried to touch her. Whatever his plans were, they didn't involve leaping on her the instant they were near a bed.

She hated that she'd responded to his kiss. Was she so desperately lonely that she'd give in to the first man who touched her? Would she have been the same if Toosun had done it, or Captain Khan?

Okay, she thought with a return of sanity, she definitely wouldn't have encouraged Khan. She had no good answer for Toosun, partly because she had the feeling that she wasn't going to have any choice even if he had been the one to pick her. Whatever was going to happen with Ryven was going to be his will. She wasn't going to be consulted.

The horrible thing was, she wanted what he wanted to do with her, but she never would have chosen him. She didn't know him enough to trust that he wouldn't hurt her. And what about her heart? She'd die of shame if he tried to make her his mistress. She'd been raised in a very conservative society and hadn't shaken the moral convictions she'd been taught. She couldn't sleep with a man who wasn't her husband.

But she couldn't marry him! She was already courting disaster for having attacked her captain. If he were traded back in negotiations, his story of events would get out. If she became married to Ryven she'd definitely be branded a traitor. She didn't want her sisters to believe that of her.

Namae rescued Xera from her agonizing self-absorption that afternoon with another intense grooming session. This one included a massage, some painless and permanent hair removal, a facial and more hand and foot therapy. It was a marvelous distraction and ate up what might have been a horrendous wait.

She started to get a clue that Namae knew more about her schedule than she did when the young woman pulled out an apple green gown of heavy, embroidered silk and said it would be perfect to wear to dinner with the lord governor.

"Dinner?" Xera asked uncertainly. "We just had lunch."

Namae smiled. "It is an honor, and an excellent sign. It's good that he likes you."

Xera supposed it was better than being stored in the dungeon, but she still worried. "Are married couples here *monogamous*?" She didn't know the Scorpio word for monogamous and used her own.

Namae frowned over the unfamiliar word.

Annoyed at herself, Xera tried again. "On my world, married couples are faithful to each other. They don't share themselves with anyone else."

A startling pallor iced Namae's cheeks. She wouldn't meet Xera's eyes. "It is that way here also, mistress," she said quietly.

Concerned, Xera got to her feet and put a supporting arm around the servant. "What is it? Are you ill? Here, sit down." She sat the reluctant woman down in her vacated chair.

"I . . . I shouldn't be here. I should go," Namae protested. "You are right—I have no business being in a respectable home."

"What are you talking about?" Xera demanded. "There's nothing wrong with you. At least, nothing a shot of brandy won't fix." She looked around, mentally cursing the lack of liquor. She hadn't landed on a dry planet, had she? She'd grown up in a bar that served the best liquor on her planet. To suddenly come against a problem that clearly called for whiskey and be dry . . . her sisters would be horrified.

Come to think of it, she could use a drink herself. Maybe she'd have a request of old Ryven after all.

Namae was sobbing now, her face in her hands. Desperate to help, Xera took charge the only way she knew how. She said briskly, "All right, that's enough! Sit up here and let's talk about this. Obviously you've kept it bottled up long enough."

Namae obediently sat up. "I'm sorry. It's just that I feel so ashamed." Tears threatened again.

"Just *talk* about it," Xera urged her. "Tears might make me dissolve into a clone of my sister, and trust me, you don't want to see that." Not that there was anything wrong with her sibling's calm, take-charge attitude, but Xera had spent years trying to be different from her older sister. The thought of becoming her was truly abhorrent, like becoming a copy of one's mother.

Namae laughed at Xera's desperation, then sobered. "I was involved in adultery," she explained.

"You, Namae? I just can't picture that," Xera said, looking over the elegant young lady. "I can see how seriously you take your duties. I can't imagine you'd be any different in a marriage."

Namae gave a watery sigh. "It was not by choice. My brother-in-law forced himself on me when my husband was away. He came home as his brother Myg was finishing. I . . ." Namae looked close to weeping again. "Tovark would not believe me."

Xera was outraged. "What! Was he stupid? They were lucky you didn't kill them both."

A sound that was half laugh, half sob broke from her. "I am not a warrior like you, and I was hurt. My heart . . . it *broke*. Myg said I had seduced him and my husband believed him. He spit on me and walked away."

Xera could only shake her head. "What about your family?"

"I went to them for help," Namae said, valiantly calming herself. "My father and brothers were outraged, and my mother and sisters held me. My brother took the matter to the judges, who ruled against my brother-in-law. He was sentenced to death. My husband was disgusted with me over the death of his brother and still believed me to be a liar. The courts granted him a divorce. My brothers cheered, and my father agreed it was for the best, but—oh! The shame of it! To be a divorced woman is almost unbearable. I have no more honor. I am treated as so lowly, so—"

"Nonsense!" Xera cried, unable to stand the woman belittling herself. "You were attacked! You were wronged! This is not your fault."

"It doesn't matter," Namae said in a choked voice. "You do not understand my world."

Xera stood up and gestured as she spoke. "I understand what honor is! I understand that your family is behind you, and that's what matters. Better yet, *you* get behind you, Namae! You're somebody special, somebody important. You deserve to walk down the street with your head high, and damn anyone who looks down on you."

"That's what we've been telling her," a voice spoke into the pause.

Xera whipped her head up. Ryven stood in the doorway, and in a flash, she understood. "You're her brother."

"Yes."

Confused, she looked at Namae. "Then why . . . ?"

"It's time to go," Ryven said quietly. "I like your hair down. The braids look nice." Namae had braided strings of milky crystals into the short hair, making it glow.

She'd also slipped away while Xera wasn't looking. Ryven answered her questioning look by gesturing her to come to him. When she was close enough, he took her arm and murmured softly, "She does not wish to be a part of the family yet."

Dismayed, Xera looked in question at him.

"We tried to force her at one time, but she only

withdrew more deeply. She has gotten better with time. I am hopeful she will take her proper place again soon."

"How long has it been?" Xera asked softly as they left the room. The world didn't need to know their conversation.

A muscle in his jaw tightened. "Two years."

"Did you beat up her husband?" Xera asked, feeling bloodthirsty. Poor Namae!

He looked straight ahead. "Something like that." She looked at him long enough that he finally answered. "We broke him financially, gelded him socially. He will not be taking another gentle girl to wife."

Hm. Not as grisly as she'd envisioned, but poetic. "It might've been nice to have brothers."

He smiled at her. "You would keep a brother busy. Who is in your family?"

"Sisters." She didn't want to talk about them right now, though. "Are things really as bad as Namae says? Could she remarry?"

He frowned thoughtfully. "Could she? Yes. Would her situation be forgotten if she did? Yes. It would take a special man to woo her, though. I think she protects her heart by hiding away. There are many who would have her, but she will not see it. Also, there are few our family would countenance. Many would marry her for the prestige of the social connection. After the last time, Namae will look to us for guidance before she chooses a man."

"You didn't like the first one?"

"Despised him. She was youngest, though, and spoiled. She would not hear no." He was quiet for a moment. "She has matured much since then."

Hoping to change the sad subject, Xera said, "She mentioned a mother and sisters."

"Our mother died of an illness some months after Namae's divorce. We have three sisters, all younger than me."

"Big family," she said, impressed. "Toosun's younger than you, too. I hope they plagued you as children."

His look was reproving, but a glint of humor sparked those brimstone eyes. "Your hopes were fulfilled, but sadly, you will not be meeting my sisters tonight. My aunt has come, though. You will judge if she is torment enough."

His words made her expect a dragon, and the woman Ryven introduced her to was formidable. The Lady Tessla was a silver-haired dowager with an upright carriage and a timelessly beautiful face. Her teal and silver robes were immaculate and draped a slender figure. Though obviously in her fifties (more noticeable by bearing than any age in her skin), she moved like a dancer, every move unconsciously graceful. She was gracious, though, and quickly put Xera at ease.

They were seated across a low table with cushions for chairs. Gauzy fabrics draped the ceilings, lending colorful shadows to the inlaid stucco walls. Little globe oil lamps in swirling, colored glass lent atmosphere to the party of four. Xera was a little surprised to see Lord Atarus reclined on a cushion. She hadn't expected it of him, nor the informal atmosphere.

"You are very beautiful to have been unmarried for so long," Tessla observed. "Is it common to remain unwed so late in life on your planet?"

Xera blinked. It wasn't often she was called attractive, let alone beautiful, but the lady also implied she was a delicacy that had been held in the oven too long. It threw her. "It can be. Even if I were considered more than average on my world, I'd still have chosen to explore a career. I wasn't happy in the family business."

"How did your mother and father feel about letting you go?" Tessla asked curiously.

"My parents are dead. My eldest sister resisted my leaving for a long time, but we had a rule about dreams. She let me go to pursue mine."

Tessla raised a brow. "Hm. Would she be happy to see you here now?"

Xera considered that. "She'd have some words for me. Ever since my middle sister ran off and got married without her permission, she's been a bit touchy about being out of the loop—not informed," she explained. "She made me promise not to . . ." She trailed off, unwilling to complete the thought. Her smile died.

"What did you promise?" Tessla prompted gently.

Eyes still on the memory of her sister, Xera said softly, "I swore I wouldn't get married without telling her."

There was silence at the table. Xera took a deep drink of her beverage. Turned out they did have booze here after all.

"Well, then. You must keep your promise."

Uncomprehending, Xera looked up. "What?"

The aunt looked at Ryven and his father. "She must keep her promise. She has given her word."

Lord Atarus frowned and opened his mouth.

"I agree."

Xera looked at Ryven in shock. His eyes were on his father. "It's possible. She doesn't have to meet in person. A video conference would suffice." He looked calmly at Xera. "It is knowledge she needs, yes? You don't require permission."

"N-no," she stuttered, shocked by this turn of events. She never expected to be allowed to keep her word. That they would go to this length to allow her to do so . . . she was going to owe them. Big time. But . . . "I hadn't planned to marry for some years yet." It was the closest she could come to a protest. By law and custom, she was still a war prize. Though she'd been treated very well, she still knew that Ryven considered her life his to do with as he pleased. It was obvious that his father and aunt were of the same mind. Pitching a fit over it would only demean her in their eyes. She was being *honored,* she thought with inner rebellion. She must *behave.*

Her words were ignored.

"Very well," Lord Atarus said at length, as if she'd never spoken. He looked rather grumpily at his son. "It will delay events, though.We do not have a communication relay set up that can bounce a message that far. One will have to be set up. It will take time. There is also the issue of security—pin beams are not the most secure of media. Something will have to be done about that."

"Yes," Ryven said calmly. "I will bear the expense. It will be my bride gift."

His father sighed. "It will be arranged, then."

Xera stared at them until she remembered herself. "Thank you." The lord governor nodded regally, and then returned to his dinner with an air of resignation. Ryven merely inclined his head.

Xera couldn't eat, so she sipped her drink instead. Turmoil whipped her heart into a storm. She thought she'd never see her sisters again, never speak to them. The chance to tell them she was alive, was okay, was a golden gift. She didn't ask for more, didn't even hope. She understood these people more every day, knew what a concession she'd been given. Even aside from the distances involved, there was the political hostility.

She didn't want to think too deeply on it, but she knew their plans for her. They wouldn't let her go. What she didn't understand was why. Why her? Ryven was the son of a powerful family, and quite a force in his own right. Surely he could have any one of dozens of women.

She glanced up as the lord governor's words caught her ear.

"Your brother has made my heart glad. This promotion he's earned is just the thing."

Ryven grinned. "I see how you are. If your sons make commander you think you will see marriage in their near future."

His father looked pleased with himself. "My theory would seem to have merit. Once you stop thinking of your careers, other needs hold your attention." He glanced at Xera, transparently pleased. "He leaves on his first mission shortly. Make no mistake; his mind will turn to a wife of his own once the thrill has settled. It is the next great challenge."

Xera studied her drink, faintly annoyed at being

classified as a challenge. To her mind it was no reason to get married.

"Come, my dear," Tessla interrupted her thoughts. "They've degenerated into discussing starship specifications, and you look as bored as I am. We will take a walk and I will show you around the staterooms." The men nodded congenially to the women and went back to their discussion.

The floors were all tiled in marble or elegant woods. Long drapes of silk and velvet framed the arches between rooms, dampening sound and giving the rooms an inviting, exotic look. There was a great deal of stained glass art and lamps, interspersed with scrolled metalwork in the style of wrought iron. Portraits and landscapes hung on the walls in gilded frames, inviting Xera to stop and look. A particularly arresting one made her pause and study it. The landscape had been painted at sunset, with the light glinting off the lake. It wasn't light in full bloom, but the last throes of dying sun that cast shadows on the mansion in the center. It managed to be poignant and moody, beautiful and exciting at the same time.

"This is amazing," she said at last, aware that the aunt was watching her. "Caught between the old and new, life and dying. I feel so sad for the past, yet hopeful for the future when I look at it. I didn't know a painting could say so much."

"Thank you," Tessla murmured. "It took me days to find just the right light to portray the mood."

Surprised, Xera sent her a questioning look.

"Of course it is my work. I have done several of the portraits here as well."

"You're very talented," Xera said honestly. "I wish I could capture feelings like that."

"Have you ever tried it? Art, that is."

Xera laughed. "I don't think I have that kind of talent. To be honest, I never tried. I was always better at physical things."

"Dancing?"

"Never tried it. Martial arts were more interesting. Seemed more pertinent to my future, too."

"Hm. You will try the dancing now, then. I will arrange for you to view several different styles. It is best not to let a figure as trim as yours waste away for lack of exercise."

Reminded of her present situation, Xera's mood dimmed.

The lady looked at her knowingly and linked their arms. She led Xera to a small alcove and bade her sit. "Come. We will speak of this thing. You have no female elder of your family here to advise you, so I will listen and tell you my thoughts."

It was a generous offer, even if it was, like so many of the Scorpio statements, voiced as a command. Xera decided to take advantage of it. "Why does he want to marry me? Surely there are lots of willing women here."

The lady smiled. "This is the heart of your confusion? You have not asked him, then?"

Xera grimaced.

"Very wise," the lady agreed sagely. "Men do not know their own feelings. I do know his father is delighted he has finally chosen *anyone*. He has despaired for years of seeing his son wed. The man is obsessed with seeing grandchildren, though of course he wants his son happily settled as well. For years he has shoved young women under Ryven's nose, until he finally realized he was killing his own cause. Ryven has been more inclined to choose his own women, and not for honorable purposes. You were right in saying he has his pick."

Xera looked down, embarrassed.

"I tell you this only that you may understand what an . . . interesting thing it is that he has brought you here to meet his father. Amorata are never given such an honor, of course. It can only mean that he has met his match. But of course, he is marrying you, isn't he?"

Xera folded her arms. Sourly, she said, "Apparently. We are accustomed to being asked where I am from."

"Would you say yes?"

"Of course not!"

The lady smiled. "Then why would he risk his heart? Our men seem very fierce, but they are tender enough when a woman finds her way inside. You could wound him very easily."

"He doesn't love me."

"If you have any sense at all, do not pose such a question to him until your first child, at least! My own husband would not speak of his love until we had been married twenty years! He was a very stubborn case," Tessla confided. "Ryven will lie to protect himself, just as you would now. Admit that you would not speak the truth if asked about your feelings for him."

Xera was silent. She didn't even know enough about her feelings for him to do more than lie about the obvious.

"He will be good to you," Tessla said with an air

of finality. She rose gracefully to her feet. "Come. It is time for tea."

They finished off the meal with "small bites" that were spicy or savory rather than sweet, and then Ryven walked her home.

Xera didn't want to talk. She'd only known Ryven a week. That wasn't much time to understand the man with whom she was now expected to spend the rest of her life. He'd stood up for her, though, and that had touched her deeply.

"Thank you," she said, after he'd closed the door to her suite behind them. "I appreciate what you did."

He made her a short bow. Very formally, he told her, "You realize we are betrothed. That much I insist on."

She looked at him sidelong and chose an overstuffed chair to sit on. In spite of her emotional fatigue, she tried to choose her words carefully. "That is your prerogative."

He studied her. Whatever his thoughts, he said only, "You're tired."

"I am."

"Tomorrow, then. I'll give you the night to . . . think."

He was letting her be for now, then. Grateful for the space, she said simply, "Thank you."

He inclined his head in farewell and let himself out.

Chapter Nine

Lady Tessla hadn't been kidding—she had Xera in a dance class first thing in the morning, and Xera was finding it hard going.

The thing was, Xera had always liked sports. She had a natural talent for martial arts and enjoyed things like rock climbing and hiking. Unfortunately, none of that gave her any grace on the dance floor. Of course, that may have been due to the style of the dance: belly dancing was nothing like the fighting arts she knew. The movements were soft, circular, and oddly relaxing, even when she fumbled. Undeniably sensual, the hip circles and graceful arm movements—well, the other women were graceful, anyway—drew her attention to body parts she usually lost track of in sports.

Tessla led the class, which consisted of perhaps twenty women of all ages. Dancing was a highly respected pastime for women here, and considered not only excellent for posture and bearing, but a wonderful conditioner for childbearing as well. Xera could tell from her own aching abs that yes, such toning might be useful on the birthing stool.

Not that she wanted to think about children—
definitely not yet.

"Relax, Xera. The movement should look as if
you are waving your arms gently through water,
not as if you had sticks attached to your shoulder
sockets," Lady Tessla chided. A few of the other
ladies grinned at her in a friendly way. There was
no rivalry here.

It was a pretty room, too. There were three walls
of mirrors and one devoted to a lovely pink sunset
mural. Burgundy curtains hung from a ceiling
medallion and were gathered at the corners by tas-
seled ropes, giving the room the look of a luxurious tent. Pillows were scattered at the edge for any
who wished to watch the class, and candles were
generously distributed. Xera could enjoy having
frequent workouts in a room like this.

She couldn't seem to get the hip shimmy right.
When Lady Tessla demonstrated, Xera saw hips
shaking but was told the movement came from the
knees. Unfortunately her version of the move left
something to be desired. Her lower back and sides
were aching by the time she was done, and she still
couldn't get those hips to swivel on command.

Ryven was standing in the observation area when
she came off the floor. His arms were crossed and
he was watching her intently, his head slightly lowered. "Interesting," he commented.

She raised an eyebrow. Everyone else was filing
out toward the showers and locker room. "That's
one word for it. I'll say this for dancing—it's very
relaxing. I don't think I've ever been refreshed after a workout before."

His eyes scanned her sarong skirt, cropped top

and formfitting tights. "You've made me curious. I'd like to see your fighting art."

"What? Now?" She glanced around the empty studio. It seemed kind of a girly setting for an impromptu *dojang*.

"You're not intimidated, are you?" he asked lazily.

"Oooh . . ." She mock glowered at him. "Play dirty do, you? I hadn't intended to show you any of my skills. I've already seen your men practice, and I don't measure up." There was also a part of her that didn't want him to know what she could do . . . just in case.

"Tell that to your captain." He circled her, his body relaxed yet menacing.

She turned to face him, her hands up, prepared. "I'm human. You're not. You're going to be faster."

"I'll try not to fall asleep." He chopped at her head, but slowly, softly enough that no damage would have been done even if he had connected. A baby could have blocked him.

She returned the favor with a controlled kick.

He shifted and her foot slid past him. His eyes took on a hot gleam as he aimed for her throat.

Slowly the dance got faster, more complex. She didn't fool herself that she had seen a tenth of what he could do, but this session didn't seem to be about fighting. The more they moved together, the higher their pulse, the hotter his eyes blazed. Soon they were fever bright, burning with an excitement she shared. When his hand lashed like lightning and seized the back of her head, the other her waist, she was not shocked. The way he looked at her, the slow way he brought her mouth to his as if about to devour her whole, *that* shocked her. That self-control of his was devastating.

Sparks started in her brain. Soon a white-hot fire obscured her vision, spurred by the heat of his tongue, the fire of his touch. Dizzy, hungry, she clung to him as the heat ate her marrow, her strength. Ah, if this was what it was like, if this was how he made love, she had nothing to worry about in his bed.

The thought triggered a sudden panic. She jerked away as if bitten by ice water. "We're not married."

"Not my fault," he murmured, making for her lips.

She wrenched away, aware that he allowed her to go. He didn't look pleased, though. "We are not married," she repeated, stronger this time.

He crossed his arms and regarded her.

Discovering her hands were shaking wasn't pleasant. She hugged herself to disguise it. "Look, I don't know what your morals are here, but we don't do certain things before we're married on my world. A woman can be ruined if anyone even thinks she has. I've no interest in becoming a whore." Ah, but it had not always been true. She'd been tempted as a youth, had nearly brought her family to disaster, all for the price of a few kisses. If it had been anyone other than her sister who had discovered her, she would have disgraced them all. The memory burned. She cared about her family. It wasn't all about her.

"You haven't been with a man before?"

His blunt question made her cheeks burn. "No. I choose to wait."

He blinked slowly as his eyes swept her. "How inexperienced must you remain to satisfy this honor of yours?"

Her neck got hot. She hadn't been deaf, dumb and blind while she'd been offworld. She knew what he was talking about. "No, Ryven."

He ignored her, took a step closer. "I assume kissing is innocent enough."

She didn't trust herself, didn't trust the fresh sweat that broke out on her skin. "It's not innocent when you do it."

He grinned. "Thank you, sweetheart. You haven't answered my question, though. Perhaps you could trust me to stop before that line is crossed." The last was murmured against her lips. He brushed them softly and withdrew enough to look in her eyes. "I hold honor as strongly as you do. Though I have no qualms about taking you now, I will respect *your* sense of honor. I can wait for the final moment." He curled a finger in her hair, gently pulled her closer. "There is so much more we can do."

She ducked his kiss, nearly moaned at the feel of his lips on her temple instead. "No, Ryven."

He withdrew, laughter in his eyes. "I'm going to enjoy changing your mind." He slapped her butt on the way past. "I'll wait while you shower. Don't be overlong or I may be tempted to come looking for you." He cast her a look over his shoulder as he walked out.

Xera shuddered. She closed her eyes. The man was going to kill her.

He didn't say anything when she came out of the showers. He took her to a restaurant and ordered something he thought she might like, since she wasn't familiar with the food. In public he was aloof, in command, but there was something in his eyes, his touch, that had her uncharacteristically flushed. Chills would strike her, and she actually felt faint. Her condition made her clumsy, and she nearly spilled her wine. His hand settled over hers as she struggled to right the glass.

"Easy," he murmured. "The cause is also the cure, *hiri'ami*. I could ease you." He let go slowly, a certain look in his eyes.

She glared at him. "Your aunt is right. You are a rake."

He raised a brow. "And?"

"We don't respect them much where I come from."

"You are not on your world."

"I don't want to marry someone who won't keep the vows."

He regarded her steadily. "You know I am a man who keeps his vows. I even keep yours . . . when it can be done."

Direct hit! She drew a breath. "I apologize. You have done much for me."

He looked unsatisfied. "It has not all been honor."

Did he want her to ask? "Which part?"

Their food arrived then, and he chose not to answer. Perhaps he'd already revealed more than he was comfortable with, but he'd left her curious. She waited until the waiter left, then looked at him with troubled eyes. "Do you *like* me, Ryven? I've known you for such a short time, and I don't understand you very well. I don't . . ." She shook her head, unable to organize her thoughts.

His mouth turned up in the faintest of smiles. "You'll find asking Scorpio men about their feelings a lost cause, *hiri'ami*. I will admit I like you. I would not marry you if I did not. That is not being done to cause you pain."

His answer bewildered her, but she wasn't sure why. She finished her meal in silence.

He waited until they had both eaten, then leaned back in his chair. "There will be a small ceremony tonight to introduce you to our society and to incorporate you into our family. It is not difficult. Namae will instruct you."

"What exactly is the meaning of the ceremony? Not that I would accuse you of leaving out any details," she said wryly. Better to ask than to be condemned for her ignorance later.

He looked amused. "It's a public show of approval by my father, telling those of rank that he approves of my choice of bride. Believe that he has no intention of refuting you."

"And it's not a marriage ceremony?"

He shrugged. "We do not celebrate the actual 'wedding' of the couple in any public ceremony. My father will give his public approval and we will celebrate with a feast after we have had our private consummation."

Her eyes narrowed. "That sounds like a wedding."

He shook his head. "Only the preparation. The bedding completes the act, but we will wait until you have spoken with your sister."

She felt uncomfortably like squirming. "Is there any chance of that happening soon?"

"Eager?" he teased her.

She rolled her eyes. "Just getting information."

"You'll speak to your sister soon," he assured her. He rose and offered her his hand before he pulled out her chair. "Come. You must practice."

Practice, she found, did nothing for one's nerves when one was expected to walk down an aisle in front of hundreds of spectators. The only consolation was that she was not expected to give a speech. As gracefully as she could, she walked down the sage green, tiled aisle, careful not to step on the hem of her coral silk gown. The empire waist dress had short tulip sleeves and parted down the center to reveal a gorgeously embroidered underslip of pale pink. A golden clasp was centered just below her breasts, at the point where the underskirt parted. Matching slippers with a ridiculously dainty heel adorned her feet, making the walk that much more challenging.

The room was huge, and although she knew she was indoors, a blue sky chased with clouds arched overhead, enlivened by the occasional bird. Trees grew out of the floor and collections of potted plants lined the walls, giving the room the feel of a hothouse.

Ahead of her, the lord governor waited on a raised dais with a single throne, though there was room enough for three others. If this had been a normal Scorpio wedding and her family had been here, her sister Gem would have sat on a chair next to him, and Ryven would have had his turn climbing the steps to receive her approval. As it was, he and his family watched in a circle below the dais. She chose not to look at them, afraid she would lose her concentration.

Carefully she climbed the black crystal stairs, raising her hem just high enough to assure her safe ascension. She raised her eyes to meet the lord governor's, then carefully knelt at the left side of his throne. She raised her hand and let it rest on the arm of his chair, careful not to touch him.

This was the place where he could reject her, could refuse to touch her. She swallowed down a sudden qualm, but the five-second pause that came before he touched her hand and bade her rise was nerve-racking. She made her bow and then met his eyes. He wasn't quite grinning—too undignified! The LG would never grin—but a fierce light shown in his eyes, a mixture of glee and pleasure.

"Rise, daughter, and be welcome in our family," he told her in firm, ringing tones. He looked at Ryven, who climbed the stairs as soon as his father had spoken. The LG then put Xera's hand in his son's. "All joy to Lord and Lady Ryven Atarus!"

A great cheer rang out. In spite of herself, Xera colored. She glanced at Ryven, who looked pleased. He winked.

The reception was a dizzying round of introductions and congratulations. As proud and fierce as the Scorpio were, they still threw themselves into a party with great enthusiasm. Xera was a little shocked at the sensuality of the dances displayed on the dance floor. She was reminded of salsa and various Middle Eastern dance, and these Scorpio varieties were both similar and altogether different. She prayed Ryven would keep her away from the dance floor—he knew she was helpless out there.

Her wish was not granted. "I can't dance!" she hissed at him as he led her out with the other dancers.

"I can make it seem otherwise," he assured her, a gleam in his eye. "You will be my reluctant bride. I want you to resist me. Show me that, cross your arms and glower at me, and I will show *you*."

She'd never seen him like this—so wild, so completely uninhibited. He made her his centerpiece, danced around her as if showing her off. Wow, but the man could move his hips. He did a hip thrust that actually made her shake her head to clear it. Enjoying herself despite the attention, she fanned herself. He grinned and moved closer, teasing her, sculpting the air around her without actually touching her. She found herself following the movement of his head, tracking his lips until, as the song ended, he bent her backward with a flourish and and kissed her.

Wild cheers broke out around them. Drunk with kisses, Xera laughed and tried not to stagger as he stood her upright. Dangerous man.

She had wine as well: bubbly, intoxicating stuff that fizzed in her blood and messed with her judgment. She was giggly and subtly leaning on Ryven by the time he took pity on her and made their excuses.

She was a little fuzzy about how they got to her front door. On closer inspection, the room wasn't hers. "Is this your place?" she asked, confused. She was going to have to watch that wine. She'd had hard whiskey that hadn't knocked her on her tail so fast.

"Hm. Since I didn't want to fight tonight, I

thought I would settle for giving you a massage . . . and kisses. I demand kisses."

She laughed. "Kisses are innocent enough, I guess."

His expression was angelic. "Perfectly innocent, wife." The room was lit with candles.

She let him undress her. In her current state it didn't seem alarming. He even had a massage table covered with soft saffron linen, and he drew a sheet up to her shoulders. Nothing alarming there, but it made her wonder. "Have you done this before?"

He took his time replying as he poured a subtly scented oil over his hands. "I've had many massages and have learned something of them. You'll enjoy this."

"This isn't your table, though."

"I could purchase one," he murmured as his hands began to work their magic. "You'd like that."

Maybe she would. Those deep strokes he was using on her back certainly felt good. He even found some knots in her left lattisimus dorsi that had her moaning with the release of a tension she didn't know she'd carried. He stroked her arms all the way to her fingertips before moving down her back, eventually slipping aside the sheet and working his magic on her firm, round tush. It felt good, but not in a sexual way . . . not at first. Not until she began to think about whose hands were doing the work. It felt so good, though, especially when he worked out the tension in her thighs and bent her knee to relax her calves.

Oh, yeah. More people should spend their wedding night like this!

He set her legs down and reached for a bowl. She was surprised to feel a hot, wet washcloth moving over her skin. It felt heavenly, but—"You're going to get the sheets wet."

"It evaporates," he murmured. "It is already steamed off." He drew a hand down her clean, dry back to demonstrate.

"Oh." She relaxed again.

He washed all of her, allowing extra to stream down between her legs, she thought just to tease her. The feet were the most devastating, though. The nubby wet cloth made her feet tingle, and the hot wet tongue that followed made her squeak in surprise.

"Kisses only," he reminded her. "What harm can it bring if I kiss you here?"

Reasonable harm, she thought as waves of pleasurable lassitude swept her. How had she never known that a sweep of a tongue between her toes could send a shiver right up her leg, or that having her toes suckled could make her moan? No one had ever tried it. If they had suggested such a thing, she would have laughed them away.

Shivers wracked her. His tongue caressed her instep as his hands glided over her calf, and sudden sensation made her cry out. It felt like someone had poured champagne right between her legs. Her head came up and she shot a look over her shoulder. Ryven looked pleased. He also looked . . . well, she didn't want to think about that too closely.

"M-maybe we should . . ." She puffed out a breath as he switched to her other foot, and lowered her head. It just didn't seem worth the effort. She'd stop him soon.

He made her cry out again before he covered her with the sheet and told her to turn over. She did, and began to wonder if there had been more than wine in her cup.

He started on her toes again. This time he massaged his way up her legs, inching the sheet higher as he did until it just barely covered what it ought. She moved restlessly, whimpering. A peek through her lashes showed his mischievous grin as he lowered the sheet over her legs and took one of her hands.

His mouth felt every bit as dangerous on her hands as it had on her toes. It swirled and suckled, then made its wicked way down her arm, dragged across her chest above the sheet and licked its way back up to the opposite hand. Shivers wracked her and she occasionally cried out with the hot pressure between her legs. Sometimes it would culminate in a burst of light that raced through her body and exploded behind her eyes. She didn't know what it was.

He lowered his head and took a nipple in his mouth. She cried out and grabbed his shoulders, her nails digging deep. Instinctively turning away from the intense pressure, she pushed at him, prompting him to snag her wrists and hold them over her head. He made a leisurely feast of her breasts, then raised his head and kissed her until heat burst like rifle shells between her legs. She cried out, desperate for some relief.

He slid down her body. Down and down. Kissed, nipped, until his head settled between her legs and his tongue thrust deep.

She screamed. Frantic to dislodge the source of

torture, of pleasure, she grabbed his hair and yanked. That got her hands flattened to the bed, his hands on top. All the while she cried out as her thighs grew damp and heat drizzled between her legs.

He loved her until she was weak, until the pleasure stripped any resistance from her body. She didn't remember "no," didn't care what her sister would say. He could've taken her with impunity. . . .

But he didn't.

She slept naked with him that night, curled with her back to his front. She slept through the night undisturbed and woke to the feel of his mouth on all the places he'd taught her to love, but he did not take her. They even bathed together at his insistence and she got an eyeful of unabashed, aroused male, but he didn't take her virginity. His hands didn't even stray past her thighs.

She felt . . . resentful.

It was crazy. He'd made her climax—that's what those bursts of light were—so many times she was exhausted. She ought to have been satisfied, even grateful that he'd kept his promise, but she could only watch him with hungry eyes and dream.

He noticed. That he said nothing, only watched her with those brimstone eyes, made it worse.

She deserted him for her own room only to discover it was no longer hers. Her clothes had been moved to his chamber before she'd returned last night. How had she not noticed that? She still felt the need to be alone, however. Sharing a room with him only made her affliction worse.

She shouldn't have gone so far, but they were married . . . almost. The qualification didn't settle right in the light of morning. She was confused, afraid that the source of her confusion would do what he had promised—guard her sense of honor. Even if she went to him and asked for him to finish what he'd started, she knew he would refuse. It was a lowering thought, that she couldn't even guard her own honor anymore.

He shouldn't have seduced her. Her mind was a mass of confusion now, and she blamed it on his carefully planned trap. She'd been loved all night, enough to ensure her devotion, but she wasn't a wife. Why had she promised her sister anything? Why couldn't he have left her alone?

Chapter Ten

She wasn't left alone long. Namae soon came for her and conducted her to a small reception of Ryven's family and friends. She met Ryven's other two sisters there and their families. Toosun and Shiza were present, along with the LG and the Lady Tessla. Namae only stayed because Xera collared her as she tried to slink away. "I don't think so."

"Mistress—"

"Sister, you mean. Whatever else you are, you are also my aide. That means you stay by my side and try to keep me from embarrassing myself unnecessarily. It's your job, Namae."

Oddly enough, defining the action of staying with her family as a job seemed to relax Namae. She stood up straight and made no further protests, though she did move a respectful distance away.

"Cleverly done," Toosun said in her ear. "I never would have thought to use that approach." Ryven was talking to one of his sisters an arm's length away and didn't comment, but he glanced their direction.

"Too much sympathy is like eating too much

candy—it sours the stomach," she told Toosun. "How would you like to break your arm and then have the world treat you like you were made of glass?"

He blinked. "Interesting thought."

Xera shrugged. "I was a younger sister, too, and probably overindulged."

"You think we spoil her?"

She frowned at him. "You're letting your sister pretend to be a servant and hug the wall."

He stared at her. A reluctant smile tugged up his mouth. "You have a way with a rebuke. I think I'll go and talk to her." He shook his head as he turned, either at her or himself, but the smile remained. He leaned on the wall by his sister, a determinedly casual expression on his face as he chatted.

"What mischief are you up to?" Shiza asked her. His eyes lingered on Namae as he sent a curious glance her way. There was something guarded, pensive there. He handed Xera a drink. "You may want this—these family gatherings can be hard on the nerves."

She accepted the glass but didn't smile. She still didn't like him. "But you're not family, are you?"

"I grew up with Ryven. We are old friends."

"Hm." She looked around for someone else to talk to.

He wasn't disturbed by her cool attitude. "How are you finding married life?"

That caught her attention. "We aren't married yet. I haven't informed my sister about it."

"Ah. This is some custom of your people?"

"I made her a promise. Ryven is letting me keep it."

Shiza looked at Ryven and smiled enigmatically. "How like him. He has far more patience than the rest of us. Or does he?"

Was he baiting her? The innuendo sparked her temper. She didn't have to raise her voice to make it vibrate with fury. "You're lucky I wasn't your captive—I'd have slit your throat in your sleep."

He leaned closer, amused as only one who loved to bait others could be. "You assume I would use force."

"You'd have to," she retorted.

He smiled. "I know my friend very well. You've had something of a wedding night. Was it so bitter?" He waited until the color in her cheeks betrayed her. "We're brothers in that, sweetheart." He sauntered away.

Xera was left feeling stupid and a little breathless. She glowered at his retreating back and went in search of a distraction. Since Shiza was heading toward Ryven, she went the other way.

Ryven looked meaningfully at his friend as Shiza joined him. "You've tormented my wife."

"She is unaware I helped you move the table into your chambers," Shiza said blithely. "She insists you are not married yet."

Ryven's expression was bland. "We reached a compromise."

"I thought so." Shiza looked at him curiously. "What's it like, being married? Any regrets?"

"No. I doubt I'll ever be bored with a woman like her."

"Hm. How do you think she'll hold up to her

ambassadorial duties? It's rare to have a woman in that office."

"She'll have help. Speaking of which, it looks as if my sister is haranguing her. Excuse me."

As her husband extricated her from his sister's clutches and moved her to a more private space, he asked Xera, "Tired yet?"

She gave him a look. "Your sisters are very like mine." They were giving her qualified approval, but she sensed she was on probation. They hadn't accepted her yet. Nobody said it, but maybe they wished he'd married one of his own kind.

Part of her was glad. She hadn't given up on going home. Ryven might be working hard on changing her mind, but this wasn't where she belonged.

"Headstrong, bossy and full of unsolicited advice?" he suggested. "I can see why you left home."

She laughed, but the mood didn't stay. "Tell me the truth—are we married?"

He looked thoughtful. "If I were to die this moment, yes, you would retain your status as my wife. This is to your benefit, of course. There is no requirement of pregnancy, for instance."

She frowned. "Is that even possible? Our species may not be capable of reproduction together." She was surprised she hadn't thought of that before this, but all of the main bits of their anatomy were the same.

His brows lifted. "It won't be for lack of effort."

She exhaled in reluctant amusement and looked aside. After last night, she had no doubts he would go above and beyond the call of duty in that regard.

Lucky her. However she felt about being stuck here, she had no doubts she would enjoy his tender ministrations.

"We won't have the official reception until after you speak with your sister," Ryven told her softly, breaking into her reminiscence. "We will use pressing business as an excuse for the delay."

She looked at him in question.

"I and a small group leave tomorrow for the border. A fleet of warships is coming to parlay with us. You'll step into your ambassador role very soon."

She drew a breath. She'd be close to her people soon, as close to a ride home as she would be for a long time. She knew that all the while, he'd be watching her like a spy satellite.

"How many days is it to the rendezvous point?" she asked.

"Three. It's another eight months travel to reach your world, isn't it?"

"Yes." They had never discussed it, but she knew he'd salvaged information from her wrecked ship. The distance depressed her. What had she been thinking, to travel so far from home? Her sisters were literally billions of miles away. Even if she could steal a ship and head home, she'd have a hard time reaching them. Traveling alone for such long distances could be deadly.

"We will be able to receive a message, though it is a vast distance to cover. Fortunately, communications are far swifter than ships, and while the communications relay won't be done for a while yet, I think we can persuade the GE to pass on a message using their relays, this once." Wormhole technology made possible for messages what was deadly for a man. No one knew how to send a live body through a wormhole yet. Somehow, it was harder to be hopeful when they were so close.

He seemed to realize that. "Come. My aunt looks lonely."

Xera snorted at that bold lie, but she let him distract her anyway. Brooding wasn't helping anyway. She did offer a word of warning, though. "The GE are not to be trusted."

He raised a brow in inquiry.

"They don't always keep their word." She didn't know how to caution him further without betraying old loyalties, so she said no more.

He seemed content to drop the subject, for he said no more about it. He did look at her thoughtfully from time to time, though.

If she had been nervous or excited about the night to come, Xera never had a chance to explore it. A courier met them at the entrance to their room with an urgent message for Ryven.

"What is it?" Ryven asked grimly. He must have known what was coming.

The courier looked at Xera.

Ryven glanced at her, too. "Would you excuse us, Lady Xera? I won't be long."

"Sure," she said in her own language, forgetting to translate. Deciding it would be explanation enough just to exit, she entered their quarters alone.

Ryven came in shortly afterward. "I'm sorry, *hiri'ami*. There is something I must attend. There is no need to wait up for me."

"Trouble?" she asked, following him into the

bedroom. "It's nothing to do with our upcoming trip, is it?"

"No, the other border," he said as he rapidly changed out of his civilian clothes and donned his military uniform.

"What's on the other border?" she asked curiously. It had never occurred to her to wonder what the Scorpio boundaries were, or what lay beyond them; her world had been a smaller bubble for the last week, and an absorbing one at that. Did they have more enemies, then?

He noticed her disturbed expression and gave her a comforting kiss as he took her hand and towed her into the living room. He picked up a remote and turned the viewing wall on, then thumbed through the programs. "Here. There are some shows about our northern border, and plenty of entertainment videos to take your mind off it after that. We'll talk about things when I get back." He really did look imposing. Putting on his uniform was like donning a mantle of war for him—his whole demeanor changed. It would have to, wouldn't it? He was a leader and a warrior, and he'd only been a husband a short while.

She felt a twinge of intimidation, reminded of how they first met.

His eyes softened and he gave her another lingering kiss. "There will be another evening for us, *hiri'ami.*" He strode from the room.

A twinge of loneliness struck her. Surely she wasn't becoming emotionally attached to him already after all he'd done, all he'd forced upon her—albeit pleasantly, and in her best interests? Shaking her head at herself, she settled down on the couch to learn about her new world and what Ryven faced.

Hours later, she was feeling decidedly chilled. The Khun'tat were a predatory race of flesh eaters who lived beyond the Scorpio frontier. Seven feet tall, leather-skinned and fanged, the aliens dressed in metal body armor and slit-eyed masks only a little less hideous than their faces. They had hoselike tails at the back of their skulls tipped with sharp spines that could stun prey, making it easier to devour them at leisure. The females laid eggs. Their hatchlings required fresh, warm blood to thrive, and the Khun'tat were not farmers. They seized whatever beast or person they could lay talons on to feed their monstrous appetites.

They had moved into Scorpio territory over a hundred years ago. Only the ferociousness of the Scorpio had kept them at bay, plus the Scorpio's slight technological edge. It was scary to know this race was what the human race would have been facing if the GE had succeeded in pushing back the Scorpio borders. Humans had yet to encounter anything like it, and Xera hoped they never would.

Namae had told her once that her brothers were skilled pilots, some of her people's best. Xera wondered how many battles they must have fought to develop those skills, and how often Ryven would fly into battle now. Would he be called away often, as he'd been tonight? Did he lead the missions in person, or did he call the shots from a battle cruiser? Not that a cruiser couldn't be shot down: the Khun'tat reportedly swarmed around those ships often, knowing the big score of blood that could be had inside. It was more economical than taking pilots ship by ship, especially when a pilot could trigger a suicide explosion rather than be taken as food.

Xera felt a hollow ball of fear settle in her gut. She'd seen Ryven in the field, knew what he could do, but his ship had been shot down along with her own. He was vulnerable. She could lose him.

She laughed at herself, at her misty eyes. She'd known him for so little time! How could she be feeling like this? Love had to grow, didn't it? Didn't she want to go home? What about her sisters? Her world?

She shoved those questions aside as a new thought occurred to her. The Scorpio didn't need the hassle of the GE. What they needed were allies. If she herself were any indication, humans and Scorpio were compatible races. If she could use her position to help foster peace between them, it could help them both enormously. If the Interplanetary Council could be convinced to rein in the GE—or at least send them exploring in another direction—this could work. Her life could count for more than she'd ever dreamed.

With a renewed sense of purpose, Xera settled down to think.

Ryven found his wife curled on the couch hours later when he returned. A glance at the main view screen showed a video about the Khun'tat still playing. She must have fallen asleep watching, instead of switching to lighter fare. As he scooped her up and carried her to bed, he wondered if she'd had nightmares.

She stirred, saw it was him and relaxed. He smiled to himself as he helped her undress and slide under the sheets. In moments he was with her, curled around her sleeping body.

Xera woke to find herself in a heated tangle with her lover. Ryven had surely gotten less sleep than she, but he had woken first and was presently kissing her neck. She sleepily arched to give him better access before reality trickled in.

"Hey," she rasped, giving him a half-hearted elbow. "We shouldn't be doing this."

"Why?" He licked his way up to her ear and suckled, sending chills down every nerve. Even her fingers tingled.

Not for one moment did she think he didn't know why. "We're waiting to be married."

"Compromise," he murmured. It sounded more like a command than a suggestion.

She sat up and frowned at him, the sheet clutched to her chest. "You don't compromise—you sweep in and take over."

He smirked. "So far that's been to your benefit."

She ignored his comment. "Look, this is a weird situation and I'm blaming you for that. First we were engaged, then virtually married in that ceremony I had no control over. You seduced me, too, which to my mind constitutes a verbal breach of promise."

"Next time get a written contract," he advised her, his head propped up on one hand. He looked sleepily entertained and deliciously mussed.

Her eyes narrowed. She was not going to laugh at him when she was trying to make a point, or she'd lose this argument . . . though so far it had been an argument of one. "The point is, I'm not about to give up any more of my seriously strained virtue."

"Then take mine," he suggested before she could continue her harangue.

"What?"

Those brimstone eyes sparked with mischief. "You can hardly sully what I no longer possess." When she just stared at him, uncomprehending, he took her hand and brought it to his chest. He leaned back against the pillows. "I like it when you touch me, too."

She blushed, unable to meet his eyes. In all their interactions, he'd always taken the lead, had always made love to her. Put on the spot, she didn't know quite what to do.

He wasn't inclined to make it easy for her, either. He crossed his arms behind his head and looked up at the ceiling like a lazy cat. "Coward."

She gasped indignantly. "It's not like I've ever done this before!"

"Hm. Well, you have a willing victim."

"Victim," she muttered, and got distracted by all that bare chest. Miles of hard muscle stretched out under her fingertips. Her mouth went dry. Her fingers twitched, and suddenly she was trailing her fingers over him, exploring all the grooves and planes. He hummed when she traced his nipples and growled when she trailed her fingers over his belly. It was a powerful feeling, watching all that powerful animal flexing under her hands. She even trailed her fingers up to his neck and buried them in his hair, the better to lean over and breathe in his scent.

"I can't help but notice you're avoiding looking

below the sheets," he said huskily. "Aren't you curious?"

She muttered something, avoiding his eyes.

"What?"

"I'm shy!"

He grinned. "I won't bite."

She half laughed even as she sent him a look of rebuke. After a moment her hand edged toward the blanket.

Ah, his wife was killing him, Ryven thought as he closed his eyes, but he didn't want to be saved. He looked through his lashes as she lowered the sheet, saw her eyes dilate. She'd seen him before—he'd seen to that—but she always averted her eyes. This time she was looking, trailing a tentative finger down the length of him.

"It's so hard," she said, as if she couldn't help herself. "I've never felt anything like it."

"Enjoy it," he encouraged her. "You'll never see another one."

"Arrogant," she chided him, but her hand circled him just the same. He inhaled sharply and she started to let go. He grabbed her hand before she could. "Don't stop. Feels good." He curled his hand over hers, firming up her grip, then showed her how to move up and down. After all, she was driving him mad.

He was not tame in his passion, arching and moaning his pleasure. A glance at her showed how his voice made her cheeks flush, her lips part, but after that he stopped analyzing her reactions. She took instruction very well—he couldn't wait to see what else she took to.

He showed her how to speed up when he needed it, let her watch to the blessed end when the climax took him. Let her watch . . . let her want.

She fetched him a washcloth and herself a robe. She sat quietly on the bed, seemingly unsure what to do with herself. He fixed that by pulling her down into his arms for a kiss. "I'm not in the habit of leaving a woman hungry," he told her, his hand trailing teasingly over her hip. "Say the word."

She groaned and pulled away. "Your brand of satisfaction is torture."

He caught her hand before she could slide off the bed, brought it to his lips. "For now, I will let you rest. It won't be long before we'll be spending days in bed . . . and there will be no resting then." He bound up and swept her into his arms on the way to the shower, where, in spite of himself, he did get a little carried away. Soap and hot water and a naked woman could do that to a man.

He did not, however, take her virginity. She did not thank him for the favor.

Chapter Eleven

Ryven kept his hands off her on the diplomacy ship. It helped that he was the captain and chose to keep long hours, but the situation was also deliberate—the love play without consummation was difficult for him, too. It didn't help that the last time he had touched her, she had begged him to finish. His own physical torment he could take, but her begging was another matter. It did things to him, things he was unwilling to examine.

He didn't want his wife to beg.

He treated her with courtesy, though, and gave her a tour of the ship. To her delight, he even took her to the hangar where the star fighters were stored. She looked around the huge space with appreciation, and stroked the nose of one fighter with something approaching reverence. Her eyes were wide, hopeful. "Can we sit inside?"

"It's a single cockpit," he told her, but gestured indulgently toward it. He helped her in, then stood outside on the retractable step while she settled into the seat. There was no danger of her getting into mischief with the power off—and just as well. That look in her eyes would tempt him to give her far greater liberties. It was best he never tell her.

She looked startled when the seat adjusted to her body. "It moves!"

He grinned. "It's a pressure sensitive seat—very helpful when gravity tries to flatten you."

She murmured her appreciation and touched the control yoke. "This is similar to our controls, but your displays are very different. If I remember my studies, this panel is touch sensitive?" Her fingers delicately traced the dash before her. She touched the thin brow band resting there. "These are the mental interfaces, aren't they? The ship adjusts to your thoughts."

He considered her. "I see those hours you've spent reading are paying off."

She flushed. "You've been checking up on me."

"I like to know what interests you," he said smoothly. "Didn't you think someone had to approve the flight manuals and schematics you've downloaded?"

Her face grew hotter. "I like to fly."

"I remember you telling my father this. It's the reason I indulged you," he admitted.

It wasn't arrogance that made him sure she'd never try to fly a fighter alone. It took many months of intense training to learn all the basics and become certified, even if one had trained on another kind of aircraft. They were complex machines, and he'd no more be able to intuit one of her ships than she would this one, not without study. Take off and landing systems alone could be very different, potentially lethal to the uninitiated. That didn't even touch on the computer guidance system or weapons. One never knew how a strange ship would adjust to space versus atmospheric flight, and she was experienced enough to know that.

She wouldn't be able to sneak it past security, anyway.

"You can fly this model in the simulators, but we will stick to shuttle craft when we get back home." He waited until she looked at him and steeled himself against the disappointment in her eyes. "I thought I could take you up when we returned." Because there was no way he was letting her fly any farther away from home, not alone.

She bit her lip. Disappointment flickered over her face, but she said hopefully, "But I can fly this one in the simulator?"

"Yes." What harm could it do? Though she'd fly a real fighter when he was stone cold dead. They were not toys.

So he took her to the flight simulators. Any regret she might have felt seemed to fade as they entered the room. She examined the different models like a woman shopping for holiday gifts. Her eyes were shining as she climbed into a double cockpit with him. "Can we install one of these in our house?"

He grinned at her. "There's no need. I can show you where to go to find them when we get back. Better yet, I can take you flying with me and train you on a live craft."

On a live craft?

Xera badly wanted to kiss her soon-to-be husband, but she knew he wouldn't allow it while he was in uniform. He was surprisingly stuffy for a man who went wild in private. Instead, she took his hand and silently squeezed, very hard.

His eyes warmed. "You can thank me properly later."

Xera was so excited she missed some of his explanations of the controls and he had to repeat them, along with an admonishment to calm down. She took a deep breath and focused. It wasn't like she'd never been in a simulator, or even a real craft, before. Still.

He had chosen a shuttle craft for her first "flight," and it didn't take her long to adapt to the controls. Compared to a fighter, the craft was much more intuitive, built for simplicity. Even so, her take off was gruesome and the flight clumsy. The differences in the ship from what she was used to made turns tricky. He watched silently as they cruised over virtual hills and joined a flight pattern above a busy terminal. She never got to find out how the landing would be. With the anti-collision system turned off, she managed to collide with another shuttle in midair.

She sat silently watching as the world burst into flames around them.

"You could have been worse," he said thoughtfully.

She shot him a look, then laughed at herself. "It *is* an unfamiliar ship. I'll adjust. I've got to admit to being embarrassed, though. It's been a long time since I crashed and burned." She was thoughtful for a moment then said, "I hear you're a pretty good pilot."

"Do you?" His expression was enigmatic. "Have you ever flown a fighter simulator?"

"Yes, and I'd love to try one of yours. What I'd really enjoy more right now, though, is to see you fly one. I admit I'm very curious."

"Hm." He unfastened his safety harness and joined her outside the simulator. He then directed her to a viewing area along with the simulators' technicians while he chose a fighter simulator. It didn't look like much from the outside, of course—just an egg-shaped pod like all the others. He climbed inside and sealed the door.

Xera sat in a chair and watched the view screens come up. The room dimmed slightly to focus more attention to the screen. She would see everything he was seeing.

"Run simulation Yega-zero," one of the techs said to another. "Level ten." The tech setting up the program looked surprised, but he did as ordered.

Maybe that program was rarely run? Xera thought to herself, but she kept quiet and watched the alien glyphs run across Ryven's screens.

Ryven calmly ran through his preflight as they talked. "Ship one, ready for launch."

"Go, ship one," the tech cleared him.

Ryven's fighter cleared the docking bay and glided outside the hangar, then took off in a burst of speed as two alien fighters charged him. Ryven fired, hit one, disabling it, then banked right, dodging a barrage of return fire from the remaining ship. He took an impossibly tight U-turn upside down and destroyed the remaining ship as two more appeared behind him. Enemy craft came in fast with a hailstorm of laser fire, swarming Ryven's ship like mosquitoes around a nudist. He'd roll to avoid three only to surface facing two more. He was fast with his attacks, snapping off shots and rolling away before they could hit him.

He took some damage, though. No one could fight so many and not be grazed, but he took his ship past the limits and made it do things that left Xera in awe. All told, he took out eleven ships in a pitched battle that should have killed him in the first minute. That kind of fighting took years of experience. She had to hold herself very still when he came out of the cockpit to keep from throwing herself at him. She could feel her eyes glowing with pride and the love she felt for him.

Love? Scary, but true. When had that happened?

The way his eyes sharpened on her, he must have seen it. He linked arms and escorted her out of the hangar and to the lift. They didn't say anything all the way to their room, didn't communicate until she shoved him up against the closed door and kissed him hard. That lasted all of three seconds before he reversed positions and flattened her against the door, her mouth under his, his thigh nudging her higher. They didn't say a word, just kissed until they were both dizzy. He finally broke away and rested his head against her neck. "Woman . . ." It was rebuke and hungry regret. He finally backed up and set her away from the door. He had to steady her a moment before letting go. "Stay here," he said, pointing a warning finger. "Decide what you will say to your sister when you speak. It may be short, and this may be your only chance for quite a while." He turned on his heel and quickly left. Maybe he didn't trust himself, either.

Xera was ready to speak, all right. She might trip over her tongue in her haste to tell her sister everything. She was starting to think her promise didn't matter under the circumstances. Ryven wasn't going to wait much longer, and she couldn't. What she felt was becoming a need, and went much deeper than touch. There was something he could give her that she desperately needed, something she could only experience in his arms. She wanted that joining, that closeness. They were past the point where merely snuggling would work—they couldn't touch without catching fire.

She groaned and flopped down in a chair. She needed this to be over.

Xera sighed and took up her electronic tablet. She had to review what she'd say to her sister. After that she might study the shuttle flight manuals. If she wanted to master the fighter, first she'd have to start at the bottom.

Anything that kept her busy was good.

It was late when Ryven entered their shared room. He'd been tense for hours and hadn't looked forward to another night on the floor. Much as he wanted to see his wife, she was hard on him. He wasn't sleeping well, and he'd had nightmares of his wife going back to her people, leaving him.

She wasn't there.

He checked his automatic concern. Although it was late, she was on the ship somewhere. A simple question on the security net told him where.

He glanced at the simulator technicians as he

entered the control room. He nodded in response to their salutes and checked the screen. Xera had made progress since that morning. The log showed that she'd done nothing but practice takeoffs and landings for hours, with the result being that she'd become quite smooth. An unusual approach to learning, for most students became bored with that kind of repetition and wanted to run the entire program through. She had more patience than he'd realized. He told the techs to signal her, and went to stand by her pod.

She blinked at him as her eyes adjusted to the light spilling through the open door. "Hello. Am I in trouble?"

He extended a hand. "It's late. You need your sleep."

She stifled a yawn and accepted his help. "I guess." Perhaps his face showed his annoyance, for she glanced at him and said, "I'm sorry if I hogged the machine. They didn't tell me that anyone else needed it."

He looked at her sideways. "I gave you permission to use them."

"But you're unhappy about it now."

He looked straight ahead. After a moment he admitted, "I'm unhappy with your preoccupation." He privately wondered at her motivation as well. After all, they would soon meet up with GE ships. If she thought she might find a way to leave him . . . But he would never say as much aloud, and she was monitored at every moment during this trip. His concern was unreasonable, but it made him touchy. The entire idea of giving her ac-

cess to a ship was difficult for him, but he chose
not to discourage her . . . at least, not until he'd
found some way to distract her.

Part of the fault lay with him. He'd been so determined to use his duties as a distraction from his
frustrated desire that he'd often left her alone. By
now his crew probably wondered why their captain didn't spend more time with his new wife.
The thought of such speculation made him frown.

She looked irritated. "There's precious little to
do on this boat. It keeps me out of trouble."

"Hm."

She sighed, but waited until they reached their
room to comment. Once inside, she braced her
legs and told him flatly, "I couldn't fly off if I
wanted to. You know that. If that's what's worrying
you."

"But the notion has occurred to you." He stared
her down, his heart suddenly racing.

Her jaw worked. "I'd be a liar if I told you no."

Suddenly he was tired. It had all seemed to be
going so well. Whatever he'd thought they were
making of their relationship, she hadn't given in
yet. Perhaps she was still holding out hope against
their union. Was it possible?

But such hope was irrelevant. There was no
point arguing the inevitable. Even if he felt unusually dispirited.

Quietly, he said, "Go to bed, Xera."

His lack of argument seemed to deflate her. She
actually looked sorry, but he wasn't going to feed
her need to resist him. He had better tactics in
mind. Yet, not tonight. He spread his pallet on the

floor and shed his clothes, heedless where they fell. He slid under the blankets, his ears attuned to her own as they rustled. Tired as he was, his arousal grew.

They couldn't cement this marriage fast enough for him.

Xera stood at the Lord Governor Atarus's left hand, her face carefully neutral. Heavy kohl extended in a line from the corner of her eye to halfway down her nose, bracketing it like the painted eyes of cheetah. Her lips were carefully lined in darkest red, and a golden diadem topped her brow, holding her thick and glossy tresses off her face like a cresting black wave. Her robes were black and gold, held snugly to her ribs with a golden obi.

She kept silent as the lord governor addressed the commanders of the Galactic Explorers' and Interplanetary Council's ships.

A line of cold sweat trickled down her back, distracting her from her presentation of professionalism. It was the first time she had seen her own people since being captured. It was a dizzying experience. So close, with all they represented of home, of the familiar, yet they were also impossibly far.

Ryven stood at his father's right hand. She couldn't see his face, but she knew it would be impassive, perhaps even arrogant like the time she'd first seen him. A flashback rocked her equilibrium. For a moment she felt a little sick, surrounded by aliens for all she'd come to know them.

Her *people* were out there, and she couldn't go to them. She closed her eyes and ruthlessly tamped down the emotion. This was here and now. She'd deal with it.

She was not the lord governor's mouthpiece. He used his computer to translate for him as he stated his case to the Interplanetary Council and the GE. Her former crew members were to be a gift, a statement of intent, as well as proof to the Interplanetary Council of the GE's trespassing. Lord Atarus had a long discussion with her over that prior to this meeting, over how their government worked, which authorities to cultivate. He was very firm over what would happen to any more GE ships that trespassed in Scorpio territory. Then he introduced her.

"The men from the trespassing GE ship are being returned to you. We have kept for ourselves our new ambassador, Lieutenant Xera Harrisdaughter, formerly of the world Polaris. As a concession to her betrothal to my son, Ryven Atarus, she will be allowed to contact her family to inform them of her impending nuptials."

All eyes turned to her. The screen was split to show the captains of two ships looking at her, but there were many more on both sides who were listening in. The commander of the GE's ship looked at her intently. "Lieutenant. I remember your file. You graduated with honors from our translator program. You seem to be well." It was a question.

"I have been well treated, sir," she answered, strained.

"You agreed to marry the lord governor's son, then?"

"I was chosen for the honor," she said carefully.

It was a fine line to tell the facts and yet tell the truth without offending anyone.

The commander's eyes glittered. "And were you chosen for the role of ambassador, too?"

"I was," she answered.

There was a beat of silence. "How were you chosen, Lieutenant? The rest of your crew seems to have fared very differently." It was clear what he was insinuating.

Ryven stepped forward, and his expression was not kind. "The officers of Xera's ship were uncommonly stupid. Initially I was inclined to kill all of the crew we captured. Be grateful I found anything worth redeeming." He sent an arrogant look Xera's way. "The woman is a war prize, as are all of that crew. It is our custom to choose our own ambassadors from our captives. They are not given a choice once they belong to us."

"Ah." The commander's expression wasn't friendly, but it was difficult to argue with the kind of arrogance Ryven projected.

Xera understood his feelings—she wanted to hit Ryven herself. While she understood his defending her, she hated being referred to as a war prize, a thing.

The commander went on, "In the spirit of your generosity, we will establish a link to the lieutenant's sister. I can't guarantee it will last long—it will be a vast distance, even for a wormhole. We don't have many signal boosters this far out."

"A few minutes will be adequate," the lord governor assured him. "We will prepare our . . . guests . . . for transport."

Xera was given a brief respite as both sides adjourned to assess the situation. She knew it could be less than an hour before she was speaking with Gem if the commander was prompt. In this situation, she assumed he would be, for it was unlikely the LG would complete the prisoner transfer until he got what he wanted. If the commander didn't understand that now, he soon would.

Ryven conferred with the LG, then came to her side. "Come. I will escort you to our room. You will want to speak with your sister in private. You prepared a message burst?" It would be easier to send off a prerecorded message in a quick burst than to count on the conversation lasting in real time.

"Yes." She'd included a picture of Ryven and a recent image of herself, sans ambassadorial make-up. Her sister would want the pictures. She'd asked the LG for permission to describe her new home with the lavender snow and the crystal palace. She'd thrown in a brief description of the culture at the LG's suggestion. Perhaps he didn't want his daughter-in-law's family to think she was exiled to a barbarian wasteland.

She'd given an abbreviated version of how she came to be where she was and assured her sisters Ryven wouldn't beat her. It wouldn't stop them from worrying, but at least they'd know that Xera would have a comfortable future. She'd said she loved them.

It wasn't nearly enough, but it was all she could do.

After a little thought, she washed her face. It would help if her sister could recognize her. She left the hair, though. It was too much trouble to let Namae dress it again.

Namae was handling being on the warship as well as could be expected. She kept her eyes downcast when she had to travel the corridors, intimidated by so many men. If she kept it up, Xera was going to start poking her soon. The girl had experienced hardship, yes, but there was no call to slouch around like a beaten dog. The girl was the equivalent of a royal princess—she should start acting like one. If she walked like a princess and looked like a princess, she would be treated as such. As far as Xera knew, the only one who had ever tormented the girl about her attacker was the accuser in her own mind.

Unbeknownst to her, Namae had become Xera's private project. Xera understood fear and worry. It started with a small thought and grew, circled around and came back stronger, like the first wisp of smoke in a still, quiet house. It had to be stamped out while it was still a whisper, before it gained strength and flashed over. It was so much easier to smother the spark than the full grown, ravenous fire.

Fear was the one thing that could break the laws of physics—it could feed on itself and still keep growing.

How did she know? Fear had been haunting Xera since the moment her ship had picked up the Scorpio on sensors and decided to engage. On the planet it had been fear of death, then of the men around her, of the uncertain future. Now she had a good idea of what the future held, and it was grief she battled. She missed her sisters, hated the circumstances that would separate them. It had been one thing to ship out with the GE, knowing she had the chance to go back one day. But this . . . it hurt. She wanted to be the one in control.

The wall screen flicked on without warning. "Stand by," a computerized voice informed her. "Prepare for transmission." There was a long lag, long enough to make her shift uncomfortably. Would it go through?

Chapter Twelve

"Xera!" Her sister Gem's face appeared. She looked older, eager to speak but worried. The GE must have briefed her on the situation. Xera wondered what they'd said. She also knew this conversation was probably being monitored by both sides. They wouldn't take the chance of missing out on any information that might give them an advantage.

No pressure, Xera thought wryly.

"Sis," Xera said, fighting the constriction in her throat. "Hi."

"We thought you were dead," Gem said softly, as if she also had trouble speaking. "The GE said your ship was shot down. What happened? Are you all right?"

Xera took a breath and sat up straight. "I'm getting married, sis. I promised I'd tell you. Check the message burst for details—I don't know how long we have."

Gem's eyes glittered with the tears she fought. "Are you happy about it?"

How was Xera to answer that? There was so much she wanted to say, to confide, but there was no time. "He's a good man. I think, given time, you might like him."

"He hasn't hurt you?"

Xera forced a smile. "I'm only hurting that I can't see you again. I'm sorry, sis. I didn't mean for it to end this way."

"It's not ended! You're still my sister," Gem said fiercely. "If they won't let you come home, I'll find a way to come to you."

Alarmed, Xera said quickly, "No! You have a family. Even assuming you can find a craft, it's an eight-month journey and a hostile border—you don't belong here."

A muscle jumped in Gem's jaw. "Then I'll send Brandy."

"She's married!"

"Not anymore."

Confused—Brandy's hasty marriage had been only months old when Xera was captured—Xera still protested. It was a nice thought, but the two of them were not known for playing well with each other. If Brandy showed up, there would soon be a war of galactic dimensions. Age had not mellowed them out. "Not if you love me, sis! You know I love her, but *no.*"

Gem looked slightly cheered. "Your independent streak is showing."

"Maybe I needed reminding of it," Xera said, feeling grateful. She and her sibling might be very different, but it was good to draw strength from her family and she had needed this connection more than she could say. "Thank you, sis. I love you. Trust me. Believe in me."

"Done," Gem said. "I . . ." The screen went blank.

The communications computer attempted to re-connect, but it was useless. The beam had broken.

Xera leaned her head back against her chair and closed her eyes. It was disappointing but okay. They'd said all that needed to be said. Gem would worry, but that was her nature as an older sister. Better she worry than grieve.

As for Xera, she felt much better. Gem couldn't have planned a better resolve booster than to threaten to send Brandy. A visit wouldn't be terrible, but the chances were too great that she would get stuck with the girl. She couldn't be an ambassador while bickering with her sibling. Who would take her seriously?

A tone sounded at her chamber door. "Enter," she called, and was surprised to see both Ryven and Namae come in.

"I'm sorry to disturb you so soon. You are needed on the bridge," Ryven informed her as his sister set to work repairing Xera's makeup.

Xera tried to keep eye contact with him in spite of Namae's ministrations. "What's up?"

Ryven's eyes glittered. "Your former captain is making accusations."

"Ah." Xera sat still as she thought about that. "What's he saying?"

"He accuses you of treason, us of torture. He's a pitiful little man."

Suddenly unsure, she frowned at him. "You didn't, did you? Torture him?"

He raised a brow. "He is intact."

She distrusted the gleam in his eye. It looked too much like satisfaction. "What did you do?"

"Withheld pain medication and healing accelerators for his knee. He was allowed anesthetic for the operation on it, however—mostly for the comfort of the attending surgeon."

She sighed. Scorpio justice was rough stuff. "What about the others?"

"Also intact. They were interrogated, but not with force. We have other means."

She grunted, glad he didn't elaborate. There were some pathways her mind just didn't need to wander. "They're looking for a scapegoat, then."

"What?"

"Someone to blame," she translated, rising from her chair. "Let's see if we can head this off."

He waited until they were in the hallway to ask, "Would she really send your sister?"

She looked at him, silently acknowledging what she had assumed: her conversation with Gem had been far from private, with both sides listening in. "You'd better hope not—Brandy can be a terror underfoot."

He considered her thoughtfully. "My brother is yet unwed."

A crack of laughter surprised her. "Don't wish that on him! Whatever sins he's committed, he doesn't deserve that."

Ryven frowned at her words, but she didn't care. He had no idea. She elaborated, "Brandy is moody, solitary and cranky. I think it's her frustrated mothering instinct that bothers her. She ran off and got married a few months ago, and now it seems she's not. I don't know if the guy got scared and ran off or what, but one crisis at a time is enough. Let's see what our good captain has to say, why don't we?"

He had quite a lot, as it happened.

Captain Khan's image on the screen was pale. As a concession to his injury, he was seated in a wheelchair. New lines were deeply etched around his mouth and eyes, lines of pain and hatred. That hatred was focused on Xera as she entered the bridge. Immediately he launched into a snarled tirade. "You—"

His words were abruptly cut off. They could see the commander to whom they'd first spoken reprimanding Khan, but they could not hear the words. There was a great deal of gesturing and flying spittle on Khan's part, though.

Little man syndrome. The thought flashed through Xera's head and she had to clamp down on a smile that could wreak havoc if seen. Any hint of mockery on her part might rile the GE, and they didn't need that. She could feel Ryven's deadly focus as he moved subtly closer to her. For his sake, she was glad Khan wasn't here in person—he would be dead. Ryven had no qualms about covering his hands with blood. She didn't share his sentiments.

Finally Khan calmed down. His fists were clenched, but his posture was more subdued as his commander reactivated the sound. "In light of his emotional investment in the proceedings, I will speak for Captain Khan. He has accused the former Lieutenant Harrisdaughter of treason." He glanced down, consulting his notes. "He claims the Lieutenant seduced the alien leader." He glanced up, "That would be you, Commander Atarus—in order to save her own life. He further claims that she shared information with you and assisted in the capture of his crew. Several of his crew members agree this is true. Furthermore, they report that the Lieutenant was already known for her 'sexually generous nature.' "

"Have they been isolated and individually questioned?" Ryven inquired calmly. His coolness was strange in the face of the charges, almost as if he knew more than he was saying. "You'll see the conflict in their testimonies soon enough if you do.

"As for the claim of my seduction . . ." His mouth tipped up. "You may be interested to note that my bride is still a virgin, as any physician could tell on the slightest of examinations. We anticipated this line of questioning and took steps to preserve the . . . *evidence.*"

The commander looked taken aback, but it was nothing to Xera's chagrin. She couldn't help staring at Ryven. He quietly touched her shoulder as he informed the commander, "With my bride's permission, you may send a medic to confirm the truth. I will guarantee their safe return if you do. Of course, we will demand the satisfaction of the captain's execution in return, along with his lying crewmen."

"That's a freaking lie!" Captain Khan snarled. "You're no more a virgin than—" His portion of the screen suddenly went dark.

The commander looked strained. "We will get back to you on that. Excuse me." The screen went blank.

Even Xera was surprised by the abruptness, but it didn't stop her from glaring at Ryven.

He looked innocently at her. "You'd have suggested the same if you'd thought of it first."

Her eyes narrowed. "Then you weren't really planning this all along?"

He looked at her patronizingly, but his answer

was soft, for her ears only. "You've been in my bed, woman. Do you think I would bother to save any evidence for *him*? I waited for you—no one else."

She relaxed under his reassuring gaze. "You know, for an alien, you're a rather nice guy."

He smirked. "One who's planning to bed you thoroughly at the very soonest convenience."

She flushed, understanding that this was now a matter of pride as well as desire. No man liked to admit publicly that his wife was untouched. Even for the best cause, that had to chafe.

"Do you think they'll accept the invitation?" Ryven asked.

She laughed without humor. "I doubt it. My guess is that they'll try to wiggle out with some diplomatic maneuver. The GE isn't much into beheading these days. If anything, they'll court martial him. He would be demoted and jailed."

"I should have gutted him when I had the chance."

She couldn't help a smile. "Barbarian."

"Efficient," he countered.

"Ruthless," she added, just to see his eyes glitter.

He bent closer to murmur, "You will soon see how much."

Invisible flames licked her, and she shivered.

It took over an hour, but the commander finally contacted them. He looked grim. "In light of further investigation, we have decided to dismiss Captain Khan's accusations. It seems his testimony conflicts with that of several of his crewmen. The lieutenant's . . . medical examination won't be required. The captain aside, none of us here in command are interested in questioning her honor."

"Very wise," Ryven's father commented, speaking up for the first time in a while. "I suggest we take a recess from our discussions. If there is nothing urgent, we will recommence in twelve hours."

Fatigue set in as the tension drained from Xera. She glanced at her husband—or soon-to-be husband, or whatever he truly was—and saw him nod at the lord governor. "We will retire, then. Rest well." He linked arms with her and escorted her from the bridge.

Their masks of unaffectedness did not last past their stateroom door. Ryven cupped her jaw in his hand. He and Xera simply breathed, simply existed as their tension drained away. After a short period of relaxation, however, Xera grew restless.

She stirred. "How do you do that? Calm me that way?"

He nuzzled her temple. "It's a talent," he whispered. "Like so very many other things you have yet to enjoy." He kissed her, demonstrating another. This one left her breathless. He kept his touches light, teased her until she made a sound of impatience and attacked his mouth. He laughed and took over the kiss, ramped up the heat, the seriousness, until the laughter died in flame and passion.

They were too raw to take it slowly. She'd been hurt; he hurt for her. This demanded a vengeance that found its expression in the bedroom. They were both more clothed than not when he mounted her, took the virginity with which he'd taunted the captain.

The first act of love in a woman's life is never comfortable—there is pain, and very little stars and comets, despite what the poets say. There was desire, yes, but they unwittingly turned the act it-self into an expression of violence. It was an act of pride for him, pride of the conqueror taking his rightful due, with little memory of how much he wanted the woman herself.

Xera was . . . not herself. Her sister's call, the ac-cusations, the reminder of her status—they all were too much. No matter that she could now put "beloved" in front of "war prize," a new rebellion was born in her heart. A shell of anger formed around the new hurts and focused on the nearest target. She was glad and sorry when he reared above her with a cry. She waited a moment as he lay there, supported by his elbows on either side, and then subtly nudged him off.

He glanced at her and moved away when he saw her wince. "I'm sorry."

"I need to clean up," she growled as she slid off the bed. That should have been his first incontro-vertible indication that something was wrong. Be-fore he might have been excused for thinking it was merely the loss of her innocence that disturbed her. His judgment was understandably clouded.

The bathrooms on the warship were tiny, little more than closets, even for those of rank. Xera forced herself to be strong as she cleaned herself. The tears were too close. Rage shimmered just un-der her skin. But if she lost it in front of him, he would insist on trying to talk, and she wasn't ready to be that naked in front of him.

She looked in the mirror, saw her glittering eyes and hard mouth, and knew he'd never believe she was all right. Lying wasn't an option, but strength might get her what she needed. "Be strong," she hissed to herself, showing her teeth. "Be *strong*."

"Xera?" Ryven's quiet voice came through the door, very close.

She took a breath and opened it. "I need some time alone." She had never seen him look solemn. It disturbed her.

Those brimstone eyes moved over her face, took in the tension of her body. A hint of sadness entered his gaze. Slowly, gently, he raised a hand and touched the curve where her neck met her shoulder. He did nothing else, simply let the moment be.

Slowly, the absence of pressure caused her shoulders to loosen. Bewildered, she stared at his chest, unable to understand why. He wasn't forcing her, wasn't demanding. He simply stood there and offered silent support. Without the touch, the moment couldn't have drained her resistance, stolen away her anger. With it, only moments passed until tears gathered in her eyes, tears of relief and sorrow. She didn't want him to go, didn't want him to take his comforting presence away. She stepped close and wrapped her arms around him on a sob.

Chapter Thirteen

Her new husband made a low humming noise as he gathered her close. *"Azie hiri'ami."* My sweetheart. "I was a boor with you."

Xera shook her head against his chest. The insignia on his chest scratched. "We were both stupid. Maybe there is no best time."

He sighed and picked her up in his arms so that her feet dangled in the air. "Whenever these things go wrong, it is the man's fault." His eyes crinkled. "My sisters say it is so."

She laughed, surprised at his humor. He took her to the couch and sat down, arranging her with her head in his lap. He stroked her hair. "Rest, if you will, *azie ami*. I will listen and keep you safe."

She blinked, faintly astonished. From what she'd seen, human men just didn't act like this, being so concerned and kind. She'd expected demands and pressure, and perhaps some egocentric questions. Weren't the Scorpio a warlike race? Was this some kind of underhanded psychological trick? But after a moment she decided she trusted and liked it. She'd expected to kick Ryven out and indulge in a fit of tears. She'd gotten something much better.

Still, her previous thoughts were enough to dampen her eyes. "I'm never going to see my sisters again." He stroked the hair from her face, and she felt the bite of rage. She wanted to hurt him. "It's your fault!"

"Yes," he said simply.

A little of her anger slid away, undermined by his continued calm. Her throat got tight. "I hate you."

"Yes," he agreed softly.

That made her cry. It was long minutes before she could admit, "I don't. I just hate . . . everything that's going on."

"So would I."

That loosened the mortar that held together her fortress of sorrow. She poured out her anger, her heartbreak. She even told him how she'd felt during their time on the desert planet where they'd crashed. There was no one else to tell, and she needed it out so badly. "I was as scared of my crew as I was of yours. I thought we'd be stuck there for years, that it would become a prison. I thought being the only woman there would make me . . . you know. Vulnerable. A commodity. I think Khan's attitude might have been part of what made me so scared."

He curled a lock of her hair around his finger. "I would not let you be hurt."

"I didn't know that. You seemed scary yourself," she admitted.

He smiled. "Even then I wanted you for our ambassador."

"That was all?"

His eyes were hooded as he looked down at her. He traced her cheek. "No. That wasn't all."

"Why? Because I was the only woman there?" She laughed wryly.

His smile held secrets. "I knew a ship was coming for us. It would only be weeks before I was home again."

"Surrounded by women," she said, a bit sourly.

"They had lost appeal. I'd found what I'd been looking for."

"What was that?" she asked softly. She stared at him. His eyes had that certain glow.

He brushed a finger over her lips. "A fierce heart. You thought I would kill you and you faced death with courage. You didn't complain as we marched through killing sands and men fell around us. You're a survivor, a fighter. All that and gemstone eyes, flame red lips . . . I could not believe such beauty was allowed to serve in such a dangerous position. I wanted to kill your captain just for allowing it."

"Our cultures are different," she mused, even as he brushed her lips with his.

"I will never understand it," he replied, his voice a murmur against her temple.

He straightened, even though she could clearly feel his arousal with her head in his lap. His hands remained soothing, stroking her arm. After a moment he said, "Tell me about your family." He seemed genuinely interested, and she was quietly pleased by his questions.

"My sisters?" She thought about it. "Moody, head-strong, infamous . . . and that's just my younger

sister, Brandy. Gem is the oldest and . . . motherish."
She made a face.

He laughed. "Motherish?"

"You know, always trying to steer us in the right
direction. Bossy, though she tries to rein it in. At
least having kids has given her someone to un-
leash the instinct on besides us. She's married to a
cop. He gets bossed around by her, too." Not that
Blue seemed to mind. He'd once said there were
compensations, then had given his wife such a hot
look that Xera blushed. She'd stopped teasing
him. Truth be known, he could hold his own when
he needed.

"Do you fight much?"

She shifted to get more comfortable. "Not really, not anymore. At least, not with Gem. Brandy
drives me crazy. She's so stinking moody. She'll
snarl at you for nothing when she gets in one of
her snits. It doesn't help that she's always holed up
in the brewery, tinkering with formulas."

"Brewery?"

"We make the finest beer on Polaris. Make a
mint, too, now that offworld exports have gotten
more affordable. We own a bunch of inns," she
confided. "My dad started the first when he home-
steaded the place."

"He sounds enterprising."

"Yes." She abruptly clammed up.

When she said nothing more, he asked, "What
was your home like?"

"Clean, busy, happy mostly. Business was always
good, but it's taken off during the last few years.
Gem really came into her own. She knows how to
manage people, resources. I swear, all she did for

years was breathe through the business—it was like a third lung. Nobody did it better. I think she'd have had an aneurysm or something if Blue hadn't found her and dragged her away from the office. She kicked and screamed then, but she doesn't seem to mind now. She's in love." She ducked her head slightly, the mention of love making her self-conscious.

Ryven smiled. "You must have had some lonely years in space, judging from the quality of men who were in your crew. What did you dream of doing when your time was your own again?"

She blinked, a little surprised. How had he known she was lonely? For that matter, it was a little arrogant of him to assume that she'd never fraternized with anyone in a romantic capacity, even if that were true. "Actually, I served with a couple of decent guys. No keepers, though." Let him chew on that. It might keep him from taking her for granted. "What did I dream of though? Little things, mostly. I dreamed about eating at home again—we always had the best cooks."

"Space rations are not always enough," he agreed. "What else?"

"Sunlight. A garden to snooze in. I was never much for weeding, but my sister always grew the best flowers. Windows open to the breeze, good beer, good neighbors."

"The home you knew," he said.

"Yes. I'd gotten my fill of exploring by the time we crashed. The GE soured it for me."

"You don't like them," he remarked carefully.

She was silent for a moment, held in check by old company loyalty, then admitted with irritation, "No.

No, I don't. They're greedy, corrupt and have really lousy benefits. It's a wonder they haven't started a war yet instead of skirted around it. Even then, if they had more money and better leadership . . . but they don't. They're a bunch of land-grabbing investors ruled by a board of nincompoops. I'm glad I'm out of that mess."

"So I rescued you, did I?"

She huffed at him, trying not to laugh. "Please! My ego can't take much more."

He kissed her. "Take a transfusion from mine. I have enough to share, according to my sisters."

"They would know," Xera retorted, but his kiss distracted her. He really had a talent for it.

The mood was light-years different than before, but still he only teased her and retreated. The mischievous smile he gave her only made Xera want to chase him. "Come here," she demanded at last.

Mock regretful, he shook his head. "I don't think I should."

She frowned and sat up, wincing as she did. "Another kiss won't hurt."

He obliged, and then said breathlessly, "Anything else will hurt. I'd rather not cause you pain."

"Then don't." She pulled his head back down, still hungry from his clever, enticing kisses. At this point, *not* having them would be worse.

"Such a lot of work you are," he complained huskily. "You'll have me start all over. I'm exhausted from your demands, wife."

"Tough luck." She grabbed his head in both hands and shut his mouth with hers. It felt good, powerful to be in charge. She wanted to control him, but oddly enough, the feelings brought back the anger. She became more aggressive, almost hurting him.

His head snapped back and he gave her a warning look. His old command surfaced. "No! Not again. We will not follow that pattern. This time, we will be soft because it is best. You will be soft for me." His lashes swept down and screened those volcanic eyes as he kissed the corner of her mouth.

She turned her head, sulking. "You don't always know what's best."

"This time I do," he said softly, and cupped her breast in his hand. She didn't have time to object before he palmed it, delivering a jolt of pleasure. "Be soft for me, wife, soft where a woman should be soft, and I will be your rock."

He was asking for trust, for openness. Though he was remaining dominant.

It was difficult. She didn't want to let go, but he had ways of persuading her. In the end it was his gentle yet commanding patience that won her over. Somehow his touch was soothing yet exciting, light and fiery, like ghostly flames licking over her skin. He made her thoughts spin away in her head, her vision dulled with passion. Even the clothing sliding from her skin was an unbearably welcome caress; the hands that followed, nirvana. It was, "Oh!" and, "*Jai tai, kdi ahn,*" as she moved against his fingers. "*Tomou,*" he murmured breathlessly, his mouth open and hot over her nipple. And "Yes!" and, "*Xeinxi.*"

Each forgot any but their native language as the passion swept them, but Ryven did not change his plan. This time he took her gently, slid with utter care into her slick core. This time she shuddered with passion before he slowly rocked her, deaf to the urging of her nails, her hot anxiety. He knew better, knew to guide their bodies slowly. He rode out her impatience, took her past the first burst of light and guided her into a second, even more powerful.

Her scream almost deafened him. He clamped his teeth gently on her neck and growled his own release.

It was a while before she recovered enough to see their surroundings. They were on the carpet next the couch. Her backside was raw from the carpet. Ryven was heavy on top of her and deep within. She shuddered with lingering pleasure. Hot seed trickled between her thighs.

"Mm." He suckled her neck. "We should move to the bed, little one. This carpet looked softer than it is."

She laughed. "My backside is raw."

"I'll put balm on it. You can attend to my knees . . . and other parts that ache." He brushed a kiss over her lips and reluctantly withdrew his fullness.

She blinked and sat up. "I thought . . ." She gestured at him, averting her eyes.

He smiled rakishly. "Yes?"

"Shouldn't that be . . . ah, taken care of?"

"Meaning?" He sounded like he was enjoying himself.

She couldn't bring herself to look, so she gestured. "You know. Down."

He grinned. "Wife. You're naked at my feet. Your thighs are still wet with my essence, and you think I should be '*down*?' We have much to teach you, little one."

Ignoring her hot blush, he scooped her up and

carried her to the bed, then fetched the balm. He wasn't shy about rubbing it all over her body, even deep between her legs. She gasped as his fingers slid deep with a generous dose of cream.

"S-should you . . . be . . ." She ended on a moan.

"This is what it's for," he murmured, enjoying himself. He spread the cream all over the inside of her thighs, held them wide with his forearms as he teased the petals of her femininity. It was necessary—she would have twisted out of his hold with pleasure otherwise. At last, when she was far gone to passion, he eased her up and handed her the jar. "Your turn."

She blinked at him before obediently smoothing it over his knees and thighs, forgetting to cover herself as she worked. Her hands grasped him, sweetly stroked as her generous breasts squeezed between her arms, the nipples tight little peaks. She cast him a heated, hungry look.

He smiled and leaned back. "Come here." He turned her when she would have lain down so that her back met his front. He used his own legs to spread her thighs wide, then sent his fingers sneaking, seeking. One hand toyed in her curls as the other played with her breast then slid up and between her lips. She moaned as she suckled him, and climaxed.

It was as if sudden fever ignited his body. He flipped her over, facedown on the mattress, and slid into her, though careful, ever careful. She responded with a deep groan. Baring his teeth in triumph, he rode her to their reward.

Chapter Fourteen

Midmorning of the next day found Xera seated at her desk, perusing a report on the wallscreen while Namae silently dressed her hair. Their meeting with the GE and Interplanetary Council representatives had opened up talks, and she had to be ready to participate if called upon. She was also doing research to see why relations between the races had failed—from a Scorpio perspective. Apparently the Scorpio had taken a dim view of a GE captain's aggression when he was discovered nosing around a section of space they claimed. The captain had pushed, tried to bluff, only to discover that Scorpio didn't bluff. The GE vessel limped home minus its captain and delivered the terse message, "Stay away from Scorpio space." The GE hadn't listened.

Fast-forward to Xera's day. The GE and Interplanetary Council were talking, and the IC at least, pushed for peaceful relations. The Scorpio were talking. No blood had been shed. She was hopeful that they could work things out, or at least part with civil nods. She was working on a way to introduce cooperation. What they needed was neutral ground, a place to interact face-to-face. Someone had to suggest that.

Outside the window she could see a large planet. The orb itself was a pale lavender and dark purple swirl of deadly gas, inhospitable to life. Seventh in its solar system, it had sixteen moons, one of which was slightly bigger than Earth's and had rings of its own. Its name was Betlefixh. The closest she could pronounce it was "Bettlefish."

"Namae," she said absently, still staring at the moon on her computer screen. "What do you think it would take to convince your brother and father to set up a moon station there?"

Surprised, Namae blinked the screen. "What? There? Why would they want to?"

"They claim this solar system, don't they?"

"Yes, but no one lives this far out. We haven't needed to colonize it yet, as this isn't a fertile system."

"Yes, but it's on the border between our peoples. Imagine how convenient it would be to start . . . oh, a trading post here. The land doesn't have much value yet, but what if people of both races were stationed in the area, lived and worked together? What do you think would happen then?"

"War?" she said doubtfully.

Xera grinned ruefully. "Maybe. Maybe, though, something better would happen. Our races aren't that different, you know."

"Hm," Namae offered, noncommittal. "What would we trade, though? What would be worth coming all the way out here for? Your world is a long way off, isn't it?"

"Information, for a start. My people are curious—that's why we explore. I bet your people would like to know what we do about our section of space as much as we would love to see what lies inside yours. If nothing else, the Interplanetary Council should know about the threat of the Khun'tat. They would also make a better effort to police the GE if their allies were threatened. You would be one of the herd, after all."

"I don't like that analogy."

"You're right. What would be a better one?"

Namae thought. "Best leave it at allies. If you say anything else, it will definitely sour my brother. You mentioned information. Are you planning to send scientists here?"

"Good idea. Astrographers, people who want to study wormholes—imagine if they learned to send drones through!—maybe even artists and musicians. Of course there would be all the other people required to support a moon station, too. This could really work." Her eyes gleamed with excitement. Her family could actually visit her in a neutral place like that.

What would her husband think of her idea?

He listened attentively when she presented it. She made sure to use her most businesslike approach. It wasn't difficult. She'd been honing her bargaining skills on tradesmen while working at her family's inn. This was just another type of sale.

When she was finished, Ryven sat back in his chair and considered silently. She knew the value of silence and waited. She tried not to let her cold sweat distract her. Either the idea had merit or it didn't. Maybe he wouldn't think they needed a whole moon base. Maybe he'd think an annual summit meeting would be enough. Maybe he'd scotch the whole idea and continue as they were, with ships patrolling both sides of the border and the GE playing chicken with them.

Finally he looked at her. His expression warm but shuttered, he said, "The idea is worth bringing to my father. He may take it into consideration. It would depend greatly on the reaction of the GE and Interplanetary Council, however. If they are not in agreement . . ." He shrugged. If it didn't happen, he would not be heartbroken.

She gave a small smile. It was a start. "Thank you. That's very open-minded of you." It couldn't hurt to give the compliment, and she was aware of the stretch this was for him. "I can only hope all parties are as reasonable."

His father found the idea, "Palatable, but only just." The Interplanetary Council was cautiously eager, and the GE expressed neutrality, not quite willing to let go of its grudge. Of course it took a full week of negotiations to arrive at this agreement. Things promised to get even more sticky as they hammered out who would pay for what, how the station would be designed, policed and executed. Xera bargained with tact or fierceness, differing based on need. By the time an agreement had been hammered out, she was exhausted.

"You need to go home and rest," Ryven informed her the night they signed the treaty. "This constant wrangling is leaving you pale." He tucked the bedclothes over her shoulder and lay down beside her.

"It's the lack of sun," she told him, snuggling close with a yawn. "We all look pale. Besides, you wanted an ambassador. It's demanding work, but I think I'm doing a good job."

His frown was fleeting, but she saw it. "What?"

He glanced at her then looked away. "You have done well. It's only that I can't picture you working this hard once we have children."

That banished her sleepiness. She sat up. "Gee whiz, what's the rush? We haven't been married a month! Who cares if I work hard right now? At least I'm doing something useful with my life. That's more than a lot of people could say." For that matter, she wasn't ready to have children, but that was a subject for another time. Surely they had contraceptives here. She'd just quietly use them when her biannual dose of birth control wore off. Ryven wouldn't need to know.

"Being a wife and a mother *is* useful. Who do you think shapes the destiny of the next generation? Having a mother close is vital in a strong society. You can't work yourself into the ground and still expect to give the best of yourself to your children, your family." He held up a hand to forestall her protest. "As for your contributions now, though, I am well pleased. My father has also mentioned his pleasure."

Mollified, she asked, "He did?"

Ryven kissed her temple. "He said I chose well."

"Huh!" She relaxed into the mattress. "I like him pretty well myself." She looked at her husband in consideration. "For a man who worked so hard to make me an ambassador, you already sound as if you've planned a retirement. What do you plan to do for the next ambassador, kidnap another woman?"

He frowned at her.

She gave a half shrug. "It's a fair question."

There was a long pause. "I suppose you'll have to remain in an advocate position. As you're married into the lord governor's family—to his heir, no less—that shouldn't be a problem," he said drily.

Startled, she looked at him. "You're his heir? As in, you'll be lord governor someday?"

"Of course."

She stared at him. Somehow, she'd never dreamed of that. After all, the man was a starship commander and people didn't inherit titles where she was from. She wasn't excited about being the wife of a ruler. What did she know about such a lifestyle?

"This bothers you?" he said carefully.

"It's very unexpected," she temporized. "I'm not sure what to make of it."

He raised a brow. "The lord governor's wife has much influence. There were women who pursued me just for the hope of such status."

She grimaced at him.

He shook his head with the hint of a smile. "I'm not trying to mock you, wife, just understand you. You are here and they are not. It's only that I expected more enthusiasm."

She cleared her throat. "I'll see what I can do. I have to get used to this, though. I'm unsure what to expect of such a life. It's . . . daunting."

His brow cleared. "Ah. You're frightened of the unknown. That's not unusual."

Was he being just a touch patronizing? She frowned at him. "I'm concerned. It's a reasonable reaction."

"Of course."

Her eyes narrowed. "You're being a little too soothing. I don't like it."

Ryven's lips twitched. "Moody, aren't you?" He blocked the pillow she swung at him. "Temper, O governor's wife. Dignity."

Xera snorted. "You're not the governor yet." She attacked him.

He didn't even pretend to wrestle. He flipped her neatly on her back and rolled on top. It put him in an interesting position. "Little fighter. Let's see if I can tame you." He slid inside her.

She gasped. He held still, to let her fully absorb the sensation, then sharply thrust. Her sharp inhalations soon mixed with his slower, heavy breaths. These sounded like a doe in a thicket being devoured by a lion. And there were similarities of situation. Xera was the doe, pinned by the weight of the hunter. His mouth was on her, over her, *in* her, tasting and devouring, her mouth, her breasts, her—

"Oh, yes! Ohhh, *Rye!*"

Oh, yes. There were similarities.

In the end Xera just lay there, too spent to reach for a blanket as her lover lapped her in the afterglow. She enjoyed the slow caresses of his tongue, the languid sweep of his hand. She fell asleep with his fingers tucked inside her, the feel of his naked skin under her cheek. Maybe he had a point, she thought hazily. Being a full-time wife might have its advantages.

She was in a fog most of the next morning. Her husband's insistence of sleeping with his fingers intimately in her had caused a very restless night. They'd awoken several times, and now she was tender and too sated to do more than stare fuzzily at the Scorpio version of tea. She held her cup's warm weight in her hand and looked dreamily into nothing.

Ryven leaned over the back of the couch and growled in her ear as he kissed her. "Those kind of looks will land you right back in bed."

"You have to go to work," she scoffed with a smile. "You said so yourself."

He grunted. "Spoilsport. I might take a long lunch, though."

She looked at him archly. "And I might take a long nap. You didn't let me sleep last night."

He grinned. "You slept—just not for long."

"Your fault."

"You didn't mind." He kissed her quickly. "Rest today."

"Hm." She planned to, but she had other things to do as well. She wanted to start a journal so she'd remember things when she got another chance to send her family a message through the wormhole. As much as she liked to daydream, it was unlikely that her family would ever visit the proposed moon base. She'd probably have to heavily edit the journal when she was done, but that was all right. She'd read that journals were good therapy, and she could use the introspection.

She also needed a list of goals. What did she want to do with her life? Things had changed radically for her and she desperately needed a point of focus. The moon base had provided that, which was one of the reasons she'd thrown herself into it. But where was she most needed next?

An opportunity arose as she observed Namae in the officer's mess. The whole habit of her sister-in-law playing servant grated, and she was determined to change it. Xera had been forced to order the girl to sit at the table and eat with her as she had tea. Now the girl sat with her shoulders hunched and avoided the eyes of anybody who looked politely their way. The whole thing was just sickening.

Xera had enough. "For pity's sake, sit up straight, will you? Even monks act like they have a spine, and they are far more penitent than you are. Though, if it will make you feel better, we can see about getting you a hair shirt. Why you feel like serving the sentence for someone else's crime is beyond me."

Namae looked up with wounded eyes.

"Don't try that on me," Xera said in exasperation. "I'm not your father or your brothers that puppy dog eyes will convince. I'm sure they enjoy the way you punish them."

Namae sat bolt upright. "Punish them? How am I doing that?"

"Please. Do you think they enjoy the impression you're leaving? You make it seem as if they're punishing you for what your brother-in-law did. You make them look bad." She didn't bother to keep her voice down. A few of the nearby men slanted looks at them.

Namae sent her a hushing look. "Please!"

"Then sit up and act like a princess. If you've

forgotten your lessons on how to be one, I'll be glad to let you join me in the deportment classes I asked your brother to arrange for me. They are almost as much fun as boot camp, but one of us ought to come out of them looking as if we learned how to behave in public." She took a disgruntled sip of tea. "Really girl, have some pride! I thought princesses were supposed to be snootier than this."

"I am not snooty," Namae said in stiff-backed outrage.

Xera smiled with satisfaction and sipped her tea. "Now that's more like it. I was beginning to think your brothers had inherited all the moxie in your family."

"What is that?" the young woman asked suspiciously.

Aware that she had to maintain appearances, Xera lowered her voice. She waggled her brows and leaned forward slightly. "Manly bits."

Namae looked positively offended. "That's awful!" It was hard to say if it was the sentiment or the description she disliked.

"It would be if it were true. I'm happy to say I don't believe it is." Xera set down her cup. "Come on, let's go." She waited until they were in relative privacy in the corridors before asking casually, "So, who's your fancy?"

Namae looked at her suspiciously. "What do you mean?"

Xera smiled. "Who do you like? Which men do you think are handsome? Don't be shy, we're sisters now. Who else am I going to have girl talk with?"

Namae looked nonplussed. "I suppose we are sisters."

Xera pressed her advantage. "That's right, so spill. Let me guess—you like Shiza."

She made a face. "Ew! You aren't serious."

"He watches you."

"He watches *all* women. He acts like an *onta* who is never fed."

Xera wasn't familiar with the reference but understood the gist. "He has a special look for you."

"Probably annoyance," Namea retorted. "I don't fall under the spell of his commander's star and pretty eyes. I grew up with him, you see. It's difficult to take seriously anyone whom you've watched pee off a balcony when he's eleven."

An unexpected laugh made Xera choke. "You spied on him?"

"He was out there in the open for the world to see," Namae said indignantly. "I told him as much when he saw me."

"What did he say to that?"

Namae blushed and refused to answer. She took a corner of her skirt and flicked it out of her way, as if annoyed.

Undaunted, Xera said slyly, "But you think his eyes are pretty."

"It's a fact. The sky is blue. The Khun'tat are our enemies. Shiza's eyes are pretty." Namae's expression was determinedly blithe. "Are you pregnant yet, sister?"

Xera stumbled and looked at the other woman in disbelief. "That was dirty! I didn't think you had it in you."

Namae sent her a superior look, clearly pleased with herself. "I have sisters, too. Aunts, brothers, uncles, a father. Did you think I would be unde-fended?"

Xera shook her head with new respect. "Silly of me. As for whether I'm pregnant . . . no, there are no babies here. I know your brother wants to have them, but it may not be possible. As far as I know, our races have never interbred. To be honest, I don't mind—I don't have much mothering in-stinct. Incidentally, will the line go to Toosun if we don't produce an heir?" Oddly enough, she hadn't been worried about becoming pregnant prior to this. She'd faithfully taken her biannual dose of contraceptive just in case, and by her cal-culations it should still be in her system for an-other . . . she frowned, suddenly unsure of her math. What month was it?

"Perhaps, though I doubt Ryven was concerned about it, since he wed you."

"But I'm an alien. Would that be taken into con-sideration?" She didn't want to be held responsi-ble for messing up the noble lineage. Ryven may not care, but her new relatives might shun her. Families could be touchy about that sort of thing.

"It might, but don't worry." Namae patted her shoulder. "You won't be held responsible. We like you well enough. If Ryven hadn't chosen you, we might have ended up with some hideous foreign princess. Far better to have an alien sister than one of *those*." They had reached Xera's quarters. Namae gestured for her to move first through the door.

Xera entered, unsure whether to be comforted or not.

Chapter Fifteen

Xera was in the ready room, talking with her father-in-law, when the alarm claxon sounded. They broke off their conversation to exchange concerned looks and hurried to the bridge, which was nearby. Ryven snapped terse commands as he scanned proximity readouts from his command chair. He stood and surveyed the forward screen. A magnified view of an embattled space station showed a large Khun'tat warship parked close by. A great deal of the outer ring of the spoke-shaped station was damaged, and the smaller, ovoid Khun'tat fighters swarmed everywhere, dodging its sputtering weapons.

Ryven turned his head to send an order and spotted his wife and father. He finished a series of rapid commands and came to them. "We investigated the station's unnatural silence and found this. Other warships are on their way, but we're point for now." They'd originally had two other warships with them at the meeting with the GE and Interplanetary Council, but he had sent Shiza's to investigate a distress call and the other on a border sweep. They had expected an easy journey back to

Rsik; the Khun'tat should never have been able to penetrate this deep into Scorpio territory.

Ryven put a light hand on Xera's shoulder. "The bridge is too busy right now—you'll be safe in our quarters. I'll send a link there so you and Namae can watch what's happening." He shot an inquiring look at his father.

"I'll wait with them," Lord Atarus assured him. "Be victorious, son."

Ryven flashed him a smile, kissed Xera quickly and turned his attention back to the battle.

The kiss rattled Xera. If he was being so demonstrative in public, he must truly feel the need to comfort her. It didn't bode well.

"Come, daughter. He will be a better commander for knowing his wife is safe." Lord Atarus placed her hand on his arm and escorted her from the bridge. Two guards she didn't recognize fell in behind them. Two others joined them on the way and stationed themselves outside her room.

Ignoring them all, Xera told Namae what was going on and turned on the view screen. Scorpio fighters engaged the enemy in a bloody game of tag. The screen split into two sections. The smaller portion showed a Khun'tat transport already docked with the space station. Scorpio fighters concentrated their fire on the transport. Xera felt a chill as she realized the aliens were already taking prisoners.

There was a sudden flash from the alien battle cruiser, and the ship shuddered slightly around them. Xera blanched. "What was that?" Namae cried, wide-eyed.

Lord Atarus frowned. "The battle cruiser fired on us. That's unusual. Normally, they would get out with as many prisoners as they could and jump for hyperspace, with or without their fighters. There might be a breeding queen on the ship, which would make them more aggressive. They're very demanding when they're hungry. If I'm right she'll have a hatching chamber full of developing larvae."

Their warship's laser cannons returned fire on the Khun'tat battle cruiser. Both ships' shields stayed strong—for the moment.

"Wouldn't it make more sense to have the food before she laid eggs?" Xera asked. Not that she approved of the Khun'tat method of grocery shopping.

The LG shook his head. "They aren't logical like that. The queens especially are at the mercy of their instincts, and drones follow her lead. If she's hungry, they get food. She won't back off until her own ship is endangered."

"Why can't they just start a farm or something?" Xera demanded.

He ignored her question, knowing it was rhetorical.

Namae had a better one: "How long until her ship is endangered, Father?"

He was silent for some time as he stroked his long mustache. He seemed to be calculating as he watched the battle. "The station didn't have fighters of its own, but it was not defenseless. Many of the enemy fighters are disabled . . ." He indicated the floating wreckage.

Another blast flashed nearby, and he widened his stance to retain his balance. Calmly he went on: "But the mother ship is whole. They will not stop trying to take the prisoners—and Ryven will not stop trying to prevent it. We do not ever let our people be taken."

Which put them in a dangerous spot. They had to disable the mother ship before it beat them. The good news was that there were friendly ships coming. The aliens didn't have that advantage.

Xera opened her mouth to say so . . . and two more Khun'tat battleships jumped out of hyperspace. Namae went white. Xera saw her face and helped her sit down, feeling shaky herself. This was not good.

Even the LG looked grim. He watched as their ships opened fire on the two new arrivals, but they were grossly outgunned. The Khun'tat targeted the single-man fighters first, decimating their numbers. They also soon had the battleship's shields down. They began to take out its cannons, destroying any chance the Scorpio had to fight back.

The battleship was rocked by blasts, its engines trying to keep its shields and stabilizers working, and things seemed desperate. Then the situation took a turn for the worse. The Khun'tat battleship began to launch fighters. Minutes later, it launched a prisoner transport.

Xera felt the blood leave her head. They were coming for her. They were coming for them all.

"Come." Lord Atarus collected the two females and headed for the door. "Now is the time to go to the bridge." Their escort of soldiers closed around them, looking tense. Xera didn't have to ask why they were going to the bridge. It was time for a last stand. She did not want to end up on the meat wagon.

Trouble was, the Scorpio felt the same way. She knew from the videos she'd watched that they would blow the whole ship rather than be taken for food. They'd fight to the bitter end first, though. "Never lay down arms" might as well be the motto of the race. She was proud to be a part of the group and terrified at same time. It was an ugly way to die.

Ryven gripped her shoulder as they entered the bridge, and he sent a grim look at his father. Without a word, a warrior came up and handed them each a laser rifle. He showed the women how to use it.

The waiting was tense. Ryven positioned his family far away from the doors and stood by them. Screen after screen showed armored Khun'tat getting closer, taking prisoners. They shot out the cameras as they came, but those on the bridge could see the fighting getting closer. Big and ugly, with their hoselike tails at the back of their skulls, the Khun'tat crushed anything inanimate that got in their way but only stunned their other victims, either with guns or the venomous spines on the end of their head hoses.

The Scorpio resisted but were being swarmed. In twenty minutes the Khun'tat were amidships. A quarter hour more and they were past the galley.

Xera closed her eyes and faced the fact that she was going to die.

The Khun'tat were suddenly at the door to the bridge. Loud noises came from the other side as they fought to dismantle it. All the defenders could do was brace themselves and aim for the hole that would soon appear. Anything coming through would be greeted with lasers.

Xera looked at Ryven. He appeared very grim and very alone. She believed he was preparing to order the computer to blow the ship. Or perhaps she was wrong; maybe he'd already started the countdown and was just bracing against death.

She caught his eyes. A wordless symphony passed between them, sweet and doomed. She closed her eyes. His fingers curled around her arm.

The blasting at the door suddenly stopped.

Everyone froze. There was a variety of noises, sounds of exchanged gunfire. Shouts. Someone was battling outside the door! Tense minutes passed until suddenly the ship's com crackled to life.

"Ryven? It's Shiza. I don't mind telling you that you've got lousy hospitality." He had to repeat himself twice over the shouts of relief on the bridge. "Open the door, will you?"

Xera's muscles went liquid with relief. Ryven put his arm around her and kissed her hair. His grip was crushing, but she didn't care. Lord Atarus had his daughter in his arms, hushing her shuddering breaths.

They had to work a bit on the door controls before they could oblige Shiza since the mechanisms had been disabled in the attack. Even afterward, the door would only come halfway open before it jammed.

Shiza hunched under the vertically rising door and stood in his stiff battle suit, his head still covered in a helmet. He nodded to Lord Atarus and clasped forearms with Ryven. "Getting into trouble without me, are you?"

Ryven flashed him a grin. "What's our status?"

His bridge crew hurried to their stations and got to work while Shiza filled them in.

"The distress call was a decoy. A small ship was attacked, but by the time we got there, it was already destroyed and abandoned. I was already concerned when we got your message."

Shiza's battleship had taken out the original alien craft and rescued the prisoner transport. He'd then engaged one of the remaining battleships while the backup cruiser he'd summoned took out the other. He'd launched fighters as soon as he could to dock with Ryven's ship and stop the boarding process. They'd almost been too late.

Ryven's ship was heavily damaged. They had no shields left and no working defenses. The hull had been compromised in several places and would not stand a jump to hyperdrive. The engines had not been harmed, though. The ship would have to fly straight back home as they made repairs, a lengthy and dangerous proposition with Khun'tat popping in at will.

It was Ryven's ship and he wouldn't abandon it or his crew, but he refused to permit his family to remain in danger. Shiza was tapped to take them home, along with the survivors of the space station and any wounded. More ships would be arriving within the hour to escort all of them.

While everyone else was working on logistics, Xera happened to glance Shiza's way. He'd removed his helmet and was caught in an unguarded moment, his gaze on Namae. Quick, piercing and quite revealing—he wouldn't have wished anyone to witness that glance, she was certain. Xera let her eyes slide away, pretending not to notice his secret heart. Perhaps she pretended too hard. He sent her a warning glance then looked away.

Xera felt in the way on the bridge. Namae looked strained. Xera didn't want to divert necessary manpower, but she wanted to give herself and Namae a chance to recoup. Namae particularly needed it. She lightly touched Ryven's sleeve.

He glanced at her, alert. "Yes?"

"We're underfoot here. Is it safe to go and pack? We'll need a few things, and it will hurry us along."

He followed her gaze to his sister's strained face. "I see. Let me check the security scans." He looked over the surveillance data and sweeper reports. "You may go. Your bodyguards will go with you. And, Shiza . . . ?" He looked inquiringly at his friend.

"Of course. I'll stay in contact as I transport them." Shiza touched his communicator as a gesture.

Ryven looked subtly relieved. "Thank you." He brushed Xera's hand. "I'll say good-bye before you leave."

She nodded, eyes downcast as she pressed his hand. She longed to hug him, but understood his feelings of reserve. He would hold her when they were alone.

It was nerve-racking, traveling the hallways where Khun'tat had recently roamed. Not all the corpses had been removed. The bodies made grizzly mile markers for the journey.

She and Namae packed lightly. The docking vessels didn't need any extra weight, not with the need to quickly haul the wounded, and they didn't want to linger. Xera was done before Namae and went to check on her. She was pleased to see Na-mae subtly relying on Shiza, allowing him to help her pack a travel case. She was doing her best to seem serene, but it was obvious the shocks of the day had taken their toll.

He was subtle in his concern and matter-of-fact in its exercise. His practicality was a good mask for the glint of worry in his eye.

Ryven entered the room just as Shiza was seal-ing Namae's travel case. He hugged his sister and murmured assurances, then took Xera in his arms. He didn't say anything. Fiercely, she returned the hug. "I'll miss you. I'm glad we're alive." She breathed in his scent. "Hurry home."

He breathed deeply, his nose in her hair. "Woman . . ." He shook his head. "Shiza will keep you safe. Hurry home yourself—I want to know you're away from harm." He would never say, "I love you" while others looked on.

He released her. "It's time."

He, Shiza and an armed escort took them down the grim corridors to a crowded transport ship. Xera solemnly clasped hands with Ryven and watched as his father and sister said good-bye. Their bags were stowed in the webbing, and they settled into their seats. Their ship was sealed, the docking clamps disengaged. A glance out the port-hole showed Ryven's battleship getting smaller.

Xera looked away, unable to dwell on it. Already she missed him. It was depressing, the thought of leaving him behind, but she also understood the need: he didn't dare to be worrying about his fam-ily at a time like this. She wasn't wild about staying exposed out here anyway, not when there was nothing she could do. Insisting on staying with him now would be childish, even if she felt lost and adrift in his world without him as an anchor.

Funny, she hadn't realized how dependent upon him she'd become.

Chapter Sixteen

Ryven had little time to think of his wife. With his ship so badly damaged, he had his hands full directing his crew. Thankfully, Shiza had loaned him extra men to make up for his casualties. Some of those men he put to making repairs. Others went with him to explore the remains of the Khun'tat craft.

He was grateful his wife would hear about this exploit later—if at all. Women were touchy about that kind of thing. The reconnaissance had to be done, however, and he wanted to be a part of the exploration team that tried to discover why the Khun'tat had behaved so erratically and gotten so deep in Scorpio territory. None of them wanted a repeat of the situation.

The second-in-command of the other Scorpio battleship joined him as he docked his troop transport with the Khun'tat vessel. Scans showed life-forms inside the ship, some of which were humanoid—probably some survivors from the space station. Getting to them would be a challenge, though. Even after they forced the docking hatch open, they were faced with bigger challenges. The Khun'tat ship was a series of honeycombs; layers of phosphorescent orange cells stacked on top of one another, formed around a hollow core. Each comb led to a warren of tunnels organized in an obscure way known only to Khun'tat. Stairs linked the different levels, but there was precious little cover while they climbed them. Any enemy who wanted to take a shot at them would have easy pickings.

The humanoid readings were all coming from the third level—the brood area. Mouth set in a grim line, Ryven led his troops in. Oddly, they encountered no resistance. Apparently the remaining Khun'tat were content to guard their queen, deep in the center of the ship, their most protected location. He almost wished he'd had more to shoot when they finally entered the brood chamber.

Stunned and helpless, a few people lay piled on the floor, awaiting attention. Others hadn't been as lucky. Several had already been sealed up in brood chambers. They'd had no defense when larvae had attached to them and began to suck their blood. Some of the grotesque worms had attached to legs or engulfed hands. Others had chosen stomachs. One was sucking greedily on an eye socket. And if Ryven and the others hadn't come, the adult Khun'tat would have been feasting on the drained bodies by suppertime.

Ryven swallowed to settle his gorge and ordered those who couldn't be saved to be shot, mercy deaths being preferable to being savaged. The rest of the victims were taken to the transports for evacuation. Only when the last had vanished did they proceed with phase two.

Their goal was to take the queen alive for questioning. Interrogating a drone would be useless, as they were little more than puppets, but to succeed they first had to get past the twenty or thirty drones guarding her. They couldn't get a more accurate body count, as the room was heavily shielded.

They shot a spike through the door with a high-powered gun that also was loaded with a special gas to incapacitate the Khun'tat nervous system. Ryven gave the signal, and everyone moved back as a magnetic charge was affixed to the door. Specially designed to spend its energy in one direction, it emitted a sonic blast that shivered the door to hot molten pieces.

Thanks to the nerve gas, the aliens inside reeled as if they were roaring drunk. A few got off shots, but the battle was hopelessly lopsided. Ryven's men captured a few and shot the rest. The captives would be used for experiments, to develop things like the nerve gas. The Scorpio had no qualms on treating these prisoners like animals, either. An eye for an eye, blood for blood . . .

The queen snarled at them. She was much larger than the males, with features set in a broader head. She had no hands or feet, just a wormlike body covered in rounded, glassy blue plates. Her head hoses were harder looking, almost like horns trailing down her neck. She had no purpose other than to eat and breed, but she was revered by her race.

Ryven took satisfaction in knowing that he'd just killed and captured all of her favorite drones and breeding partners. This monster fed on the bodies of his people. This queen had probably eaten hundreds of his kind, for the queens were always given the best food. For Khun'tat, the best food was always Scorpio.

He turned and casually fired on the slimy green eggs piled next to her. There was an explosion and a horrendous stench of burned goo.

The queen roared.

Ryven casually looked at her. "A lovely smell, no? I know you can understand me. I want to know why you chose here and now to attack. If you deny me, I will destroy your eggs one by one—then I will see to you."

The queen gave a guttural snarl. She looked behind her.

Ryven's men all tensed and aimed their guns. Were there more Khun'tat hiding back there?

What emerged next was a surprise. A slender young woman appeared from behind the queen. Unmistakably humanoid, she was as pale as a corpse and dressed all in burnt yellow. The garment's bright color made her pallor even more ghastly.

Ryven's men looked to him for an explanation. He had none. Khun'tat ate people; they didn't let them run loose in the queen's egg room.

Not that the girl looked capable of running. If anything, she seemed likely to faint at any moment. Nevertheless, she parted her lips and said faintly, "The queen says, 'I will not speak the language of food.'"

Ryven's lip curled, though his disgust was not for the girl. She did not look Scorpio, not with that hair the color of toasted sugar tipped with black. She couldn't be human, either, unless they came with pointed ears and cat eyes. Where had she come from?

"Is that what you are, her food?" he asked.

The girl's eyes were so old, so weary. "I am of the Leo-Ahni. We are . . . allies with the Khun'tat."

The pause in her voice made him wonder. "Yet they feed on you." That had to be the source of her pallor. He'd lay odds that the girl was blooded, and often. "It would seem to make you their slaves, not their equals."

The girl was silent.

Ryven studied the queen. Perhaps he didn't need her after all. "I have never seen your kind, girl, yet you speak our language. Why?"

"We are taught. The queen does not speak the language of food, though she understands all things. You are food."

He laughed. "Is that so?" Before she could blink, he'd grabbed her and pulled her out of the reach of the queen, who roared angrily. The Khun'tat monarch started to charge, but quickly drew back as laser fire scorched her hide.

Ryven thrust the girl at a medic. "Do a med-scan, quick. I don't want her dying on us." He looked back at the angry queen. "Now we will talk—without your mouthpiece this time. You have things to tell me."

The girl lay in sick bay, barely conscious and severely anemic. The Khun'tat had installed a shunt in her arm and bled her quite often, judging by her condition. She was dehydrated, her hair coarse and her heartbeat patchy. There was no doubt they'd saved her life by taking her from captivity.

Ryven was fatigued from questioning the queen. Her answers had not come easily or without pain, but she'd told them enough in the end. The queens had used the Leo-Ahni to study the Scorpio, taking a few of them on as slaves and translators. While ostensibly an honor, very often those servants ended up as food. The Khun'tat truly couldn't control their appetite, which made Ryven speculate on the condition of the Leo people. Had the Khun'tat tried to be farmers and found themselves unsuited to the task? Unable to keep from consuming their stock?

Whatever the case, the Leo were behind the Khun'tat's recent change in tactics. It did not bode well for their relationship.

Unfortunately, the only one of the Leo Ryven had met now lay in his sick bay on the verge of a coma. The doctors were working to replicate her blood for a transfusion, but it was going slowly. He could hardly interrogate her in her current state. There was no telling what damage may have been done to her mind, either. It couldn't have been easy serving on that ship, watching the queen feed on the captured. The girl might not be quite sane.

Reports of similar attacks were now coming in, including one on Toosun's ship. Toosun acquitted himself well, but another battleship was destroyed. The captain had self-destructed his ship when it was obvious all was lost. Unlike Ryven, he'd had no last-minute rescue.

Communications with several outposts and smaller ships had been lost. All were in a state of emergency. Already demands had come back from the lord governor's emergency assembly to do everything possible to heal the Leo girl, and *now*. Further escort and more doctors were being sent to make sure she reached safety. Survival depended on it. The Scorpio wanted to know where her home world was, fast. Her people would be given a chance to talk, to cease hostilities. After that, there would be no mercy.

Knowing it was useless to wait around sick bay, Ryven went to see the ship's status on repairs. The sooner they were patched, the sooner he could get home.

Xera's ship had arrived on Rsik the previous day. She didn't feel much like company. Ryven's family was grimly focused on news of the Khun'tat's surprise attacks that were now occurring with alarming frequency. Xera had thought about it until her mind began to chase round and round, and she was done.

She'd gotten Lord Atarus to send a message to her people concerning the new dangers. Thanks to the new relay station he'd agreed to help set up during their talks with the GE and IC, the message wouldn't take as much effort as the initial contact had. She was grateful: as long as the two sides maintained a truce, she had a real chance of sending occasional messages to her family. And that benefit paled in comparison to the importance of informing her people about the Khun'tat threat. She didn't see how a moon base could possibly prosper in her intended location now, as she didn't want responsibility for innocent people being hurt.

She was a little worried about the GE heeding
the warnings. If they continued their pattern of
sneakiness, they might use the Scorpio's preoccupation with the Khun'tat to continue snooping
around, maybe even on the planet she'd been ma-
rooned on. That might make continued communication with her family difficult, for although the
Scorpio relay station was powerful, it relied on
other stations in human space to bounce her messages home. If her signal was intentionally interrupted because the GE started a war . . .

She sighed. She'd mention her concerns to
Ryven, but that was really all she could do.

The stress had driven her out of her rooms and
to explore. She'd sent Namae on an errand, accepted that she couldn't do the same with her
bodyguards and chosen to tune out their silent
presence—except when she had to ask directions,
of course. Happily, the guards were like very well-
trained department store clerks: they had a gift for
showing up only when she needed them; the rest
of the time they were remarkably unobtrusive. As a
result, she got to tour the marketplace virtually
carefree.

It was surprising what a low-tech, cheerful place
the food market was, with open stalls of vegetables
lining the main road. Many eating establishments
were just a short walk away, and all took full advantage of the abundant supply of fresh fruits and
vegetables available in the market. She chose one
at random and ended up having a lovely meal.
The waiter, who introduced himself as Apal, listened carefully to her list of allergies and recom-
mended a dish. It turned out to be a lovely braised

meat in some kind of savory purple sauce. She'd been so pleased she'd let him choose dessert, too, and was rewarded with an incredibly light yet crispy cookie filled with a delectable cream that oozed out with every bite.

She grinned at him and licked her fingers—a compliment in the Scorpio culinary world. "I can't wait to tell my family about this place! Your chef is a magician."

He bowed slightly. "You honor our humble establishment, dear lady." There was a twinkle in his eye. She wondered how often newsworthy guests came in and whether she'd start a trend.

Afterward she went shopping—Ryven had set her up an impressively stocked bank account, though she was shy about spending anything. She didn't make a purchase from the hopeful vendors. Children were not given gifts on their birthdays here. Instead, a child was expected to give his mother a flower and to prepare a special tea or drink for their father. If their parents were deceased, that honor was transferred to another near relative, such as an aunt or uncle, grandmother or grandfather. Adult children might prepare a special meal. Spouses and friends did not give each other gifts to mark the day. It was a rather nice custom, but she still planned to celebrate Ryven's birthday in her own way, with a gift—whenever it was. She'd have to find out the date. He could adapt to her customs, too.

She wasn't sure what he would like: a hazard of knowing him for such a short time. She had seen his collection of weapons—of course he had one— but she didn't know much about Scorpio blades or the like. Toosun might be helpful there, might have further suggestions. She wasn't opposed to going with a simple gift, either. There might be a favorite dish she could learn to prepare, or she could give him a massage. She smiled, considering what fun that might be. If only he would return!

She'd been thinking and walking, and her feet had taken her to the front of an elaborate building made of polished black tiles. Silver-tiled steps led up to an impressively carved crystal door. "What is this?" she asked her escort.

"An art museum. Some of the Lady Tessla's paintings are displayed here."

"Really?" she asked with interest. Of course she had to check it out. There was nothing like being related to a famous artist, after all.

She paid the admission for herself and her escort, and entered the museum. The place was huge, and set up as a box within a box, so there was plenty to see. She'd gotten about a third of the way through and was admiring a sculpture of a creature so alien, she wasn't sure if it was real or a fantasy of the artist's mind, when a harsh laugh caught her attention.

Her bodyguards closed rank before she could even identify the origin of the mockery. "Leave and you will not be hurt," said Xtal, her chief of security.

"This is a public place," a broken, harsh voice insisted. "And I have something to say to the woman."

Curious, Xera tried to see around her bodyguards, but was stymied by their tall frames. Where did Ryven find these guys? She'd swear half of them were a hand over six feet—at least. Sighing, she gently touched the biceps of the two in front and pushed slightly. "Two inches, please, guys."

She was reluctantly accorded six. Xtal explained tersely, "This is Lady Namae's ex-husband, my lady. Your husband would not approve of your speaking to him."

And no wonder. The man before her was a wreck. His face appeared battered, one cheekbone sunken deeper than the other. His nose had been badly broken and healed with a twist that suggested sinus problems. It had been slit between the nostrils, too, and the upper lip bore a wide scar in the middle. He had a collarlike device on his neck that allowed him to speak and breathe, judging from the grill in front. When he spoke, his lips didn't move. He opened his mouth and showed her his forked tongue. "Your husband's brand of justice, lady."

She blinked. *Ryven* had done this? When he'd spoken of breaking Tovark, it had sounded political. Now she saw it had been physical, too. She wondered if he'd been trying to spare her the gruesome details. She knew he wasn't a man to boast about things like this. She also knew he was ruthless enough to exact this kind of revenge, but she couldn't imagine the kind of beating it would have taken to cause such lasting damage.

Her stomach clenched as she tried, and failed, to visualize herself delivering such punishment. The knife work alone—she suppressed a shiver What Tovark had done was bad, but did he deserve this kind of punishment? She had no good answer.

She spoke coolly to Tovark, knowing this was no time for pity. "Then you are unwise to speak to me. He may wish to finish the job."

The man blinked. Perhaps he hadn't expected such a reply. "I wish to speak to you alone," he suggested.

"Absolutely not," she said without hesitation. Even if she'd been inclined—and she was decidedly not—her bodyguards would never permit such foolishness. They weren't the kind of pansies to be talked into whims that compromised security. One look at Tovark would remind them of the follies of displeasing their lord. Not that Ryven would do such a thing to his own men, she thought.

"A pity," Tovark said. "I had heard you were forced to become his bride. That cannot sit well with you."

She raised her brows at his strategy. He really thought he could create fellow feeling in her? "You believed I would become your ally?" She shook her head at his folly. "You overreach yourself. I don't approve of what happened to Namae, either."

His face twisted. "She was a whoring little—" His speech was ended abruptly; Xtal had stepped forward and flattened him with one strike.

The security man now stared down at his unconscious victim and grunted in disgust. "Come, lady. Doubtless you wish to retire now." It was an accurate statement, and something of a command.

Blinking at the speed with which he'd defended Namae, and with which he would have defended her as well, Xera let him escort her away. Scorpio bodyguards didn't put up with much, apparently.

She asked him about it.

Xtal glanced briefly at her. "I'm charged with defending all that my lord holds dear. That includes you and his family. This is what he would have done if anyone spoke in such a manner in his presence."

She thought about that and decided she liked the sentiment, even if it had been a bit rough and ready. "That's heartwarming, Xtal. Thank you." She thought he colored a little, though he stoically avoided her gaze. To tease him, she added, "I'll have to tell your boss he chose well." Now the man was definitely blushing.

She sobered, thinking of Ryven. He'd sent her nightly communiqués, and sometimes over the past few days he'd had the time to establish a real-time link and exchange a few words. The situation didn't permit much more, but at least she knew he was thinking of her. She'd send him an electronic message, tell him about her day, commend Xtal and ask him about Tovark. He'd be bound to have something to say about all that. The odds were good he'd call in person.

Smiling, she started composing the message in her head.

Namae was horrified when she heard that Xera had eaten at a public place without her husband or family. Apparently it was considered extremely bold, though common women did it all the time.

"Why?" Xera asked mildly. "My family owned a tavern, remember? And several inns."

Namae scowled. "You're not on your world. People will think you're too daring to be ladylike if you do that here."

Xera shrugged. "Then I'll have to be on my best behavior the rest of the time. Maybe they'll come to think of me as merely eccentric. Alien, you know?"

Namae actually rolled her eyes heavenward and mouthed a prayer.

Xera smiled, picturing Ryven's face when he saw this recording. She had been in the middle of her message when Namae entered, and had left the recorder going. Namae didn't know. Though she was taking the girl's words into consideration, she couldn't help provoking her husband's sister. "My bodyguards didn't say anything."

"Of course not! It's not their place to correct their lady."

"Hm. Well, no harm done. I'll try to have you along in the future—if you have time to spare. Shiza seems determined to have you to himself."

Namae blushed. "He asked my opinion on choosing a gift for my brother, if you must know. Toosun's first successful voyage as a commander of a starship must be celebrated. We are very proud of him."

Xera smiled to herself. "So he took you and Lady Tessla shopping? How strange. Most men would rather cut off their right hand than subject themselves to that."

Namae gave her a droll look that would have been out of character before last week. "Maybe his foster mother is pestering him to marry again. If he appears to be courting an eligible woman, she relents for a time."

Xera clapped in delight. "You just called yourself an eligible woman! I'm impressed. My work here is done."

Namae merely sniffed. "Since you're settled, I have some things to do. Good evening to you."

"And to you," Xera called fondly at Namae's retreating back. She let herself smile for a moment, and then returned to reporting on her day. Namae didn't have to hear the serious parts.

Less than an hour later, Ryven called. He glowered at her. "You shouldn't have spoken to him."

Xera sighed. She'd been sampling a glass of excellent spirits and felt relaxed. "My love, have I told you how handsome you are?"

"I will not be distracted," he said, though he visibly mellowed. "At least Xtal kept the interview short."

"I'd hardly call it an interview. Heaven only knows what Namae saw in the man." There was a short silence. "You certainly left your mark on him."

Ryven studied her. "The slit nose and forked tongue is a mark of disgrace. The rest was retribution."

"I see. I'll have to avoid making you angry, then."

His frown darkened. "You could do nothing—*nothing*—to earn that kind of punishment. Consider what the man did."

She did, and sighed. Maybe there was more to the story she didn't know. Asking Namae was out of the question, and she knew her husband didn't have time for a long discussion. There were other people she could ask. For now, she said, "I understand. I suppose I'm more squeamish than you are."

He relaxed a fraction. "You are a woman. That's to be expected."

She choked slightly. "Those are fighting words, buddy!"

That made him smirk. "Then I'm lucky you are squeamish, aren't I?"

She opened her mouth, then shut it. Sometimes a hasty reply was the wrong approach. Instead she said mildly, "So, tell me about the Leo girl. Did she tell you anything today?"

Ryven looked frustrated. "She stares at us vacantly, as if she's mind-damaged. If she is faking, it is an excellent ploy. I can't stomach it for long."

Xera looked at him sideways. "Is she pretty?"

His mouth dropped open a fraction. "Are you jealous at a time like this? She is pale and . . . *limp*. I could never desire such a—are you laughing?"

She smirked, amused and pleased that they'd developed such a comfortable rapport so easily. "Sorry. I'm just missing you. I'll try to tease you about something else."

"Please." He paused and seemed to reorder his thoughts. "The repairs are going well. We should return in the next hand of days."

She perked up. "Really? That's great! I can't wait to see you, and all joking aside, I'd really like to meet that alien girl."

"We'll see. I have to go. Keep yourself well. I'm looking forward to seeing you, too." The heated look in his eyes told her how much. He closed the connection.

She blinked at his abruptness. Well, what had she expected? He wasn't going to get sentimental over a communication line, as it were. She'd just have to coax his feelings out of him in person . . . though she did feel a dash impatient with him. Was it really so hard to tell a woman that he cared?

That night she had a nightmare about the Khun'tat. She woke in a sweat and couldn't get back to sleep, so she settled for watching entertainment programs and thinking about the day. Knowing someone would be awake, she called her security team. After assuring them she was fine, just having bad dreams, she requested a report on Tovark, starting with the time just before his marriage dissolved. If they were surprised, the men showed no sign. They said it was possible and would look into it. She thanked them and went back to watching movies until she fell asleep on the couch.

She staggered blearily through dance class the next morning and spent some time in the flight simulators, grateful that Ryven had forwarded permission. She was making a tiny bit of progress on the navigation and weapons systems. Sometimes she wondered if engineers made ships systems complicated on purpose, but learning kept her busy. She was steadily making her way through the flight manuals.

She'd told Namae about her studies, but the young woman was uninterested. She'd taken one look at the amount of information there was to learn and winced. "There are pilots for that sort of thing," she'd said.

"What if you're in a shuttle and there's a problem? Wouldn't it be nice to know what to do?"

Namae frowned at her. "I'd do the sensible thing and call for help. It could be remote flown to safety for me."

"What if there weren't time?" Xera persisted.

"You can't know everything," Namae had said placidly, and that had been the end of the conversation.

Xera told herself she'd be able to talk to the guys she knew about it. After all, several of them were pilots. She'd have to be delicate about it, though. Surely they'd share Ryven's suspicions about her hobby, even if they were polite about it.

Maybe they were right to worry. In the back of her mind, there was still the question of *what if*.

The ironic thing was that she truly did love to fly. There was a freedom to be found in the exercise that existed nowhere else. Maybe Ryven could share that with her someday . . . if he had enough trust in her.

He hadn't said anything about her joining the martial arts class. As the lone woman in the group of men, she was often frustrated. The guys were reluctant to hurt her and were gentler than they should be. She understood their confusion—after all, she'd never be as fast or strong as they were. From their point of view, she was wasting her time. She'd heard that before, and it just made her more determined. She knew when she was right. All she had to do was think of Captain Khan and push harder. The guys would adapt in time.

Maybe it had been thoughts of Khan that had prompted Ryven to give her permission. Despite the risks, he wasn't the sort of man to deny a woman the right to defend herself. As the battle with the Khun'tat proved, things happened.

When she'd finished with the simulator for the day, Xtal informed her he had the report she'd requested.

She tried to suppress a yawn as she cradled a hot cup of tea. Unfortunately, it didn't have quite the rejuvenating powers of coffee. "Hold on to it for me, please. I'm not feeling as paranoid as I was in the middle of the night. I think it will keep for a couple more hours. I'd hate to ruin a perfectly good nap over him."

Xtal actually smiled. "As you wish."

Unfortunately, her plans for a nap were derailed. Her father-in-law and Ryven's sisters invited her to share lunch with them. It was too early in their relationship for Xera to feel comfortable about not going, so she let Namae help her dress for the occasion.

"Are you well? You don't seem rested," Namae asked with concern as she brushed Xera's hair. "Perhaps you should sleep instead."

Xera grunted. "I'd probably just dream about the Khun'tat again."

"Oh! I admit I've had a bad dream or two since the attack. At least they have faded for me. I find listening to soothing music during my rest to be helpful. It keeps me grounded."

"Good idea, but I've made it this long without nightmares, so maybe last night was an aberration. Maybe I'll walk myself through some positive visualizations about slaying them. Sometimes that helps."

Namae seemed taken aback. "How . . . interesting. Perhaps you can tell me how that's done as we walk."

Xera was surprised to see Shiza present at the lunch. Though he spent most of the time speaking with Lord Atarus about manly things, he did take the time to answer the ladies' questions about the recent attacks. When he noticed Xera's unease at the subject, he told the others, "Let's choose another subject than the Khun'tat. Xera has suffered evil dreams over this and still doesn't look recovered."

Xera blinked, surprised by his perception. "How did you know?"

It was Lord Atarus who answered. "Your security team told Ryven. He spoke to us about it. We'd be amiss if we didn't look after you in his place."

She smiled. "That's kind of you, but don't leave the subject for my sake. I'm a big girl." In spite of her words, that line of discussion was closed for the rest of the meal.

When her yawns finally became too hard to contain, her amused father-in-law dismissed her. "Go, sleep. Play some sweet music as you rest—it often banishes ill dreams."

"Thank you," Xera said. As if in afterthought, she asked Shiza, "Will you walk me to the door? I need your opinion about something." She glanced at Namae and smiled at the girl's scowl. It was fun teasing her, and fine if she thought the conversation concerned her. In a way, it did.

Shiza blinked slowly but rose from his cushion. "Of course."

Once they'd turned into the entrance hall, she paused. "I have a question about Ryven. I would have asked Namae, but I don't want to upset her."

"About Tovark?"

Xera nodded.

Shiza looked grave. "You should ask your husband these things."

She sighed. "I'd love to, but he's a little busy right now. I try not to worry, but I can't help it about things like this. I don't want any more sleepless nights."

Shiza inclined his head. "What is your question?"

Xera looked at the wall while she gathered her thoughts. "When I asked him about Tovark, Ryven said he broke him financially and socially. He made the whole thing seem very bloodless, but when I saw Tovark yesterday . . ." She looked at Shiza.

He appeared disapproving. "You think Ryven lied to you?"

"I think he omitted a few details." They had a silent standoff for a moment.

Shiza watched her with crossed arms, as if calculating his answer. "The social retribution was for what Tovark did to Namae. The physical punishment concerned what he did to her maid."

Xera felt her stomach clench. "What was that?"

His look chastened her. "Doubtless he wished to spare you, but it seems too late for that now. Tovark couldn't reach Namae—her family would no longer permit it. It angered him, so he sought a less well-guarded target. He took her maid and savaged her instead. . . . Since he didn't rape her, he was not sentenced to death, but as a member of the family who employed her, Ryven was given permission to execute justice, short of maiming and blinding. You've seen the results."

She took a breath. "So Ryven hunted him down and . . ."

"Fought him, though Tovark has little skill to boast of. Did you think he was restrained for Ryven's pleasure? That isn't how we serve justice."

"I didn't know what to think, which is why I asked," Xera said, feeling sick. "Thank you, I understand now. What happened to the maid?"

Shiza looked pensive. "Namae's family paid for

the recovery, but the girl wanted nothing more to do with serving great houses. She returned home and eventually married."

At least there was that. "I can see why Xtal punched him. Ugh!" Xera shook her head as if to dislodge the thought. "Okay, I need something more pleasant to think about, and there was one more thing. When is Ryven's birthday?"

Shiza looked puzzled by the question, but after a long pause he told her. She thanked him and said good-bye.

Of course, she wasn't really able to shake the story of the maid from her mind so quickly; that sort of thing took a while to process. It was better knowing the truth than doubting her husband's restraint, though. She had enough problems on her plate without adding that.

Chapter Seventeen

Each day, Xera added an entry to a journal. She'd found the tome in a shop that sold handmade paper and bound books. She'd been charmed by some flower petal paper and amused by a selection of scented inks, but it was the tooled leather notebook with creamy, faintly speckled paper that caught her eye. She hadn't kept a journal in years, but knew the practice was therapeutic. Figuring she could use a little therapy, she bought the book. Now she used it to keep track of her thoughts. It provided a useful sounding board, and she would consult the entries to fill out messages she would send to her sisters.

Ryven had told her she could send one message a week, and he was generous at that. The cost of pin beam over such distances was prohibitive, to say the least, but she was grateful for everything she could get. It was fortunate he was such a wealthy man, and even more so that her family could afford the bill. It was an expensive way to communicate, but she certainly felt the money was well spent.

She was starting to settle into a routine—one she knew she'd use often, if this separation were usual with Ryven's job. She missed him, but also realized that even if he were there she couldn't own every minute of his day. She was thinking of getting a part-time job, something that wouldn't interfere with her studies. The whole ambassador gig was all good and well, but it made for some slow days when the people she was supposed to represent were light years away.

She smiled, thinking ruefully that she was a true working-class girl. She'd landed in the lap of luxury with few demands on her time, and suddenly the idea of owning her own tavern and busting her tail waiting tables sounded appealing. Not that she really wanted to go back to that, specifically; nor did she want to run a staff of maids as she had done. Being in charge had been an interesting challenge, even though she'd worked as hard at scrubbing as any of the others and been forced to deal with the staff, too. She wasn't sure what she wanted; she just felt restless. Maybe she needed to own her own business.

Then again, maybe it was more her sisters and less the inn that she missed. Even that was changing now, with Gem married and reproducing, and Brandy's on-again-off-again relationship. Xera wondered what the status was on that now. She supposed it didn't really matter; her sisters' world was closed to her. It was just that she missed her siblings, wondered how they were.

It didn't help that she didn't really feel accepted by Ryven's family. Oh, it had started off well enough, but things were hardly ideal. The lord governor welcomed her, but he just wanted a wife for his son. Tessla was determined to mold Xera into her idea of a lady, because that's what clan matriarchs did. Namae was all right, but Ryven's other sisters and wider family made her feel excluded. They were polite, but they had nothing in common with Xera. She had seen a faint look of horror on one lady's face when she said how much she enjoyed martial arts, and another woman had looked at her as if pained and begun another topic when Xera mentioned how she used to help toss the drunks out of the taproom. They didn't say anything negative to her face, but she'd seen her sisters-in-law exchange speaking looks. They never said anything hurtful, but they never warmed up, either. Their husbands studied Xera as if they didn't know what to make of her. Everywhere she went she got second glances. She was different. Alien.

Ruthlessly she shook off the melancholy. Perhaps it was time to assess what her strengths and skills were, maybe do a little research into Scorpio business practices. It might even be worth her while to take a class or two. It would give her something to do.

She mentioned as much to Ryven in an electronic letter.

No, was his one word reply.

She stared in disbelief at the terse message. What did he mean, *no*? She wrote in response, *I hope you didn't mean to sound rude, boy. I'm giving you the benefit of the doubt, though I admit I'm rather annoyed.* After some thought, she deleted *boy* and put in *Atarus.* She went on, *I think I would make a great business owner, and it would keep me occupied while you are away on long trips. You'd rather have me busy than moping about after you, wouldn't you?* She thought about adding more, but decided there was no need to rant.

His reply arrived twenty minutes after she sent her message. It read, *You're bored. I will give you something to do.*

She huffed. Bored? What was he planning to do, have her knit socks? She wasn't the type of woman who enjoyed sitting at home doing handicrafts. She was itching to be productive. She'd worked herself into a fine state, in fact, when the door chime sounded. Still scowling, she went to answer.

Lady Tessla looked amused. "I see the bridal days are over. Ready to take the mantle of a real wife, are you?"

Nonplussed, Xera stepped aside as the lady swept into the room. "I'm frankly grateful you're the industrious sort. Try as I might, I could not coax my nieces to assume the role of family hostess. Coercion didn't work any better on them than it did on my daughters. Spoiled, really. Too used to their amusements and projects. Well." She looked Xera over with almost avaricious glee. "And here you are, bored, trained to run a staff and host entertainments, with nothing else to do."

Xera coughed on her astonished amusement. "Ryven contacted you, didn't he?"

The lady raised a brow. "If a two sentence note counts as contact. 'My wife is bored. She'd make a great hostess, wouldn't she?' But naturally, he had to say no more."

"I see," Xera said. Sort of. Still, Tessla's enthusiasm was contagious. Perhaps this is what she needed. "What did you have in mind?"

What the woman had in mind turned out to be exhausting. She was giving a little party for three hundred close family members and friends. Everything from the selection of music for the dance, dining arrangements and menu planning would have to be arranged. Xera would be required to meet with the head chef, decorators, musicians and florists and help plan the menu. In addition to that, she was to greet the guests at the door with Ryven, who would be standing in for his father as was customary at these functions. Tessla declared it would now be her privilege to join her brother, whom she said had been allowed to enjoy himself alone for far too long.

"Youth must be trained to replace experience," the lady declared. "And one day *you* will be experienced and training youth. It's a very tidy circle, you see."

Xera frowned, her head already buzzing with endless lists of details. "You're not planning to kick off anytime soon, are you? I mentioned I'd been in charge of cleaning maids, not the whole inn. My sister Gem could likely do the whole thing without losing sleep but—"

Tessla waved her hand. "You admit the skill is in your blood. You will adapt." She smiled. "You'll have to. We have events of this magnitude at least once a month, with smaller dinners weekly. Now that Ryven is married, he can finally set up a proper household and entertain."

Xera sighed. So, she'd become a hostess of what was essentially a rotating dining hall. She supposed there were worse fates. It did throw a damper on her plans for a part-time job. Apparently being married to Ryven was employment in itself.

"Your friends will want to reciprocate, too," continued Lady Tessla. "I imagine you'll find yourself with more invitations than you can accept. You begin to see why I exercise diligently."

Xera shook her head, smiling. "You're turning me into a politician's wife."

Tessla smiled in return. "Only showing you the path, dear. You've already arrived at the door, you see." She patted Xera's arm. "You'll be wonderful. Now, about this menu . . ."

To Xera's surprise, her sisters-in-law privately confided their thanks for taking on their terror of an aunt. When she just smiled and said she didn't mind a bit, that it was actually enjoyable at times, they were even more impressed. Her status rose within the family hierarchy.

From her point of view, she was doing nothing to advance it. But Xera soon observed that those in charge of social activities were greatly respected—provided they did a good job, of course. Nobody esteemed a miserly or awkward hostess. Xera had never been shy, however, and understood that adequate portion size and an abundance of good drinks made for good business. It was the same when planning a party: treat the guests much like valued customers, remain formal with staff and rake in the admiration. She had to be satisfied with that, since they certainly weren't raking in coin. She was staggered by the amount of money these functions cost.

"I'm amazed that you're spending so much on entertainment," she admitted to Tessla. "How does the family keep from going bankrupt?"

Tessla looked surprised then laughed. "Have you no idea of your husband's income? What has he given you for allowance?"

Xera told her, and then added, "He's been generous, and there's no way I can spend it all. I like to go out and shop now and then, but I just can't see throwing money away on frivolous stuff all the time. Value for dollars and all that. It's a business class thing," she finished wryly.

Tessla studied her thoughtfully. "This is not such a bad thing. It requires no apology.

"Regarding the entertainments . . . my daughter, you've married into a wealthy house. These gatherings cost no more for us to give than if you'd invited one or two friends to share your own dinner—perhaps even less. Once you have become familiar with the process, it takes only a couple of hours to plan. Staff handles the rest, though of course you must oversee their work, for any flaws in the engagements will be attributed to you. From conception to the moment you farewell the last guest, all eyes are on you."

Xera nodded. That, too, was just like running an inn. If the staff made a mistake, management took the heat.

"As for your concern about money, I think it will be well for your husband to sit with you and discuss his finances and business affairs, since you are competent with such things. Many women are not and could care less where the money comes from, as long as there is plenty of it. Be assured that

Ryven has an astute financial mind and will not impoverish his household.

"As for your allowance, I suggest you learn to enjoy it. If you don't wish to spend it all on yourself, then use a portion to support charitable endeavors. I favor those that train the poor in profitable skills, but there are many to choose from." Lady Tessla smiled and squeezed Xera's hand. "Yours is a new life, but it can be rich and full. That is what I want for you." She patted Xera's hand and leaned back. "Besides, it will benefit Ryven if you are happy, and I do like my family taken care of."

Xera laughed, touched by Tessla's concern. "I've noticed." She was silent for a moment as she considered whether she'd enjoy the role Tessla offered. At length she decided to give it a fair trial. While it wasn't the life she'd thought she'd lead when she'd left home to start her career with the GE, it had its challenges. If she tried it and didn't like it, she could always find something more interesting to do. Besides, the things she'd learn in this role were bound to help when she put on her ambassador hat . . . when there were actually humans to represent, that was.

She frowned. There had been no pin beams from the GE or IC for her. Had Ryven known how little she'd be called on to do her job? She remembered his comment about her moving into an "advisory position" and wondered. At the time she'd had other things on her mind and thought he'd meant one day in the future, but perhaps she'd misunderstood. Had he known all along, even from the beginning, how little she'd be called on to perform her duties? But that made no sense. Why would he have wanted the position for her, if that were the case? They were going to have to talk about it very soon, but it would have to wait until he got home. This was not the sort of conversation she wanted to have over e-mail.

She was dreaming of autumn. Leaves fell all around. Bright and beautiful shades of bronze and gold, they evaded her fingers and fluttered to the ground, forming a soft carpet under the trees. Xera spun with delight and fell into a pile. The leaves felt as soft as thistledown.

She was not alone. The sun blinded her to the man above, but she knew his voice. Ryven had come home. His lips caressed her neck and praised her softly scented skin. His fingers slid into her hair, enjoying the silk of it. His body settled over hers. . . .

She awoke with a start, and froze. There was a man in bed with her. "Ryven?" she whispered, spooked.

He laughed, his breath a soft puff against her mouth. "Did you think they would let anyone else in?"

She pushed him back so she could breathe. She sat up. "You scared me!"

"I'm sorry," he murmured, and stroked her back. "I meant to surprise you."

"You did. I'm not used to men crawling into my bed at all hours."

His voice held a smile. "Saints be praised for that." He reached over and turned on the bedside light. "Is that better?"

She let out a sigh, surprised at how tense she was. "Yes, thanks." The reality of his presence hit her. "You're really home!"

He smiled. "Yes."

She laughed. "Well, then . . ." She tackled him. He went down easily, a willing victim, and laughed at his surrender.

Ryven glanced ruefully over his shoulder the next morning as he was getting dressed. His first attempt at rising hadn't been successful; they'd ended up back in bed before he'd had his shirt fastened. Not that he minded; his wife had a delightful way of making a man feel welcome. They had business to attend this morning, however.

As soon as Xera was up and dressed, he led her into the next room to eat breakfast. After she had caught him up on the family doings, he gave her an overview of their finances. And his aunt had been right—he should have done so sooner. Xera seemed amazed and reassured by what she learned. He hadn't realized what a source of concern it had been for her until he saw her shoulders relax. He was also pleasantly surprised by her astute questions. Her intelligence was pleasing . . . but he was not as thrilled when she mentioned running a business again.

"Why would you want that? We don't lack for money, and my aunt has ensured you have plenty to do."

She studied him. "Arranging a couple of parties a month is hardly a drain on my time. I'm used to doing *a lot* of work, Ryven. I've got a lot of energy."

He scowled. "Tell that to my sisters. For years

they've complained that the burden would crush them."

Xera shrugged. "They just don't have the knack, is all. It's not that different from running an inn. You just have a different customer base."

He stared at her. "You've forgotten what will happen when we have children. Raising them properly is very time consuming. I won't have them brought up by servants."

She considered that. "They could always go into the family business when they're old enough. I was helping in the kitchen when I was five. It builds work ethic."

Those brimstone eyes of his heated ominously. "I won't have my child working like a servant."

"Not like a servant—like a member of the family."

He took a breath, calming himself. "I understand your point of view on this. I know you were raised to see things differently. I also know we are not relocating to apartments above a business so that you can spend your waking hours directing it." He watched her blink, saw the frown start between her eyes. "As interested as I am in your happiness, you will have to find another way to pursue your interests. I am not an innkeeper. I command a starship and am a noble. My father is the lord governor of Rsik." And that was that.

Xera pursed her lips and willed herself not to comment on her husband's haughtiness. It was an integral part of him, and unlikely to be cured in a morning, if ever. Besides, he was unwittingly playing into the real argument she had coming. It would be interesting to see how he acted when she brought up the ambassador thing. She could be devious when necessary. She took a breath herself. "Okay. No lowbrow establishment for you. Do you have a more genteel option in mind?"

He looked off to the side as if searching for patience. "Let me share with you my dream of family, instead. I had envisioned myself coming home from work to find my family content and happy to see me. I work hard so that my wife can spend her time making our home pleasant and seeing that our children are raised right. I have no objection to her having hobbies, but I don't want to see her so consumed that she has nothing left for her family. I would hope to see her put her family first, yet find a way to fulfill her own needs as well. I can't see how running a business would leave room for this." He looked up, clearly watching how she reacted.

She considered him. "Do you feel the same about my ambassadorial duties? After all, you arranged for me to have them. Went to a great deal of trouble, in fact."

"They were not intended to last longer than our wedding," Ryven said, frustrated, then froze as he realized what he'd revealed.

Too late. She pounced on his words. "Of course, being an ambassador is a highly respectable and genteel occupation. If only it took up more of my day, I'm sure I could be content." When he remained mute, she added sweetly, "Of course, it would help if the IC and GE would communicate a bit more often. There haven't been any pin beams from them, have there?"

He studied her a long moment, his expression a

mix of frustration and stubbornness. At last he admitted, "As I said, your duties were not arranged for the purpose of supplying you with an *occupation*. I could not wed you if your rank was not closer to my own."

This was interesting. She digested that, then said slowly, "Let me see if I understand what you're saying. You planned to marry me all along, and went to a great deal of trouble to make it happen. Why? What was I to you but an alien?"

He refused to answer, simply tapped one hand on the table in silent aggravation.

She could hardly contain her glee. He might not admit it, but he was neatly trapped. Just to torment him, she said, "Well, now that I *am* an ambassador, I find I like it. I would like to see any communication from the GE and IC, please. I can't do my job if I'm not informed."

He was silent for a time. Finally he said, "Have you ever run an estate?"

She cocked her head, wondering at his change of subject. "My sister has one, but I don't know much about it. I don't see what this has to do with our discussion."

He nodded. "We have one with several dozen tenants. Many of them grow produce for the fresh market: flowers, spices, fruit. A few of them produce livestock or farm crafts. Do you know how to judge superior produce?"

She frowned. "Are you really that desperate to change the subject?"

"You didn't answer my question," he said

doggedly. It was clear he was determined to ignore anything he had no wish to discuss.

How annoying. Well, she could circle back to her point later. She, too, could be stubborn. Just to show that she, at least, was cooperative, she said, "I didn't work in the kitchen much, but sure, I could tell good stuff from bad. We couldn't accept goods from bad vendors."

"Excellent. And your knowledge of farming?"

She looked at him suspiciously. "I have none. Are you suggesting I might want to . . . what? Oversee this business? I don't see how I'll have time. An ambassador is a busy woman . . . when she's allowed to read her mail." She'd thought about it after her talk with Tessla and decided there must have been communication between the two groups. If nothing else, the IC would be very curious about the Scorpio. When word got out, the people back home would want to know everything they could about the "mysterious" race. She'd tell them for nothing that they were uncommonly stubborn.

He reached for a piece of fruit from the display on the table and toyed with it. "You wanted to be productive."

She could only bang her head against a brick wall for so long without developing a headache. If he thought they were done, however, he was dead wrong. She'd give ground now and come back at him when he didn't expect it. It was easier than keeping track of two conversations. "Who runs it now?"

"I have a manager. You can train with him, and with me when I have time."

"It doesn't sound like something I'm going to

enjoy for long, and I get grouchy when I'm bored. You might live to regret this."

Ryven raised a brow. "Then you agree?"

She snorted. "You are so manipulative."

"Then it's settled. I've already had a shuttle prepared for us. We'll leave to tour the estate immediately." He looked pleased.

Her eyes narrowed. "You had this all planned?" Granted, it was before she'd brought up her arguments, but as a distraction, it worked in his favor.

He shrugged a shoulder. "It's traditional for wives to have a hand in running family estates. Ours has been part of the family for six generations. You'll be carrying on a legacy." He offered her an apologetic look. "I hadn't mentioned it before because I wanted you to be more settled before we discussed such things. We've had an unconventional courtship."

Ryven, apologetic? Unlikely. He was just trying to soften her. She was tempted to argue just because her blood was up. It annoyed her that he'd outmaneuvered her.

There was nothing she could say, however, so she forced a toothy smile. "Great."

However annoyed she was with his stubbornness, she liked his plan to take a scenic flight in his personal aircraft before heading for the estate. She hadn't known he had a personal aircraft, let alone one with comfortable seats and plenty of legroom. It came equipped with a small galley, lavatory and bedroom. "Nice," she told him. "Can I fly it?"

He smiled ruefully. "I knew you would ask. Of course you may, since I'll be here to act as your flight instructor. I've heard some encouraging things about your simulator training. I'm eager to see you in action."

The flight went as smooth as Xera could have hoped, and Ryven soon relaxed with her at the controls. They traveled at a leisurely speed so she could admire the snow-covered mountains and expanses of farmland between towns. After they'd traveled for nearly an hour, he took over and piloted them down to a neatly terraced hill farm. A generously proportioned but welcoming mansion of brown stone trimmed in white granite occupied the side of a gentle southern slope.

They landed on a private shuttle pad and Ryven shut down the engines. "Welcome home."

Xera blinked at him. "Home? I thought that was your palace."

Ryven shook his head. "Not really. Put your gloves on. I want to show you the grounds first."

He was justly proud of the place, she thought as she walked the freshly shoveled pathways and admired the snow-cloaked gardens and stone walls. There was even a fountain close to the house that was flanked by backless benches. A current kept the shallow water ice free for the bright fish that darted through it.

Lavender snow might cover the hedges and orchards, but Xera could see the bones of a very lovely garden. The setting was tranquil, far different from the hustle and bustle of palace life. She could see why such a place would appeal to Ryven, but . . .

"That's an odd smile," he commented as they walked arm in arm. Apparently a private garden didn't forestall that kind of touching. She was still learning what was considered appropriate and when it was okay to bend the rules.

"Of all the places I've seen you, this is the first time you . . . Well, I'd just never have imagined you on a farm."

He smiled. "There's more to me than war. Come and see the house, and you'll see how much."

The entryway had a bench to one side for removing winter boots, and a walk-in closet to the side for their coats. Xera was pleasantly surprised to find slippers waiting in her size. She sent Ryven a questioning look.

"I had the caretaker prepare the place for us," he said.

She glanced around at the gleaming staircase in front of them, then at the hallways leading left and right. She chose to investigate the living room first. A copper-tiled fireplace warmed the far wall, and she thought the picture over the mantel looked like one of Tessla's. The floors were tiled in earth tones, and the walls were a lovely shade of cream. Some of the sitting pillows were made of animal hide with large black and white patches. Others were brown leather embroidered with gold thread. The accessories were tasteful and elegant. It looked like the work of a professional decorator and probably was.

"Nice," she said.

The room on the other side of the hallway was a dining area with a view of the kitchen. There were more floor pillows here, and the absent cook had thoughtfully left the table set for two. A pair of covered dishes and a plate of sweet dumplings sat on the table.

"I'm impressed," Xera said when they sat down and pulled the covers off the pots. "They're still steaming."

Ryven smiled. "Timing is everything."

She smiled in return and accepted a serving of rich vegetable soup. She didn't know how it was done, but she'd never had a broth that was so incredibly rich and satisfying, without a trace of cream. She was about to ask if Ryven knew how it was prepared when she caught him looking at her expectantly. "What? It's very good, if that's what you're wondering."

He grimaced. "I'm trying to be patient, but you're making it difficult."

"About what?" she asked, all at sea.

He seemed about to speak, then sighed and asked, "How do you like the house?"

Was that all he wanted? His look had seemed to ask more. She said slowly, "Well, it's beautiful, of course. I haven't seen all of it, but if the rest of it looks like this, I'll love it. Did you think I wouldn't?"

"No." He shut his mouth firmly and applied himself to his soup.

Wondering what had gotten into him, she finished her broth and the spiced vegetables in the other dish. She was hungry! Must be the winter air. A gusty sigh blew over her as she was reaching for a second dumpling. They were filled with a delightful brown cheese with a crunchy texture. The filling practically danced in her mouth, and she was reluctant to take her attention from it. She shot her husband an inquiring look.

"What are you waiting for?" he asked.

What? This was starting to bug her. Why couldn't

he just speak his mind? "What do you mean?" she snapped.

He looked exasperated. "The baby! I thought you'd tell me by now."

"What baby? I haven't been around any babies lately." She thought about his family, his nephews and nieces. All of them were well out of diapers. "Is one of your sisters pregnant again? Nobody told me."

He stared hard at her, then blinked. "You don't know?"

"Know what? What are you . . . ?" She trailed off as a thought came over her. "Wait a minute. You don't think I'm . . ." She laughed, but her humor was short-lived. The expression on his face was too serious. The hairs on her neck stood straight up. "Not funny, Ryven."

His eyes moved to her middle and lingered. It was almost as if he could see . . . It hit her: "You can see in infrared. But . . . there should be nothing to see yet. I-I mean, there's nothing *to* see. I haven't even felt anything yet." She was stammering, his intent expression throwing her off. She frantically reworked her mental math, calculating dates. Her birth control must have worn off. Well, it was a good product, but not infallible. Still . . . "Look, I would know if something was up, okay?"

"Apparently not." He sat back, his eyes beginning to heat with amusement. "I thought you were only teasing me by not saying anything."

She took a deep breath. "Only a doctor would know this early in the game. I can't be pregnant!" She realized she'd been depending on the supposed differences in their physiology to keep her from becoming pregnant; it had allowed her to nod and smile when he'd talked of family planning. Apparently there weren't any of significance in the matter of fertility. That's what she got for making assumptions.

"You are. I can see the color markers. I noticed it this morning, but all you wanted to do was argue. Why do you think I was so vexed?"

"Because you're a . . ." She bit off her retort and stood up. This was horrible news! She wasn't ready for something like this. She felt trapped, confused.

He stood also. "You don't like it?"

Her angry arm gesture was meant to convey extreme agitation. "No, I don't like it! I don't like these sorts of surprises. I'm not ready to be a mother."

"We talked about this." His expression was stern, a touch cold.

"You mentioned it. I never agreed," she said vehemently. "Do I look like a mother to you? Do you look like a father?" Her throat closed up as she saw him flinch. Whatever she felt, it wasn't the need to hurt him. "That wasn't fair. I'm sure you'd make a great father. It's just . . . I'm not . . ." She turned away, unable to explain what she felt, not to him. She was trapped. If she was having his baby, then she was truly trapped. Had he known that?

She felt Ryven settle a hand on her shoulder. He couldn't miss her tension, but she didn't want to relax just to spare his feelings.

"I'm sorry," he said sincerely. "If I'd known what a shock it would be to you, we could have taken more care."

She drew a ragged breath. "It's my fault—I assumed I had it covered."

"You're not alone," he murmured. He waited, his touch drawing away her resistance. Eventually, she turned and buried her face in his chest. But her hands rested on his stomach, ready to push him away.

"I'm so not ready for this. This happened too fast." Being cut off from her family, the crash, him. Maybe she'd never really dealt with all of it, had been too busy surviving. Funny, how a thing like a baby could shatter all the walls. A wave of panic rose up and threatened to engulf her.

"Breathe," he commanded, taking her face in his hands. "Xera, listen to me. Breathe!"

She tried to obey, but it was a struggle. She'd never hyperventilated before.

He muttered something, then carried her into the living area and settled them on a floor cushion. "Breathe," he coached her, and began to massage her feet.

"What are you doing?" she demanded, and tried to jerk her foot away.

"Giving your mind something to focus on." It was weird, but it worked. In a few minutes, her breathing was mostly back to normal. She began to feel tired. Worse, she began to cry.

Ryven instantly stopped rubbing her feet and moved up to hold her. "Easy, wife. Hush." He held her while she blubbered and babbled, then rose to fetch her some tissues. When the storm finally calmed, he stroked her hair. "Some better?"

"No," she groused, though she did feel somewhat improved. "I hate that I cried."

He thought about that. "I understand that's not abnormal."

She sniffed. "If you tell me that pregnant women cry all the time I'll have to hit you."

He laughed. "Have mercy! I'd have to let you win."

She growled. "It'd serve you right if I had triplets."

There was a pause. "Is that a possibility?" He had the nerve to sound eager.

"I doubt it. Oh, I hope not!" The idea of babies in triplicate was daunting. She had an appalling vision of herself as large as a shuttle. "Do you know how helpless pregnant women are? I'll look like I swallowed a moon!"

He sat up and took her by the shoulders. Sternly, he said, "My wife will look regal and lovely carrying my children. I will not accept you holding any backward beliefs about this. It's a proud moment in a man's life. I'll be pleased to see you change with the life that's within you."

Xera took a breath. No, she couldn't take this man's child away, and couldn't talk about her feelings. Even if he'd trapped her on purpose, she couldn't hurt him, not about this. "Change scares me."

He kissed her. "Change brought me you."

Chapter Eighteen

They didn't go home that night. Ryven let Xera nap. He woke her just before dinner to show her the rest of the house. He distracted her with a board game and joined her for a hot bath when she began to yawn. Most importantly, he didn't try to make love to her that night, sensing that what she needed was to be held. When they woke in the morning, he was very gentle in his lovemaking, careful that it held the reassurance she craved.

It was different, seeing her so vulnerable. After everything she'd been through, he wouldn't have thought it would be the news of her impending motherhood that would bring her low. Women were strange creatures, he mused as he escorted her back to the shuttle. Sometimes he thought his was stranger than most. Still, he liked her. It was a novel sensation, being friends with a woman who wasn't a relative. It was especially refreshing having that relationship with a wife.

He grinned, thinking of his children to be. He made sure Xera wasn't looking. It wouldn't do to have her catch him at it when she was feeling so low—she'd probably try to damage him. But, why shouldn't he be happy? This moment had been a long time coming.

He needed to find a sufficiently distracting matter for Xera. She didn't need to be brooding about this, and he suspected she'd become used to it in time. With luck, she'd soon take her situation in stride and treat it with her accustomed practicality.

Of course, he would never admit that he knew pregnancy would hobble her. As happy as he was about the baby, he was even happier to know that his wife was now welded to him. She missed her family, yes, but there was nothing like carrying a child to create stronger ties. He'd seen it many times before. He understood Xera well enough to know it would be the same with her.

And he was fiercely glad. Her strong will had given him pause in the early days, when he had first began to desire her, until he'd realized that will would probably be inherited by any children they might have. It had pleased him enough that he'd decided it would be worth it to have a wife who was a bit beyond his control. She was the only woman who had ever made him happy, and that's all he really wanted in a wife.

Not that he would tell her now. He wasn't ready to give up that final bit of reserve, not until he was certain she would stay with him, even if given the chance to leave. Since he wouldn't willingly provide that chance . . . the words would have to wait.

He kept his thoughts hidden behind a pleasant manner. "We should send a message to your family. Our first child is news worth passing on."

She looked at him with interest for a moment then settled back into her funk. "Yes. That would be good." She looked a little less gloomy than before.

That wasn't good enough. Determined to lift his wife's spirits, he told her in more detail about taking over the Khun'tat queen's ship, leaving out the goriest parts. But she was most interested in the Leo-Ahni, whom had been brought back into her thoughts.

"Where is she now?"

"I'd forgotten. I had other things on my mind—most notably, my wife."

Xera frowned in irritation, which Ryven still felt was an infinite improvement over moping. "Didn't you think I would feel for the girl? We're exactly alike!"

Surprised, he said, "You're not even of the same race! You're married; she's not. You've got rank and family and—"

"Only lately!" Xera interrupted. "We're both translators who've had sticky assignments—why are you frowning? You try translating for a bunch of hostile aliens! She's lost and alone. I was like that for a little while. Maybe I can help her."

"I don't want you anywhere near her. She was on the same ship as the Khun'tat, helping them." His face darkened. "Men died because of her."

"She didn't have a choice, though, right? She was stuck. Has she said anything new?"

This was sore spot. His crew had managed to speed the girl toward healing, but her mind was another matter. She barely ate, still sat in a room and stared blankly at a wall. She wouldn't talk to psychiatrists. They were afraid she'd try to take her own life, so they'd removed everything from her chamber and watched her carefully. There was no progress, which they badly wanted.

"No. She doesn't speak. Everyone who has tried to talk with her gives up in frustration."

"Well, were they all guys?" Xera asked.

He looked at her askance. "Why would it matter?"

She sighed. "Think of it from her perspective. Strange men, soldiers, keep invading her space, demanding answers. She's already been trapped in a nightmare, kept isolated, just as she is now. Why should she trust you?"

He considered for a moment. Some of his wife's comments dovetailed with what the doctors had said. But, "How could you know what's in her mind?"

Xera scoffed. "I have two sisters, don't I? And I keep trying to tell you, *I was in her position.* All kinds of horrible things go through your mind when you're trapped like that." Her lips tightened as memories obviously stirred in her mind. "She needs to know who the good guys are. I can help."

He thought about that for quite a while. Xera glanced at him from time to time, but otherwise held her peace. At last he said, "We can try you talking to her."

She grinned at him. "Thanks." She was smart enough not to say anything else until they reached home.

The girl sat on a mat with her eyes fixed on the wall. Her caramel-colored hair hung limp to her shoulders, the black-tipped ends partly screening her face. The tips of pointed ears poked out of her locks, proving she was neither human nor Scorpio. Her lids were half closed over dulled, catlike green eyes. She looked like the survivor of some horrific event.

Xera didn't try to talk to her at first; she just plopped down cross-legged in the girl's line of sight and began a staring contest. It was a full minute before the girl's eyes began to focus, as if she had to pull out of a deep, dark trance. At first she blinked, clearly surprised. Then her eyes widened.

"You're a woman! *Drarfiquex!*"

"Well, of course I'm a woman. I don't know what a drra-fix is, though. I hope it's complimentary," Xera replied calmly. She'd decided to treat the girl as she would one of her sisters. Hopefully that would be a good start. "My name is Xera."

The girl stared for a moment then spat out a rapid stream of words.

"I'm afraid I don't speak anything but Scorpio. Well, that's not true; I speak about half a dozen languages, but none you'd know. I can curse in nine, but I'll spare you a recital."

"Are you trapped here, too?" The girl looked around furtively, as if she guessed they were being watched.

"Not anymore. Ryven rescued me from my crew. I was a translator for a ship that crashed. We were a long way from home and my captain hated me," Xera said darkly.

"Just like me," the girl whispered. She looked barely younger than Xera chronologically, maybe in her late teens, but with her vulnerability she seemed younger.

"Yes," Xera replied. "Say, I'm hungry. Would you mind if I called for something to snack on? What do you like to eat?"

The girl looked wary. Maybe she was afraid. She said, "Food is strange here. They bury it with spices that burn. They put thick liquids on it that smell strange."

"Huh. I guess everyone likes to eat different stuff," Xera remarked. "What kind of food is best for you? I'd feel rude if I served you something you didn't like." She could see the girl was thin, and she really wanted her to eat. Besides, Xera herself was really hungry, thanks to the baby.

The Leo-Ahni looked uncomfortable. "Fish and meats without . . . I don't know the words."

"Sauces? How about some cooked meat and vegetables? Or do you like your veggies raw?"

"What are veggies? Do you speak of plants? I've seen no edible plants here."

Xera held up a hand. "I have an idea. Give me a minute." She went outside the door and asked Ryven, who was watching through a screen, "Favor, please. Could you send for some plain cooked food and a platter of raw fruits and vegetables? Maybe some bread and crackers, and that kind of stuff? Thanks."

"Fine. But stay on your guard. You're too relaxed with her."

"Sure," she said to placate him, and went back inside.

The girl looked wary. "You work with them."

"I am one of them," Xera admitted, leaning on one hand. "I married the Scorpio who rescued me. When I heard about you, I wanted to meet you. I thought we were a little alike."

The girl's eyes dulled. "Were you forced into service? Did your family make you a slave to the flesh eaters? We are *not* alike." A light like hatred blazed in her eyes. It was an improvement over apathy, but Xera went on alert. She didn't want the girl taking any rage out on her.

"So, you were forced to help the Khun'tat? The Scorpio fear that your people are allies with them, that you want war."

The girl's jaw clenched. "That's not what I want." Xera waited, but she didn't say anything else.

"So, you want to go home?"

"No!" The girl sat bolt upright. "Don't send me! They'll only make me serve again. Once a person is marked, they can never go home."

Xera held up her hands, palm out. "Okay, calm down. I'm just trying to figure out what you want. I can tell you what the Scorpio want—information. They want to know everything they can about their enemy, and whatever they can about your people. There's a chance for peace if you can work out a compromise." That wasn't the whole truth, but the stark facts weren't going to help right now. "How did you become allies with the flesh eaters, anyway? They didn't treat you very well."

The girl's lip curled. "We are not allies so much as slaves, though some people refuse to see it. In the beginning there was a treaty—we would give animals, blood tribute, the bodies of our dead and living criminals to the flesh eaters. In return they would not invade us. Our leaders said this would buy us time to find a way to destroy them. Instead it made us weak. Everyone gave blood each month. Meat became expensive, and women especially became anemic. Birth rates dropped. People began to disappear out of hospitals. People died at home rather than risk disappearing. Even minor crimes became causes to be handed over to the blood wagons. Our world is dying, and there are signs that the flesh eaters are becoming impatient. There are some who think they will attack."

"Are you one of them?" Xera asked gravely.

"Yes," the girl whispered. "But our leaders won't listen to reason. They call us rebels."

"Is that why you were sent to work on the Khun'tat ship?"

The Leo-Ahni's mouth twisted. "No. Someone has to serve. I was chosen."

The two women were both silent for a moment. Finally Xera asked, "What's your name?"

"Rysing."

"Well, Rysing, I think our food is finally here. Look." The door had opened to show Ryven himself bearing a huge platter. He set it on the floor between them and sat down.

Xera frowned at him.

He looked at her urbanely. "I'm hungry, too."

She sighed. "Oh, all right. Ryven, this is Rysing. I guess you've met."

Rysing stared.

When it was clear the girl wasn't going to say anything, Xera pointed to the platter and started naming things. "This is a fish, and whoever left the head on is just gross. This is a kind of bird, that's a four-legged beast, and this is. . . ." As she named things, Ryven sampled them and then gestured for Rysing to try. After a moment of wary contemplation, the girl did, eating only the things he had.

Watching them both, Xera had a disturbing thought. "You did test her for allergies, didn't you?"

"Of course."

"What are 'allergies'?" Rysing asked. She eyed the food with distrust.

Xera sighed and ate a piece of crunchy brown cheese. She loved the sticky sweetness. "When I first boarded a Scorpio ship, I ate a piece of purple root that made me sick. Sometimes the foods that others eat make me sick, so I don't eat them. In the case of the yur root, I don't mind—it tastes terrible to me." She pointed to the criminal foodstuff in question.

Ryven promptly ate a chunk. "You're not allergic," he told Rysing.

The Leo-Ahni looked at him warily, but sampled a small piece. Her face lit up. "Why, it's delicious! The best thing I've had since I came here." She promptly finished off the entire pile.

Xera grimaced. "To each their own, I guess."

The three of them ate in a friendly little silence, and when Rysing had sampled almost everything, Xera asked, "Find anything you wouldn't mind eating again?"

The girl nodded happily. "The yur root is especially good, and all of the meats. I think I could eat most everything—except for these and these." She waved her hand over the fruits and the cheese Xera favored. "They are very foul."

Xera grinned and shot a look at Ryven. "She'd be an easy houseguest. I'd never have to hide my favorite things."

He frowned at her, but then his face took on a subtly calculating air. He regarded Rysing with the faintest of smiles. "My wife has an interesting idea. Would you like to leave this room?"

Rysing's face lit with a terrible hope. She immediately tried to hide it with a coolly spoken, "Perhaps."

He nodded. "Very well. There is a garden I think you would enjoy. We will go for a walk after we discuss the flesh eaters. Tell me about these rebels you spoke of . . . the ones who'd like to see your alliance broken."

Xera looked at the floor. She didn't like to see the girl manipulated after all she'd been through, but she understood his reasoning. She raised her eyes to see Rysing looking searchingly at her. Xera gave a reassuring nod.

The Leo-Ahni took a shaky breath, and then told him everything she knew.

"It's almost painful to watch her," Xera said. They stood in the gardens, a little apart from Rysing. The girl stood as if transfixed, staring at the sky. There was a pleasure almost painful in her face.

Ryven just nodded. His attention didn't waver for a moment. Xera might have been jealous if it weren't obvious that he mistrusted the girl. She started to say something when the entrance of a familiar face distracted her.

Toosun caught sight of them and grinned. "Hello! How fare the newlyweds? I was beginning to think I'd never find you."

Xera grinned and readily accepted his brotherly arm clasp. Ryven received the same and a slap on the shoulder, too. He bore it with good grace and commented, "Heroism has made you bold."

"Hah! I hear you have some stories of your own. Destroying Khun'tat ships, rescuing the . odd damsel." He noticed Rysing and stared intently. "And this must be the damsel."

Rysing stiffened as Toosun approached her. She looked scared.

Xera caught up with her brother-in-law and touched his shoulder, a silent signal for caution. She stopped next to Rysing. "You haven't been properly introduced. This is my husband's brother, Commander Toosun Atarus, of the High Family. He's recently returned from his first command."

"Killing Khun'tat," Toosun put in. His gaze was hard. Obviously Rysing's reputation had preceded her.

Xera went on, slightly annoyed, "And this is Rysing, of the planet Akan in the Xhozon sector." This had come out in the talk after lunch.

Something in Toosun's manner must have triggered Rysing's annoyance, for she added coolly, "Of the family Naktoon, rulers of the Mountain District."

"And will Daddy be suing for peace when he finds we hold his daughter?" Toosun asked. He'd clearly felt the snub.

"Hardly, since he sent me to the flesh eaters in the first place."

Xera held up her hands. "Children, please! I'm too young for an ulcer. Play nice, wouldn't you? It's been a long time since Rysing saw the outdoors, and I'd hate to ruin that for her." She gestured for the girl to walk deeper into the gardens.

With a last nasty look at Toosun, the Leo-Ahni complied.

Xera looked her rebuke at her husband's brother. He shook his head. "Don't be taken in by her. We don't know enough to trust her."

"Nor enough to condemn her," she replied pointedly. "Are you forgetting how you met me?"

"You were not found on a Khun'tat ship."

"Just a GE one," she said tartly. "And I'm alien, too."

"Humans are occasionally acceptable," he remarked, with a reasonableness that bordered on patronizing. "But that is not who we're discussing."

Ryven had been silent during the exchange, but he raised his hand when it was clear the argument would continue. "You are both too stubborn to win with words alone, and you are both right. Besides, we were in the middle of welcoming you home, brother."

Toosun looked a little nonplussed. Maybe he wasn't used to his brother practicing diplomacy. "Hm. Yes." He glanced down at Xera's middle and smiled. "And I was here to offer my congratulations."

Xera frowned at him. "Does everybody know?"

"Of course." Toosun studied her face. "You are happy, aren't you? Our family is ecstatic."

She grunted and looked away.

Ryven answered his brother's sharp glance with a look that promised more speech later. "She doesn't like surprises."

Toosun had nothing to say to that.

Toosun waited impatiently until they'd "put away the pet," and then joined Ryven on a short walk to his private rooms. Toosun took out his best liquor and joined his brother at the kitchen table. He seemed surprised to see how quickly Ryven drained his glass. "This is troubling you?"

"The woman is maddening! I had no idea how emotional she could be." He felt harried, drained. He had to be if he was confiding in his younger brother, but whom else could he tell? He couldn't stand it if his brothers-in-law knew he'd joined their circle. He'd always imagined he'd dominate his wife's moods, not suffer them.

Toosun relaxed and served them both drinks. "This sounds like a familiar complaint. Men agonize because of women. I've often listened to my friends complain. She hasn't left your bed, has she?"

Ryven shot him an incredulous look. "Of course not!"

"Then you've got nothing to fear. She'll come around."

Ryven peered at him. Perhaps he was seeing double, since he was on his third drink. Generally sober, he hadn't built up a tolerance for alcohol. He asked Toosun, "How can you have that many sisters and remain so ignorant of women?"

"Who do you think counsels our brothers-in-law when they have wife trouble?" His brother shrugged. "Be understanding, I tell them. Charm them out of their hackled state. The worst is when the wife wants something that is not possible. Then they have to be charming *and* firm. I pity them." He grimaced and took a drink. "Women troubles. They make a sally against hostile Khun'tat sound appetizing."

"Charming and firm? How does that work? Why can't she just be reasonable like a man?" Ryven snapped. "Then I could duel with her and work out our differences. Afterward we'd both go out for a drink." He noticed his voice was beginning to slur.

His brother smirked. "There must be something you can bribe her with. Let her send a message to her family."

"Offered. Didn't help."

"Well, what does she want?"

"A job. She wants to own a tavern like her sister." Or she wanted to remain an ambassador. He was so frazzled at the moment, he wasn't sure which.

Toosun choked on his drink. "What?"

Ryven grunted. He knew his brother's thoughts. Toosun couldn't imagine any woman in his family doing such a thing. Scandalous, even for an alien! He was likely wondering that Ryven had been as patient as he had.

"You told her no, right?"

"I told her she could help manage the estate."

Toosun just stared at him. Then, surprisingly, he changed topics. "What about the alien? Are you going to let her roam free?"

Ryven sat up and frowned. He pushed his glass aside. "Today was . . ." He frowned in concentration. "Today was an experiment."

"In what? Need I point out that your wife is becoming attached to your 'experiment?' That's not good for her. If the Leo-Ahni is false, Xera could suffer. I know you're protective, and I don't understand why you take the risk."

"Our world is a lure. The girl claims she doesn't

want to go home, that they'll send her back to a Khun'tat ship. If she wants to stay here bad enough . . ."

"Ah. But this assumes she tells the truth."

"Yes."

"And if she's lying?"

Ryven's eyes hardened. "Then she will regret it. I'm not required to allow her out of her room. She would discover it soon enough." Harsh, his wife would say, but their need was desperate. He frowned as her imagined opinion popped into his head. His wife was not the keeper of his conscience. He would reward the girl for cooperation; that would have to be enough.

Chapter Nineteen

Ryven wasn't the only one who had plans for the Leo girl. In a shadowy corner of the palace, others were making plans.

"They took her out of her cell today." The voice was cold, calculating.

"I know, but I still don't see what use she'll be. They don't trust her. She doesn't have access to anything important."

Tovark smiled. His teeth showed through his split upper lip. "She knows much about the Khun'tat and her race. She's more valuable than platinum to them. If she disappeared, they'd be very upset. Imagine if he lost an asset like that and a wife at the same time."

He studied the guardsman he'd bribed. The man felt it was distasteful associating with him, but money spoke loudly. The traitor wanted a smooth path to a better life. What he'd get was a knife in the back when the job was done . . . but he needn't know that.

"I don't like it. It's dangerous," the guard said.

"This should boost your courage. Think of the

things it will buy." Tovark flipped the man a coin, watched him weigh it in his hand. "Now, this is what I want you to do."

Three hundred and thirty-one people attended Tessla's party. By Xera's count, three-quarters of them were women.

Her husband was quick to disagree. "Tessla always invites even numbers of males and females. You should know. Didn't you see the guest list?"

"Then why do I count nine women hovering around your brother? Where are their escorts, their husbands?"

Ryven looked amused. "You're protective of his honor? He'd never shame himself by dallying with a married woman."

"And it's okay to 'shame himself' with a nice unmarried woman?" she replied tartly.

"No, that presents a problem, too," he said, laughter in his eyes. "If he asked me, I would suggest he find some who are not so nice. Sadly, he has not asked."

Xera's eyes narrowed, but good sense kept her from starting a fight. After all, *he* was behaving himself. Unlike his brother.

She was crabby and she knew it. That morning she'd nearly bitten off Ryven's head over a trivial matter; only his even stare had brought her back from the brink of a tantrum. She knew the cause of her moodiness and resented it. One thing after another would slide out of her control because of this baby. How long before she could no longer exercise? Would she start throwing up everything she ate? She'd always been taller than her sisters, the big strong one. Now one little infant was going to turn her into an emotional wreck unable even to touch her toes.

Not that she wanted harm to come to the baby or anything. She just didn't want . . . this.

Ryven saw her dark look and gently touched her arm. "It will pass."

She exhaled moodily and subtly shook him off. "I'm going to go talk to your sisters. They've been full of advice lately." They'd also assured her that the broodiness would pass. One of them had even shared a story where she locked her husband out of her bedroom one night, then tore into him when he didn't make a greater effort to break down her door. His protests that he didn't want to alarm her and perhaps harm the babe had earned him another night locked out—or would have, if he hadn't kicked down the door the second time. He'd refused to have it repaired until after the baby was born.

Thinking about that made her smile.

Namae joined her in slowly threading a path through knots of people. It was a trick to nod and smile politely to avoid conversations, and Namae made everything easier.

"It's good to see you smile," Ryven's sister said. "The broodiness has hit you hard."

"I'm finding it difficult to believe I can be this moody," Xera agreed. "I just want to hit someone all the time." It didn't help that she'd been forced to quit her martial arts exercises. Dancing hadn't been forbidden yet, but right now that wasn't nearly as satisfying as pounding a punching bag.

Namae nodded in sympathy. "Let me take your

mind off it. Aunt Tessla has been spreading it about that you are her new protégée. You'd be surprised at the number of women who want to meet you. Some have already expressed interest on your opinion of their own party plans."

Surprised, Xera said, "Why? Your aunt really directed most of the event. I didn't do much."

"That's not what she's saying, and when our aunt speaks, others listen. You'll find yourself in high demand as a party organizer if you don't take care."

Xera stopped in her tracks. "Really?" She let the idea percolate and then smiled. "This wouldn't happen to be a socially acceptable occupation, would it?" It sounded more appealing than the estate manager option her husband had offered, if only because it was something she'd found herself. She had a feeling he'd grumble about it, which only made it more enticing. The man got his way far too often, and just then she really wanted to spike his tire. Besides, she'd enjoyed organizing this.

Namae looked at her curiously. "Well, yes. It would raise your social status immensely. Of course, Aunt Tessla has never needed such a thing. She's occasionally given advice to close friends, but nothing more. You'll see after you've attended a few gatherings that ours are something special."

Xera felt like the cat that'd discovered a vat of cream. "Do tell. Could I be paid for something like this? If I set up formally, that is."

Now Namae looked perplexed. "Well, of course. Why would you want to, though? Surely Ryven is generous."

Xera patted her hand. "Let me tell you about a wonderful thing called capitalism, my friend, and the little girl who teethed on it."

Ryven had taken a moment to answer an urgent message and found himself in a quiet corner, away from the crowd. His business hadn't taken long, but already he was anxious to return to his wife. He told himself she couldn't get into trouble in this kind of crowd, not with Namae at her side, but he had an eerie feeling that she was making mischief. Of course, that was a normal feeling where she was concerned.

He turned to exit the small sitting room and saw one of the women who'd been circling his brother this evening—a woman that he himself knew.

"Hello, Commander." Her bloodred eyes were framed with thick dark lashes, and her lips curved. "It's been too long," she said, and there was obvious flirtation in the glance she gave him.

"I think not," he said coldly. Whatever they'd shared in the past, he was married now. She knew that. If she had any sense, she wouldn't be here.

Her lips formed the slightest pout. "I'm disappointed. I'd thought you might have tired of those hard blue eyes by now."

"It shows you haven't been thinking," he said callously. "Do not approach me again."

Her mouth opened in surprise, but she made no sound as he brushed past. There was nothing she could say.

He was surprised at his own fury. Women like her had peppered his past, and he knew no regrets. Had they met under casual circumstances, he'd have been polite. He was angry that she would dare approach him now, however, would try to tempt him away from his wife. He was not a man who swayed with the wind. Now that he'd chosen his woman, it was forever. If anyone couldn't see that, he'd have to make it plain.

The best place to start was with his wife.

He found Xera speaking with a knot of women. He smiled just for her and placed a hand at her back. He looked at the ladies. "Excuse us. I need my wife *alone* for a while." His words won a blush from her and smiles from the others.

Xera chastised him when they were out of earshot. "Isn't that rather . . . obvious? You've been coaching me in the art of not showing affection so long that all that seemed rather risqué."

He smiled down at her. "Perhaps I've been too conservative. We *are* newly married." He felt a pang at her confusion. He'd gathered her culture was far more demonstrative, and wondered if she doubted his affection. He'd never wanted that.

He led her to a quiet receiving room and shut the door. He put his arms around her. "You're beautiful, do you know that? I've been a fool not to tell you."

Her eyes misted up, and she swallowed hard. It took her a moment to speak. "Thank you," she whispered.

His heart ached. He should have told her sooner. "However you came into my life, I'm glad you're here. You're the best part of me. I've never found a woman as special, as memorable, as you." She was crying in earnest now. He was afraid to compliment her more, as she didn't seem capable of taking it. Instead, he held her and tried to ignore the tears soaking his shirt. He couldn't remember the last time he'd felt such a sense of peace. He'd been right to tell her. Perhaps one day soon, she'd be able to speak of her feelings for him. Strange, how he hadn't even realized he'd been waiting for her to speak first.

There was one other thing. "You said that I had been teaching you 'the art of not showing affection.' I hadn't realized you'd viewed my actions that way. In my culture, a man proves his feelings by the things he does, not the words he says. Words can be false, but actions seldom are."

She sighed. "It's been difficult. I never know when it's okay to touch you. Even looking at you warmly feels wrong. You're very reserved."

"I regret that you feel uncomfortable. Perhaps in time we will find a compromise." Her tears were beginning to worry him. Perhaps an apology would help. "Forgive me, *hiri'ami*. I regret causing you pain."

"I think we should go home. These parties are exhausting, aren't they? Wait here while I say good-bye—it won't take long."

She nodded and dabbed at her eyes. She did look peaked.

Grateful for the excuse of her pregnancy, he went in search of his father. He was more than ready to be home.

Ryven didn't wholly understand the change in his wife, but he was pleased nonetheless. It seemed his declaration of affection had moved her to unexpected heights. She laughed, she smiled. Best of all, she no longer seemed dismayed about the baby. He was perplexed, but he liked it.

A Scorpio woman would assume that her man loved her. No declaration of sentiment would be expected, only a demonstration. His own woman seemed to be the opposite. Only now that he'd spoken of his affection did she finally seem able to accept the little things he did for her as the romantic gifts they were. He hadn't even realized how resistant she'd been to them until he saw her recent pleasure. She even showed joy in discussing the arrangements for the baby's arrival—a thing he wouldn't have dared to bring up before.

It made him wonder what would have happened if he had brought himself to say he loved her.

His father remarked on the change as well. "I hadn't realized her vibrancy was muted until I saw her today. What has her so happy?"

Ryven actually blushed. "I declared my affection." There were some things that were embarrassing to admit to one's father.

The lord governor smiled. "I see. Well done. I am pleased to see her so alive."

Xera's newly bubbly attitude even coaxed a smile from the Leo girl, who had won a more comfortable room and daily walks through the garden by cooperation. On this day she'd just finished a long run down one of the many tracks around the park. She smiled at Xera as she dried her hair. "Life leaves you sweet today."

Xera, who'd jogged a little with permission from her doctor, grinned. "It would be even sweeter if I could keep up with you. How do you do it? You run like a cheetah—that's a very fast Earth mammal," she explained. It was true; Rysing ran like she was born to it, as if she had four legs instead of two. She was incredibly graceful, moving with a kind of lope that left her guards in the dust.

Rysing snorted. "I am badly out of shape. It's been forever since I could run anywhere. Given time, I might be something to see."

Ryven, who'd joined them that morning after seeing his father, raised a brow. "I think we'll ban you from any footraces, then. There's simply no competition."

Rysing grinned. "I will have to find a pet to run with, then. Surely you have something fast enough on this planet." There followed a lively discussion on what might be wild enough to keep up.

Ryven looked at his wife and wondered if she would enjoy a pet. Her recent sweet temper had left him feeling indulgent. Anything that would keep that smile on her lips would be all right with him.

He realized what he was thinking and shook his head. He'd better be careful not to let her know just how much she'd affected him, lest he give in on something he'd regret.

Xera was still feeling the inner glow of happiness a few days later as she shopped in the market. All the colors seemed especially bright and vivid—or maybe it was her mood. She smiled ruefully at herself. She'd have sworn she wasn't a romantic, but look what Ryven's admission had done for her. She was even starting to think about baby names! Not that they'd been able to come up with anything they both liked. He wanted unpronounceable things like "Urjub" and "Werq," and her choices sounded equally bizarre to him. At the rate they were going, the kid wouldn't have a name until he was five.

A display of bright scarves caught her eye, and she thought of Namae. Shiza's circling had taken on a new intensity, and Ryven's sister was getting nervous. Maybe a gift would help to take the young woman's mind off her nerves.

Xera was looking over the offerings when a conversation caught her attention. A woman dressed like a shopkeeper was gossiping to a plain-faced man. She said, "Hear they found a human woman like Atarus's wife. Got her down in the bay."

Xera froze and looked at the pair out of the corner of her eye. Had she heard right?

The man looked intrigued. "Human! Are you sure? How do you know?"

"My husband works the space docks. He hears things. Guess her name is Harris-something. They're keeping it hush-hush."

Xera's blood began to pound in her ears, nearly drowning out the conversation. Done with pretending indifference, she interrupted the pair. "I overheard what you're saying. What is your husband's name, and where exactly does he work?" she asked the woman. "I'll reward you for the information."

The woman looked startled, then uneasy. "I didn't mean any offense, great lady. Just a little gossip."

"I'm not offended," Xera insisted. She handed over a coin. "Please tell me."

Moments later Xera hurried toward a transport that would take her to the docking bay. While she acknowledged her security detail's concerns about the lead, she would not be swayed. If there was the slightest possibility that her sister could be there, she wanted to check on it personally.

Her bodyguards contacted Xtal, her chief of security, who asked her to wait. A clever man, he pointed out it would take eight months for any of her sisters to reach her, and it had only been weeks since she had contacted them. It was physically impossible for them to have arrived already, even if they were prepared to take such a costly, perilous trip.

"You're right," she admitted into her communications link. "But I have to see for myself. It's not as if I'm alone."

He did not look happy in the viewscreen. "I'll send backup."

Xera reached the dock and took a deep breath. She knew to temper her hope, but just the thought of seeing her sisters again made her unbearably tense. Could one of them really be here?

They found the workstation the woman had told them about, but there was no one in sight. One of her two bodyguards moved off to check the far side of the shuttle—and was shot to the ground like a dog.

Xera shouted as her other guard took her to the ground, but it was too late. A man grabbed his limp body off her and drew Xera roughly to her feet.

"Tovark," she said grimly. He stood boldly in front of her, a sardonic smile on his ruined face.

"Women," he said deliberately, "are very stupid." He opened the shuttlecraft door in illustration. Rysing was lying there, unmoving. He smiled slightly at Xera's aborted attempt to get to her. "Don't worry, you'll have plenty of time to visit. This shuttle is scheduled to leave here in two minutes, and you'll jump to hyperdrive in another two. Of course, any craft unlucky enough to be too close to you will be damaged, but that's the cost of travel today." He gestured for Xera's captor to load her aboard.

Xera felt Rysing's neck and was relieved to find a steady pulse. The girl had a bruised jaw, but didn't look too banged up otherwise. Hopefully he hadn't had time to extract a more complete revenge. She couldn't think what the girl could have done to anger him.

She glanced at Tovark as he continued to speak.

"I suggest you strap in. I wouldn't want you to be damaged for your meeting with the Khun'tat. You'll come out of hyperdrive in a system where they've been particularly active. Think of me fondly when you arrive." He smiled and started to shut the door, then paused. "Of course, there's the chance that they won't be there to meet you. One can never know about these things. In that case, you might make it to a little planet on the border. You've been there, Xera. You remember the biters."

He sealed the door.

Xera felt a moment of cold terror. Biters! He was sending them back to that desert hell? Thankfully, she didn't have time to waste time in thought. She dragged the barely conscious Rysing to the cockpit and strapped her in as the autopilot fired the engines. She'd barely fastened her own bindings before they cleared the shuttle bay doors.

The shuttle controls were locked. Xera slammed her hand on the console and looked out at the rapidly thinning atmosphere. They broke out into true space and her stomach clenched. Next stop: hell.

The attacker had covered his tracks well. The shuttle bay surveillance cameras showed the bodyguards being murdered in a different location, and the bodies were found in that different place, to collaborate the story. It wasn't until the forensic examination that anyone knew for sure the bodies had been moved.

Fortunately, Xera's bodyguards had kept in touch with Xtal, so it was known where her last reported location was. Ryven knew the guards were too well trained to have claimed to be in a different spot.

What he and his crew didn't know was what had happened to the women—for the Leo-Ahni was missing, too, and one could only speculate that they were together. The pair might be held somewhere on the planet or have been sneaked offworld. But Ryven and his family didn't know who had taken them or why. An exhaustive search commenced.

Ryven knew he might only have hours. If it took them too long to locate his wife and Rysing, they might find only bodies. He tried not to think about it, but it affected all his decisions, which is

why he let Xtal lead the search. He was too involved, his choices potentially blurred by rage and
fear. His wife and child were in danger, and he'd
never felt less in control.

Chapter Twenty

Since they'd dropped out of hyperdrive, Xera was doing everything she could to unlock the controls. Nothing worked.

It had been three tense days to the frontier border. They had plenty of food and water, but no weapons. Their shuttle was a commercial model for ferrying passengers, not fighting aliens. She didn't know what they'd do if they did make it to the desert planet. Unless they made it to the shelter, they wouldn't survive long. Unfortunately, she didn't know the coordinates to the fortress, even if she could unlock the controls. . . .

She wanted to scream. Instead, she cursed. The black words were almost a mantra, but they weren't helping her much. She tried praying instead.

Rysing sat like a statue, alternating between staring at the proximity locator and Xera's dogged efforts. "Can you fly this if we do unlock the controls?" she finally asked. Maybe Xera's constant muttering was wearing on her.

"Sure. Mostly. I can land for certain," Xera said. She hoped she could.

Rysing took a shuddering breath. "What is this planet like?"

Xera bit her lip.

"That bad?"

"It wasn't a pleasure park."

"I'm sorry to hear that," Rysing said, her voice distant. She'd been watching the readouts with disturbing intensity. "There's a planet coming up, and I think we're headed for it."

Xera stopped what she was doing to stare at the display. Rysing was right, but there was something else. "There's a ship in orbit."

Rysing froze. "Khun'tat?"

Xera frowned. "No. It almost looks like . . . the GE! We're saved!" Her joy was quickly cut off as she realized what they might look like—an enemy ship closing in on their turf. Granted, they were in a shuttle and not a warship, but they weren't exactly invited to this particular party, either. According to the newly minted treaty, the GE weren't supposed to be here.

She drew a quick breath and thought fast. They needed a way to communicate, and their controls were still locked. Could they free the transceiver in time?

They got lucky. The GE ship hailed them, and while the women could not respond, they could see and understand the captain of the ship. He looked startled to see her. No doubt her face had been splashed on telecasts all over the star system—her situation would have been interesting fodder for the folks back home. She wondered what spin the GE had put on the story. "Lieutenant Harrisdaughter? What are you doing here?"

"We're trapped!" Xera tried to tell him, but it was plain he couldn't hear her, so she gestured to the controls and mouthed, "Help!"

He frowned at her. "Is there a problem with your communicator?"

She nodded, then glanced around in frustration. There was nothing to write with, so she looked at him and mouthed, "Help!" again.

"We're going to bring you in," he said, as if she might disagree with that option.

Xera nodded and gave him an enthusiastic thumbs-up.

"Who are these people?" Rysing asked.

"My former employers," Xera said bluntly. Realizing her position, she turned her back on the screen and told the girl, "They're kind of enemies of the Scorpio, so we're going to have to play this carefully. They're to think we were both held against our will—that should be easy for them to believe. If they thought otherwise it might go badly, understand? Don't tell them about the baby. In fact, it would be best if you didn't say much. Try to act shell-shocked, like you did when the Scorpio first found you."

Rysing looked disgruntled at the reminder.

Xera wasn't above pleading for a good cause. "Please? If we're not very careful, I might never see my husband again." An eight month journey was too far away for casual visits, and if the GE did take her back to Polaris, her baby would be nearly a year old before she could return to Ryven. That was assuming she could find the money and a private craft willing to take her so far out. With the Khun'tat running around, it became too dangerous to risk.

Maybe, someday, conditions might be right to

meet her sisters halfway—they could each travel for four months and meet at a place somewhere in the middle. None of that mattered today. Today, she had to choose between them.

Rysing looked at her intently. "And is that truly what you want? You have a chance to see your sisters again. I've heard you speak of them . . . you miss your family."

The ship shivered as the GE ship's tractor beam locked on. Xera had minutes to make up her mind. Her husband or her sisters? New or old? There was only one choice her heart would accept.

"Commander! You need to see this."

Ryven took the tablet from the ensign and scanned it quickly. His eyes slowed as he took in the data.

"What is it?" Toosun strode over and tried to read over his shoulder.

"One of the cloaked satellites around planet 4 Zega picked up a human ship. It looks like the interlopers are back. That's not all. An hour ago they towed one of our shuttles on board. The satellite picked up a transmission." He keyed the audio and heard the human commander say, "Lieutenant Harrisdaughter? What are you doing here?"

Ryven's heart lurched when he heard his wife's name. He listened intently to the rest of the exchange, learning all he could. If her communicator was jammed, what else might have been wrong with the ship? What was she doing on it in the first place?

Toosun looked sober. It was obvious he was considering the implications of Xera conveniently appearing near a GE ship.

Ryven looked at him. "There's no way she could have known it was there. We didn't even know until now."

His brother still looked somber, but continued Ryven's line of reasoning. "She couldn't have killed her guards, not by herself. We all watched her, and she had no one who would have helped. There was no indication she ever tried to make any allies to help her escape, either. But if a chance opened up to run? Would she have taken it? She knew how to pilot a shuttle."

"With jammed controls, through Khun'tat infested space? She's not suicidal," Ryven snapped. But it begged the question, was she put in there? If so, someone had seemed intent on an ugly death for her. Who hated her—or him—that much?

Toosun bit his lip. "We'd better get to her fast. It's three days if we leave now."

Ryven gave the order. The ships were already fueled and standing by. He prayed they'd get there in time to prevent a disaster.

It was a disaster. Xera just didn't have the patience to pretend to be downtrodden and abused. She sat in the commander's office and tried to at least look weary. That was easy enough. She'd forgotten how much she hated bureaucracy.

To give him credit, Commander Telis seemed to be trying to be sensitive. He offered her coffee and asked again if she'd like to see the medic. When she refused, he settled down to politely interrogating her. "Lieutenant, I know you've been through a lot these past months. We at the GE salute you for your bravery and daring in escaping your captors. While we know it will in no way make up for your pain, rest assured that you will receive a promotion and a substantial bonus for your suffering."

There was the bribe, she thought dispassionately. The man sounded like he was at a board meeting. "Thank you," she said into the expectant pause.

He cleared his throat and looked down at his electronic tablet. "As I'm sure you know, the Galactic Explorers finds itself at odds with the Scorpio on a number of matters. They've objected to our exploring this particular planet, for instance."

Xera maintained a polite silence. They both knew the GE was breaking the treaty by being here.

"In spite of the risks, our leaders feel it's a world that requires at least a cursory survey. There are so few habitable planets that we can't afford not to learn all we can about each new discovery."

In other words, the greedy board members were willing to risk having their charter revoked to explore this planet. They must think there was something valuable to be had. If they got in and out quickly, they could get away with samples and a cursory survey without anyone being the wiser. If they did find anything of interest, who knew how far they'd go to obtain the planet? Even if there were a movement to revoke the GE's charter, the Interplanetary Council might not have the power to stop them. After all, the IC was simply an underfunded, unappreciated peacekeeping committee. The GE had grown powerful. It might take a true war to bring them down.

His next words confirmed her fears.

"Of course, should the planet prove as valuable

as we hope, the GE may decide to press our claim on it. After all, there are no Scorpio currently living here. Why should they be allowed to claim a planet they aren't currently using?"

Why should the GE? Xera thought privately, but she said only, "That's very ambitious, sir." And wouldn't the Scorpio love to know about their attitude? Of course, the fact that the commander was telling her all this confirmed that he didn't expect her to bolt back to the Scorpios.

He nodded. "Do you have any reason to believe your escape was discovered or tracked? We'd hate to cut this mission short."

Xera frowned. He was ready to pull out if she said yes. That might make her life very difficult. If they left, she'd have no choice but to go with them. "If they had any idea they'd already be here. I have no reason to think they've discovered us." She tried to look anxious for the mission. "I'm sorry, sir. It wasn't my intention to make this difficult for you."

He relaxed a fraction. "It's certainly not your fault. In fact, you could be of great value to us all. No one else has been so deeply integrated into the Scorpio culture. Any insights you can offer would be appreciated—especially anything with military applications."

She didn't have to fake her distress. There was no way she was going to betray Ryven's people to the GE. "I'm sorry, sir. I wasn't allowed to witness much of a military nature. They didn't trust me, you know. Except . . ." She frowned as if reluctant to dredge up the memory. "I was on a ship once that was attacked by the Khun'tat. You did get the message they let me send to the IC? You know what they are?"

The commander looked uncomfortable. "We got the message. Our understanding was that they mainly existed on the other side of Scorpio space."

She let the full weight of her concern show. "We were attacked close to the site of the peace talks. That's not so far from here."

He was silent a moment. "Any additional information you have will be useful. I'd like you to file a formal report as quickly as you can.

"Meanwhile, your assessment has made me want to get this assignment done with all speed. We'll be landing on the planet shortly." Her alarm must have shown, for he added, "You don't have to worry about your safety. We'll be using the 'fortress' you know from before—we have a full report of it—and our ship is in good working order. Our force field will be more than sufficient to repel any creatures."

"Yes, sir. I . . . I won't be required to leave the ship, will I?" It was easy to act petrified. Maybe it wasn't so far from the truth.

His expression was kind. "No, Lieutenant. For now I'd like you to concentrate on your report. You may go."

She was glad to leave, and more rattled than she liked to admit. She had no good memories of this place. Finding out she was going back, however briefly, was an unpleasant shock, but not as bad as the one she got when she found out who else was sharing her ship.

Captain Khan was waiting for her in the hallway. There were people around, so he didn't pause, didn't say a word as he strode forward. He didn't have to. Though he used a cane and walked with a pronounced limp, his stare was still predatory. It intensified as he neared. Waves of hatred washed from him, as if he could do her harm with a thought, and his cold eyes promised a reckoning.

Xera held the man's gaze and tensed, prepared to defend herself, though she doubted he'd try anything here. No, he'd wait for his moment. She was going to have to watch her back.

She wondered why he was here and decided the GE would want his experience of the planet for this mission. She suspected if he'd been punished at all, it had probably been a hand slap. The GE would value his knowledge more than they would care about his "alleged" bad behavior.

She warned Rysing about him as soon as she got to their room.

The Leo-Ahni sat on her bunk in their tiny cabin and eyed her. "You have a special talent for making friends, don't you?"

Xera grimaced. They'd been allowed to clean up and change into spare uniforms when they arrived, though Rysing's bagged hopelessly on her slender frame. It was hard to say whether human space rations would agree with her, but Xera hoped she'd try to eat; the girl couldn't afford to lose more weight.

Well, they'd soon have their chance to find out. On Xera's advice, Rysing had given a blood sample to the medical technicians to test for allergies. Out of politeness Xera had waited with the Leo to eat. Fortunately the med techs were quick. Rysing tested allergy negative to most common foods, though that was no guarantee she'd like them.

The galley was just ending a shift when the women walked in. A quick glance around showed no Khan in sight. "Okay, girl. Time to try some more alien food," Xera remarked. "I'll try to steer you away from anything with teeth." She gave the girl a quick smile and handed over a tray.

This far out in space, shipboard fare was pretty dull, so Xera figured it'd be easy to keep Rysing's sensitive taste buds from rebelling. The girl's nose twitched suspiciously as they moved along the cafeteria line, and she looked less than thrilled with the globs of reconstituted mashed potatoes, hydroponic veg and dehydrated fruit. Even the tank-grown fish were met with looks of stoic determination.

They sat at a table. Rysing stared at her tray and took a deep breath. She put a tiny bite of mashed potatoes in her mouth . . . and promptly gagged.

Xera nodded sympathetically over her own bite. "You get used to it."

Rysing bravely took a sip of water to clear her mouth, then tried the beans. She didn't gag, but she didn't look happy. After trying the fish, she put down her fork. "I don't think I'm hungry anymore."

"You haven't tried the veg."

"I don't think I dare."

Xera exhaled in amusement. "I see your point, but you need to keep up your strength. Trust me when I say the food gets no better than this."

Rysing looked at her plate and swallowed hard. After a moment, she picked up her fork and dug in. She chewed mechanically, an empty look on her face, as if she were trying to distance her mind from what she was ingesting.

"I've seen that look before. You looked like that when we were dining on bugs, lieutenant," a new voice said.

Xera looked up into the face of Ensign Trevor, the man who'd once offered her a comb . . . and made her a scandalous proposition. The memory made her voice cool. "Ensign."

He looked nonplussed, then reddened with memory. "Ma'am. I was hoping we could talk. I think I owe you an apology." He looked at her steadily until she relented and allowed him to sit down.

He stared at his own tray a moment as his face became a deeper shade of red. It was an unfortunate combination with his orange-red hair and the pale skin that made his freckles stand out in glaring relief. "I, uh, want to say I'm sorry for the way I handled things in the cave. It's just that . . ." He took a deep breath and looked her in the eye. "I had a crush on you, ma'am, and I didn't want to see you get hurt. I just picked the wrong way to try to protect you."

She could see no deceit in his face. Looking back, she could see how she might have taken his interest hard, but things had been very different then. She'd been feeling trapped and vulnerable, imagining the worst. She could believe that he'd been a slightly horny white knight who bungled his approach. Here and now, he could be excused.

"I think we were all out of our element, Ensign. I can forgive you for fumbling your catch."

He grinned at her description. "Thank you. I think you had it worse than most, though." He sobered and glanced around. "Listen, you need to watch out for Khan. He was forbidden to speak to you upon your arrival, but he hasn't forgotten what happened. He's up for promotion, too—"

"Promotion!"

"Yeah. The GE sees him as a valuable asset. We're all being called heroes for surviving the crash. Now that you're here, they'll use you as an example of why we shouldn't ally with the Scorpio. If they can find an excuse to lay claim to this planet, they'll be happy to send more ships and men out here."

"Why? What can possibly be so precious about this place? You've seen it—it's one step removed from hell."

He glanced at her tray. "Finish up and I'll take you to the lab. There's something you should see."

Xera translated for Rysing, who grimly gagged down her dinner, minus the mashed potatoes. In minutes they were walking into the labs where Ensign Trevor worked as a technician. He nodded to the lone woman on staff and took them over to a bench. "We've all been taking turns bringing our buddies in here, showing them why the GE wants this 'stinking hole of a planet.' You won't be seen as unusual."

He said it in such a way that Xera wondered if he'd be questioned later. Maybe he was pushing his luck to be inviting her in, explaining. Maybe he was trying to make amends for their misunderstanding on the desert planet.

"Watch this." He put on gloves, then took a big tube full of murky water and showed it to them. "This is the toxic water from one of the oceans. Now look what happens when I pour it through this filter into this other beaker. You see this sediment forming? We'll get back to that." A clear drip of liquid was slowly filtering into the tube. He set it back out of the way and reached for another tube. "This liquid is already filtered. Now we use a nanofilter to separate out the oil and water. . . ." He repeated the process with a new beaker.

"Oil? I thought the two didn't mix?" Xera said.

"Not unless they have an emulsifier, but this is special stuff," he agreed. "Okay, this is now separated. You can see the value of the water without my explaining it. As for the oil . . ." He stuck a wick inside and set it on fire. "Ta-da! Fuel, ladies. Oceans of it, enough to power a whole civilization for a long time. But wait! There's more."

"I'm afraid to ask," Xera said. Clean water and a cheap fuel source were bad enough. Her home world of Polaris had started out with much less, dragging asteroids into orbit around a gas planet and using lunar ice to form lakes. This planet didn't even need that much effort. Sure, it was overrun with pests, but varmints could be trapped and killed.

"You should be," Ensign Trevor confirmed, "because this sludge rivals tranium as a fuel source."

Xera gasped. Tranium was the most efficient fuel source ever found for starships. If a rival source were found, the GE would shed blood to get their hands on it. Suddenly cogs started clicking into place. "You didn't just discover this. The GE has been here before."

"And lost ships to the Khun'tat," he confirmed. "Nobody will admit it, but I've got a friend on the inside who says it's true. You know what? I think those monsters are out here in this sector because they've spotted a new food source." He looked her in the eyes, his expression deadly serious. "You went through all the trouble to send a message out, but you didn't tell the GE anything they didn't know, Lieutenant."

"And they're willing to risk everything for the fuel," Xera said softly. She felt sick. Countless lives were being thrown away, and for what? So some rich guys could get richer. She also had to warn Ryven.

Rysing demanded to know what was up. Her brow furrowed in concern as it was explained, and she looked thoughtfully at the tubes on the bench. "If all this is so, why are they here now? Why not attack already?"

"Specimens," Trevor explained after translation. "They want some live critters this time, and more soil samples, weather data, etc. We also have to study the bugs and fungus we ate in the cave. Unless we find other native prey animals, future colonists might have to live on them." He looked disgusted.

Xera's lips curled in memory, too. "Ugh!"

Rysing didn't look horrified by the description of the situation, just thoughtful. "I'd like to see this place," she said when their fortress destination was described.

Xera started to argue with her, but was interrupted when the ship intercom announced their impending descent. All personnel were to prepare themselves for landing.

"I think we'll ride this out in our room," Xera told Ensign Trevor. "I've got a lot to think about. Thank you. I hope we'll get another chance to talk."

He gave her a jaunty salute. "My pleasure. Remember, stay clear of Khan. The current commander is all right as they go. Stay on his good side and you'll be okay."

Xera shook her head slightly as she left. Would she be able to stay out of trouble? Considering her goals, she doubted it would be for long.

Chapter Twenty-one

"I want to go outside."

Xera stared at Rysing like she'd lost her mind. "Why? There's nothing good out there."

"I need to see it," the Leo-Ahni said quietly, but her face was determined. At times she could be every bit as stubborn as Xera herself. "I understand if you are afraid. I will ask the commander to allow me to go with his party."

Xera drew breath. She didn't want the girl wandering around alone; she felt responsible. "You won't understand what anyone is saying. You could get hurt if someone called a warning you couldn't understand."

"So you'll go?"

Xera sighed. "I guess. I'm going to request a gun for the outing, though. It's too dangerous for even one of us to be unarmed. I don't suppose you can shoot?"

"I was never taught."

So they ended up going out in the chill desert sun. Xera felt like a bodyguard as she hovered near the small Leo-Ahni and surveyed the rocky

plateau. While Rysing looked around with curious eyes, Xera scanned the skies and ground for
danger.

"Relax, Lieutenant, we've got you covered," one
of the accompanying marines drawled, smiling a
lazy and confident smile. His big blunt face was
tolerably good-looking, but his attitude grated.

"When you've marched for a day over these
sands with things jumping out of the sky and the
sand buckling under your feet, we'll see how well
you can cover me," she told him grimly. "I think
I'll stay on guard until then."

He shrugged, thick-skinned enough not to
mind her attitude. She noticed he stayed close,
though, and she caught a subtle nod between him
and Ensign Trevor, who was also part of their
party. Was Trevor pulling favors, having his friend
watch over her?

She'd have to be careful—she was really starting
to like him.

Captain Khan was also there, cane and all. He
sent her one cold look then pretended she didn't
exist. She wasn't fooled into thinking he'd given
up his revenge.

"A woman could run for miles over this sand,"
Rysing said longingly, her eyes on the horizon. "I
need to go down there."

"Don't get any ideas about going for a jog,"
Xera warned her. "Running for miles in this stuff
is deadly."

Rysing looked at her with dignity. "I'm not a
fool."

"Thank God for that, because I must be to let
you talk me into this." Xera muttered in her own

language. She nodded to the far end of the plateau. "Look, they're getting ready to go now."

She kept her breathing even as her group moved away from their massive ship toward the nearby fortress, reminding herself that they were fully armed. It wasn't night, so flyers weren't a threat, wouldn't be even if it were pitch dark, because they didn't like the lights spraying out from the ship. She'd had all the precautions explained to her. In addition, the men ahead of the party had equipment capable of detecting the other dangers, were even setting traps for them. There was no reason for her feeling of doom.

"Easy now, ma'am. It's a short walk, and you're surrounded by guns." The marine sounded like he was calming a skittish animal.

"A happy thought," she assured him, but she made herself walk tall as if she felt no fear. There was a moment of déjà vu as she remembered her first meeting with Ryven. She'd walked tall then, too.

Rysing paused on the sand and breathed deep. Her eyes half closed as she took in the scents. She'd never looked more like a cat than when she knelt down and splayed the fingers of her right hand over the sand. She knelt very still, as if listening. "There's something coming under the sand." She pointed to the southeast, toward the sun.

Xera translated rapidly.

"Naw, the sensors aren't picking up any—whoa! Incoming! Sandworm," yelped one of the technicians manning the sensors.

"The traps aren't ready," Ensign Trevor said grimly. "Better shoot it."

Rysing watched the chaos calmly. "Hold still and it will stop," she murmured, but no one was listening. She placed a hand on Xera's arm when she tried to pull her away. "Be still. It hunts by vibration. If you are still, it is blind."

Xera didn't want to experiment, but she told the marine with them what Rysing had said.

"How does she know?" the man asked softly, but he held still, his gun trained where he thought the worm would be.

Their care was unnecessary. As soon as the beast got close, it was shot. Rysing shook her head. "Silly."

"We'd better get nonessential personnel inside," the commander ordered. "I want those samples double-quick."

Since it was built for keeping out animals, not people, the security was easy to overcome. All too soon they were entering the tunnel that led to the main room.

The fortress was everything Xera remembered, but the circumstances were vastly different. She'd expected fear, but oddly the place gave her a rush of melancholy. She missed her husband. If she wanted to see him again, she was going to have to do everything in her power to get herself back to him. If an opportunity came up, she was going to have to run for it.

Rysing didn't seem in a hurry to leave. She inspected every inch of the main cave as if it were a house on the market. She even followed Ensign Trevor below to look at the worms and mushrooms.

Xera stayed topside with the marine. There was no way she was going back down in that hole. She caught Khan looking at her once, but she knew there was nothing to fear yet. He wouldn't make his move in front of witnesses.

Rysing came up munching on a mushroom. She carried a jar full of bugs in her other hand.

Xera looked at her in horror. "*What* are you doing?"

Rysing popped the last bite in her mouth and licked her fingers with a slightly pointy tongue. "These are much better than ship's food. I'm hoping the crawling ones will be as well. At least they're fresh."

Xera gagged. She had to turn away quickly to keep from embarrassing herself.

"I know the feeling," Ensign Trevor said as he came up carrying his own jar. "Nothing like squishing through the . . . say, you're not going to puke, are you?"

She came very close. For a moment she had to close her eyes and breathe very carefully. To comfort herself, she murmured, "I could understand it if *she* were the one who was pregnant."

Suddenly it registered what she'd said. Her eyes popped open. Ensign Trevor was staring at her with a particular, frozen expression. Pity or horror? She couldn't tell, but it was time for fast decisions. She shot a look at the marine. His gaze was across the room, as if he hadn't heard a thing, but she didn't believe it.

She looked at Trevor. "Could you escort me back to the ship? We need to talk."

He nodded stiffly. "I'll take a load of specimens."

"We'll watch your back," the marine said, and he and Rysing fell into step a couple of paces behind.

She waited until they were climbing the stone stairs to the platform before she spoke. "The commander of the Scorpio, Ryven, is the father. If you saw the tapes from the conference, you must have known that."

He nodded. "Yes. It's just . . . I'm so damn sorry for you. No woman should have to suffer that."

She shook her head. "No suffering here. However he behaved with you all, he's different with his family, with women. I want this baby to have his father."

The silence was thick. The ship was getting nearer. Had she made a mistake?

"I see. What do you want me to do?" Trevor said finally. "You know better than to ask the commander to let you go."

"Can you help me? We're leaving in what . . . two days? I can't go back, and Rysing . . . I'll ask, but I think she wants to stay with the Scorpio, too."

There was a heartbeat of silence. "I'll see what I can do."

She sent him a look of gratitude. "Thank you."

He sighed. "Yeah, I'm a sucker. I know."

The time passed quickly as the GE party collected their specimens. Xera worked on her report and Rysing played games on the computer, or pestered Ensign Trevor in the lab, armed with a handheld translator he'd found for her. She was insatiably curious, particularly about the planet. She told everyone it was because she'd never gotten to see anything but a small portion of her own planet and a confined space of the Scorpio world. She was so childlike and cute, she got away with it, especially since she was free in telling anyone who asked about her own world. On a ship full of explorers, she was in constant demand.

Even so, she assured Xera privately that she wanted to return with her. She had hope of seeing her own people again someday. Not all of them were ready to let the Khun'tat rule, and she hoped to help the rebels in some way.

Xera didn't spend too much time thinking about the girl's motives; she had her own hopes and worries to occupy her—and other people's motives. Time was getting tight. She needed off the GE ship, and soon, and she needed Trevor's help. Would a man she'd once spurned really help her escape?

Ensign Trevor finally asked her if she'd like to take a walk to the cargo bay. Rysing was welcome to come, too. He asked it standing in her doorway, acting as if nothing more interesting were going on than an invitation to see some of the new things that had been collected. It was such a common sight that it didn't cause any interest.

Several crew members waved to Rysing as she passed. Cheerfully, she waved back. The girl had a sunny side when not burdened with fear, and everybody liked her.

Everybody but Khan. Xera's old captain saw the group pass in the hallway and glowered. Everyone who associated with Xera was suspect.

"There's not enough room in the labs, so some of the newest specimens are stored in the cargo bay. You've never seen anything like them, I promise," Ensign Trevor said as a cover while they passed Khan and several others. "I hope we can keep them alive until we reach home."

They didn't go to the cargo bay, though. Xera and Rysing were escorted to the shuttle bay instead. The huge doors were open as men and equipment moved in and out. There seemed to be a problem at the doors. A machine was stuck on the ramp, belching smoke and blocking the exit. Xera thought she recognized their earlier marine escort as one of the shouting men swarming over it. Nobody paid them any attention.

Trevor walked casually to the Scorpio shuttle and let them in. Once inside, he spoke quickly. "Strap in and take off. It's fueled and the controls are fixed. Preflight's done. It's now or never."

Xera took a breath. Her throat felt tight. "You'll be punished for this."

He smiled grimly. "Hit me a couple of times, will you? Make it look good and things will go better for me. Remember, I have to stumble out of here looking banged up."

She winced. "I hope you go to heaven for this." She punched him in the nose, and it was a good shot. Bone crunched under her fist. He cursed and grabbed his face, probably seeing stars.

"Now *this* is interesting," Captain Khan said. He was propped in the doorway, one hand supporting him on the wall, the other clutching his cane. "I see you're still a traitor, no matter what the commander says."

Xera stared at him. Trevor turned slowly, still clutching his nose. Blood ran between his fingers. "Sir, I tried to stop her."

Khan smirked. "I heard. Lovesick whelp! Don't you know she's been rutting with aliens?" His hand tightened on his cane as he looked at Xera.

"This time, it's my word against yours, and you're the one trying to escape on this enemy ship."

Trevor rushed him. But though a hero at heart, Trevor was no warrior. One neat blow to the side of his head with Khan's cane and he was stretched out on the floor, dead to the world. Khan looked amused.

Xera glanced around for a weapon. For her baby's sake, she'd rather not get too near Khan. She knew he'd kill her and claim self-defense. It was the logical thing, given his hatred of her.

"Here." Rysing must have raided a toolbox, because she handed Xera a heavy wrench. "Hurry. We need to take off."

"No pressure," Xera muttered.

Khan grinned and lunged for her. She ducked the cane and went to one knee, swung the wrench with all her strength. His cane connected with her shoulder and clipped her ear, but it lacked force. Her wrench didn't. It kissed the man's bad knee with gleeful fury. He screamed and went down on top of her. Somehow his hands wrapped around her throat and tightened. He was crushing her larynx.

Xera saw Rysing kicking his head, but still Khan didn't let go. But she had trained for this. Xera encircled his arms with hers and grabbed hold of her right fist, locking them together. With a mighty jerk, she pulled, breaking his arms at the elbow. There was a wet crunch as the bones snapped.

Khan screamed, a sound that was quickly cut off by another crack. Trevor stood over him, the wrench clutched in his hand. He was weaving, but still hauled Khan off Xera.

"He's dead," Rysing said.

"Yeah," Xera croaked. She crawled to her feet. She looked at Trevor. "Can you get him out of here? We've got to go."

He smiled grimly. "Better hurry. This won't go over well."

"Thank you," she said. He deserved a lot more, but she didn't have anything else to give.

He held her eyes then nodded, dragged Khan from the ship. Mercifully, the ramp was out of sight of the main door, blocked by a huge crate, so no one saw. She knew the situation wouldn't last.

"It's dangerous being your friend," Rysing said. She was already strapped into a chair and staring tensely out the windshield.

Xera grunted. Her throat was too bruised for idle conversation. Ignoring the blood on her hand, she grabbed the control yoke.

The shuttle rose seamlessly and she eased out of the bay. When people saw what was happening, they started to shout and point, but there was nothing they could do; the machine on the ramp blocked the door.

Xera cleared the machine and rose above the plateau, then punched it. The shuttle hurtled away from the desert as if shot from a cannon, and Xera and Rysing's bodies were shoved back in their seats by the g-forces. In minutes they broke out of the atmosphere and saw the blackness of space.

Rysing gave a little shriek of glee. "We did it!"

"Don't rejoice yet," Xera said grimly. "I have to figure out how to get us home."

Rysing stared at her. "But . . . you can fly! Can't you?"

Xera took a breath. "I never got to plotting co-ordinates, not for this model of ship. Oh, I can do it in other shuttles, but I have to play with these controls first."

"This is not a game! Play at nothing—get us *home.*" Rysing's voice had risen an uncomfortable octave. She was out of her comfort zone again.

"Working on it," Xera snapped. Her fingers flew over the controls, trying to find the flight record. If she could find it, she could use that to get the ship back where it came from. Easy enough . . . in theory.

"There are ships coming from the planet. Your people must have seen the dead captain." Rysing started to shake.

Fighters. Xera could see them. She swore and tried to keep her mind on the task at hand. She didn't think she could outrun their pursuers in the shuttle. Their only hope was to jump to hyper-space, but it was tantamount to suicide without proper coordinates.

"We're going to die." Rysing rocked back and forth in her chair. The hunters had barely arrived, and the prey was nearly catatonic with fear. What-ever her trigger was, the GE must have tripped it. She must have forgotten all the fun she'd had on the human ship. Maybe being pursued by fighters could do that to a girl.

So much for being everyone's buddy.

Xera had no time for pity. If Rysing couldn't help, the least she could do was shut up. She was shred-ding Xera's nerves. Without looking she hissed, "Come on, girl, get a grip! We can get out of this. Stop wilting on me."

Rysing took a shuddering breath. She stilled.

With a shout of victory, Xera found the ship log and the coordinates of home. "About freaking time," she snarled as she started punching codes. They were going back.

Suddenly another alarm sounded. "Warning! Enemy ship approaching. Aura quadrant three-oh-seven."

Xera looked at the readout and paled. It was a Khun'tat ship, and it was headed their way. Feverishly she input the commands to jump the shuttle into hyperspace, only to hear, "Please prepare while the hyperdrive warms up. You have seven minutes until this jump."

Seven minutes. Her heart stopped. They'd be dead in four.

Xera had a bad moment. For several seconds she was tempted just to give up. There was a deep, dark place in her mind that would gladly leap free and scream if she would just let it. But Xera wasn't that person. The Khun'tat and GE hadn't won yet.

Xera turned to say as much, only to find Rysing slicing open her wrist with a knife from the tool kit.

"What are you doing?" Xera yelled, and launched herself at the girl before she could do the other. She grabbed Rysing's wrist, but the girl's knife raked her free arm. She hissed in pain and pinned the Leo's knife hand, then elbowed Rysing in the jaw. That stunned the girl long enough for Xera to flip her on her stomach and put her in an armlock. The Leo-Ahni was surprisingly strong for such a slight thing.

"Hold still!" Xera put a knee in Rysing's back

and grunted as she struggled to reach the toolbox without losing her captive. There was tape there. She snatched it and wrenched Rysing to her feet, using the armlock to control her. It was harder getting the girl into a seat, and Rysing nearly got away. Fed up, Xera muttered, "This is for your own good," and she smashed her fist into Rysing's face. That staggered the girl long enough for Xera tape her to the chair. A glance at the screen showed the Khun'tat ship was much closer.

Swearing at the lost time, Xera grabbed the med kit and slapped some clotting agent and a patch over the wound before taping Rysing's arm down.

"You've doomed me," the girl cried. "I won't let them have me again!"

"Don't worry, I'll slit your throat if it comes to it," Xera promised, her mind already scheming. Not that she wanted to think about it; the sight of the girl's blood already made her nauseous. She sat down and stared at the controls. What could she do with very little time and no weapons? Would it come down to suicide? Did she know how to blow up this ship?

The Khun'tat neared. Much more and their ship would swallow the shuttle whole. Just as Xera was thinking of ramming them out of spite, she was hailed.

"Ryven?" she gasped. "Is that you?" She flipped on the communications screen and could have cried. There was her husband's face, just as she'd imagined it. How had he arrived in time? Never mind, she could ask him later. "Thank God! Get us out of here!"

Ryven's expression was controlled. There was no room for relief yet. "Easy. We will." His gaze took in Rysing's condition.

"She tried to slit her wrists when she saw the Khun'tat coming. I had to knock her down to save her life."

He actually choked back a laugh. "Woman . . . ! No, don't lose composure now. You did well," he added, when it seemed she might wilt. "Don't panic—you're going to feel our tractor beam lock on in a moment."

Xera felt a little bump and relaxed a fraction. Ryven's ship had them, but the Khun'tat were so close! They were launching ships to board them.

But so were the Scorpio! She'd never been so grateful to see warships in all her life. Even as Ryven's craft's launch bay opened to receive them, she saw glimpses of explosive battle.

Suddenly, the shuttle rocked as the blasted remains of a Khun'tat fighter slammed into it. The tractor beam was no protection, and alarms suddenly flared.

"Xera!" Ryven shouted. Her screen grew fuzzy.

"Busy!" Xera shouted over the alarms. Her hands flew across the controls as she assessed the damage. Life support was failing. The hull was heavily damaged and threatening to buckle. The toilet . . . She actually laughed. "Hey, Rysing! Our toilet is off-line. Man, but that would be a problem if we planned to live very long." She shook her head, amazed at the detail and insignificance. Who designed these systems, anyway?

Luckily for them, they were swept inside Ryven's ship. Medics were waiting to escort Rysing to sick bay. Xera was sped to her husband's side. Uncaring of proprieties, she threw herself against him in a hug, which he returned with crushing force.

After a long moment, she drew back and told him solemnly, "I'm having a bad day."

He laughed, but it was strained. "We will make it better now. Will you stay with me?" He gestured to an empty chair.

"Absolutely." She parked her tail in the seat, grateful for the chance. She still felt very unsettled. "What about the GE? You do know they're here, right?"

Her husband nodded. "They are running as fast as they can in the opposite direction. We will deal with them later."

She opened her mouth to defend at least two of them, but decided now was not the time. They could discuss it all later.

Ryven began to issue commands, and she knew better than to distract him. Her husband would get them home.

Chapter Twenty-two

Since theirs had been intended to be a rescue mission, Ryven and Toosun didn't stick around to finish off attacking the Khun'tat. They were too deep in the alien race's territory to risk it, since recent developments had ceded the area to their foes; enemy reinforcements could arrive at any time. The moment they retrieved the women, they fought their way clear and jumped into hyperspace.

Xera was relieved to arrive home, though it was late before she finally crawled into her bed. Ryven joined her, leaving his brother to relay the news to their family of the mission's success and of the continued interloping of the Khun'tat. He wrapped his arms around her and held tight.

"I don't want anyone to build a moon base there," Xera said into his shoulder. "I don't want anyone to go through what I just did." She didn't want her sisters, if they visited, to be so close to jeopardy. Such a situation wasn't likely anyway, what with the GE breaking the treaty at will. They'd be lucky if the Scorpio didn't annihilate them on sight.

He kissed her hair. "I know. Be at peace."

She sighed. "Thank you for rescuing me."

"Always—though if you don't mind, I'd rather avoid more incidents in the future. I think I lose a year of my life every time I see you in danger."

She smiled slightly. "I'll see what I can do."

"Beloved," he began with mock sternness.

She looked at him in surprise. "You called me *beloved*!"

"Yes," he said simply. "I meant it."

She still looked amazed. "You love me?"

Now he was annoyed. What had she thought this was about? "I said so, didn't I?"

"Not in so many words."

His noisy exhalation was all the answer he gave.

But then she grinned, and it was like the sun peeking out of a fog bank. "You love me!"

He was ready to give a flip response when he noticed the tears still standing in her eyes. His annoyance softened. He caressed her cheek with the back of his hand. "Almost from the first. Haven't I shown you?"

"I'm a human, dummy! I need words." She tried to glower at him, but her smile kept glimmering through, as though her chest were filled with sunlight. "You love me," she said in wonder.

He was going to blush if she kept saying it, so he offered a distraction. "I've been thinking . . . you've really proved yourself. Not just with the last situation with GE, but with the way you handled Rysing. If you still wish to be an ambassador, I will permit it. It will no longer be an empty role."

She sat up and stared. "You mean it?"

His smile was self-mocking. "You've made many

sacrifices for me. I think I can give up my idea of a 'perfect family' for this. You do want it, don't you?"

She grinned and threw herself at him to deliver a jubilant kiss. "Yes! You are such a sweetie."

That did it. He blushed. To take his mind off the embarrassment, he took his wife in his arms and soon caused her cheeks to glow, too.

At least they had one less worry. Tovark's body had turned up at a hospital with a knife wound in his back. He'd been pronounced dead on arrival. A search was being made for the culprit, whom authorities assumed was his accomplice.

Whoever he was, Tovark's killer had done them all a favor. Xera was glad he was dead, and Ryven was almost inclined to let the man go. Almost.

Rysing was inclined to hold a grudge over Xera's rough handling, but reluctantly admitted it had saved her life. Xera thought the moodiness was lingering fright over the near disaster and decided to give the girl time to get over it. Rysing soon began to resume some of her former ease.

The experience changed Xera. She sent off a carefully edited message to her sister of her adventures, then decided it was time for a rest. She and Ryven moved out to the country house and met the neighbors, commuting back to the palace whenever needed. The more time she spent at the estate, the happier she was. In the privacy of the country, Ryven relaxed. It was easier to demonstrate her love when she was allowed to touch him.

Spring had come, and she enjoyed walking in the gardens. She'd had her fill of adventure for now, and was able to enjoy simple pleasures like strolls in the sunshine. She no longer felt so restless.

It was also fun to plan her child's future, though she tried not to map it much past the fifth year—the kid needed some room for spontaneity.

The child arrived in due time, and Xera was surprised to find out he was a she. "You didn't tell me," she chided her husband after she'd caught her breath.

He smiled at her. "You were so sure it would be a boy, I didn't want to ruin the surprise." The nurse handed him the child. Swathed in a towel, the tiny bundle looked absurdly small in her husband's arms, but the look of tenderness in Ryven's eyes . . .

Xera had to swallow tears. She didn't even mind her sisters' absence now, not with this kind of love here for her child. She had no doubt the baby girl would earn similar looks from her grandfather and uncle. Toosun had a special soft spot for children, and his brother's child would be especially dear to him: he'd want to vet all her suitors. The poor child was going to have a terrible time dating.

"Time to meet you mother, little love," Ryven said, gently placing the baby in her arms.

Xera gasped. "She has your eyes!"

"The next one will have yours," he soothed.

She frowned at him. "I like her eyes. I like *your* eyes. They're very pretty. Don't get any ideas on starting another one anytime soon, though."

He ignored the last part of her statement. "You never told me you liked my eyes."

"You're arrogant enough as it is."

He smiled wolfishly. "We'll continue this when you've regained your strength. Rest. Let me show her to her family. I think Aunt Tessla and Toosun will storm the room if they have to wait much longer."

"Perhaps a wash and a clean diaper, first, my lord?" the nurse suggested. She practically had to wrestle the child away from her frowning father. Ryven gave way, but stood nearby and waited impatiently for the nurse to finish, carefully watching her every move.

"Fathers," the nurse tending Xera murmured wryly. "They're all alike."

Xera smiled. She was tired, but more content than she'd been in a very long while. With him by her side, she was comfortable with whatever the future had in store for them. Let him hover—her child would know the full measure of her father's love.

With Ryven, she'd learned, no words alone could ever demonstrate the depth of his heart, but his actions were all in the language of love. They required no translation.

New York Times Bestselling Author

LYNSAY SANDS

THE ARGENEAU NOVEL AT THE START OF IT ALL!

Single White Vampire

Roundhouse Publishing editor Kate C. Leever's first letter to her newest legacy author was intended to impress upon him the growing demand for his "vampire romances." Though he'd expressed little to no desire for publicity, book tours or the like, it was clear that this was a writer waiting to be broken out. Correspondence with Mr. Lucern Argeneau tended to be oddly delayed, but this time his response was quick and succinct.

"NO."

But Kate was adamant: Luc was going to attend a romance convention to meet his fans. By hook or by crook, despite his reclusive nature, odd sleep schedule and avoidance of the sun, the surly yet handsome Luc was going to be recognized as the real charmer a nationally bestselling author should be. But soon Kate would learn that his novels were more biographies than bodice rippers, and it'd be her neck on the line.

A sweeter surrender, or more heartwarming love story—his own—Luc has yet to write.

ISBN 13: 978-0-8439-6188-1

ELISABETH NAUGHTON

STOLEN FURY

DANGEROUS LIAISONS

Oh, is he handsome. And charming. And sexy as all get out. Dr. Lisa Maxwell isn't the type to go home with a guy she barely knows. But, hey, this is Italy and the red-blooded Rafe Sullivan seems much more enticing than cataloging a bunch of dusty artifacts.

After being fully seduced, Lisa wakes to an empty bed and, worse yet, an empty safe. She's staked her career as an archaeologist on collecting the three Furies, a priceless set of ancient Greek reliefs. Now the one she had is gone. But Lisa won't just get mad. She'll get even.

She tracks Rafe to Florida, and finds the sparks between them blaze hotter than the Miami sun. He may still have her relic, but he'll never find all three without her. And they're not the only ones on the hunt. To beat the other treasure seekers, they'll have to partner up — because suddenly Lisa and Rafe are in a race just to stay alive.

ISBN 13: 978-0-505-52793-6
